THE LARK'S CALL

JENNY BOND

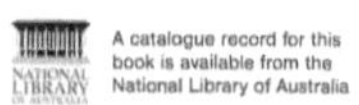

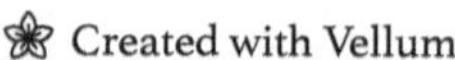

Created with Vellum

SUFFOLK COUNTY, MASSACHUSETTS

1719

As Bellamy staggered to his feet, he tasted iron with a hint of salt. Blood. It was a taste he had grown accustomed to. He gingerly ran his tongue across his teeth; all were there, but inside, he could feel his lip had been cut wide open. His tongue probed the shredded flesh.

Through the cheers and jeers of the onlookers, Bellamy heard O'Leary, his opponent, grunt loudly as he swung back his beefy arm once more. Bellamy instinctively ducked, then seemed to glide to the opposite side of the patch of dirt the woodsmen called a ring, stunning his rival with the deftness of his movement.

He waited for his vision to clear.

As he did, he took in the height and breadth of the man he was fighting. Thick through, like the trunk of one of the surrounding chestnut trees, but slow, flat-footed. Clumsy for a man who wielded an axe and piloted a crosscut saw for a living.

Bellamy spotted John among the crowd, straight-backed, the tilt of his jaw expressing his objections.

'O'Leary, O'Leary ...' the bystanders chanted, urging their fellow woodcutter to finish the fight. The pulsing sound of their voices, the amber lanterns burning in the dark and the masculine smells that sheeted the air reminded Bellamy of his previous life, one long lost. He garnered courage from the memory.

Spitting a large crimson glob of saliva into the dirt, he ran at his rival, burying his shoulder into O'Leary's girth. To his surprise, the man was soft as a goose-down pillow. O'Leary stumbled just a few inches before hoisting Bellamy off him, ramming his fist into his challenger's stomach. On his knees, coughing and bent over, Bellamy's jaw ached as he sucked air through his swollen lips.

He caught sight once more of his eleven-year-old charge. John's serious dark grey eyes pleaded with him to stop, but he couldn't. Despite the ache and the blood and John's imploring eyes, there was something deep inside him urging him forward. A fire as hot and as furious as a wounded bull blazed in his core.

He straightened and rose, the ache in his abdomen slowly dulling as he waited for O'Leary to come to him. There was confidence in the hulking woodsman's eyes, a surety that the bout would soon be finished, that this 'Captain Grand' the men talked about would soon be done with. Bellamy had seen that look too many times before. Tightening the scarf he wore around his head, he waited. He knew how to win a fight.

O'Leary clomped towards him.

Still Bellamy waited.

'Go at him!' a voice in the crowd shouted.

'He's a skitterbrook, to be sure,' another cried. The onlookers roared, fuelled by gin and the freedom that comes from living solely among men.

When the air had closed between them, O'Leary hoisted and crooked his meaty arm again. Bellamy darted around him and, rooting his feet into the ground, delivered the woodsman four mighty blows to his kidneys, his fist burying deep into flesh, the force of the blows ricocheting like a thunderbolt up his arm. O'Leary's great mass wavered slightly and Bellamy took the opportunity to stamp his foot heavily against the back of O'Leary's knee. He heard the wind rush from the big man's body as though his lungs were bellows. Observing the change, Bellamy ran at him and, with his feet leaving the earth for an instant, brought his elbow down forcefully against O'Leary's neck.

O'Leary collapsed to the ground, the great woodsman felled by Captain Grand.

Bellamy exhaled. The fire in him was finally out.

JOHN SAW to Bellamy's wounds as he usually did, dabbing the cuts and scratches with barbary. An Indian they had once met during their travels had showed him how to make a poultice from shepherd's purse and field horsetail to ease swelling. John applied one now to Bellamy's jaw.

'Stay still,' the boy instructed as he fixed the compress to Bellamy's face with a strip of cloth torn from an old outgrown shirt.

Bellamy looked at the boy who had become his son. He admired John's tenderness and concern. He was a gentle lad. Still, Bellamy had insisted on teaching John to fight. If Bellamy were ever to be recognised, or they became cornered, he needed to depend on John to hold his own. He had explained to John that there was no reason a boy couldn't fight as well as a man if he knew where on the body to target. Eyes, toes and balls were the easiest marks for a boy. Fortunately, John had never needed the skills Bellamy had taught him, a fact that was both a relief and a minor disappointment.

'Our winnings?' Bellamy said through gritted teeth, wincing. His jaw was stiff making it difficult to for him speak.

'Shush,' John murmured in concentration. 'I think your jaw might be broken.'

John's thoughts flew to the crimson buffaloberries in his case that, when ground, were a ready cure for broken bones. He had never had to use them before. Worry etched fine lines on his smooth brow. *Bellamy is all I have*, he thought.

It was a warm evening for October. John could feel sweat trickle down the sides of his face. They had been camping with the woodcutters for some weeks, following the first of Bellamy's fights as Captain Grand. Bellamy had suggested they stay put in the camp where the fight had taken place but John had been concerned, troubled that the defeated party would retaliate. It turned out that the woodcutters were a genial bunch of fellows who viewed the fight for what it was, an entertainment. And Bellamy had comforted him at the time by explaining that to his knowledge, nobody had ever shot the winner of the Newmarket Town Plate. As a good-natured victor, he was sure to be safe.

Fires dotted the camp. John could hear them hiss and crackle as fat billets were laid upon them. The evening chill had a habit of stealing upon the slumbering woodsmen. He wiped the sweat from his face.

'Well?' Bellamy pressed. He was never to be quieted where money was concerned.

'You did well, seeing that the odds were stacked against you as they were.'

John tied the final knot in the cloth that encased Bellamy's head with more force than was necessary, making the patient wince again in pain. Bellamy gave him a look. In his dark eyes, John read that he was in no mood to be chastised tonight. The boy sighed.

'You were lucky. My guess is 3, maybe 4 pounds. I haven't counted closely. Or made the conversions and so forth.'

Their takings were typically a mix of English and Spanish currency. Occasionally there might be a florin, daalder or thaler thrown into the mix, even wampum sometimes; all were accepted as legal tender in the colonies.

'And there's this,' John added, producing a small leather case from the bag of winnings.

Bellamy took the object from the boy and released the fingernail-sized clasp. He held the compass for a time, spotting north, remembering the piece he used to use long ago. The one in his hand was a handsome instrument, with a sight. He clapped it closed, noting the letter 'K' embossed in the tan leather as he did so.

Typically, Bellamy triumphed. While woodcutters were generally tough as whitleather, they lacked skill, finesse. They were not fighters. John glanced at the warrior he was tending to now. Although Bellamy had spoken of a home, a place to settle, John had grown increasingly anxious in the past few months, concerned that his mentor was just a fighter and always would be.

Finished with his ministrations, John packed up his medicine chest. It was, in fact, a small, finely carved mahogany box which Bellamy had won in a prize fight six months before. He was unsure of its original purpose, but John liked to fill it with the herbs, nuts, seeds and roots he collected. When needed, he ground them into powders and combined them to make the tinctures that cured

Bellamy. Some of the ingredients came as far away as St John.

Over the years, he had learnt how to make potions, ointments and salves to treat everything from bruising to broken bones. He'd gleaned much in the way of cures from the people they had encountered on their travels and felt his array of medicines was a thing to be proud of. *At least there's something to be said for moving around*, thought John, as he secured the box's lid.

The feverwort tea he had prepared earlier was now cooled and ready. The boy had brewed the remedy some time before the fight had begun. An Indian had told him it worked better if the leaves were left to steep until their healing powers infused the water and turned the tea a deep shade of moss green. Now, he poured a small amount of the brew into a mug.

As he did so, he watched Bellamy gaze at the blackened heavens visible through the canopy of the forest. He wondered what this man, his father in all but name, was thinking.

'Drink this. It will help with the pain.'

Bellamy eased himself upright. Poking his nose into the cup, he grimaced in distaste. *It does taste of sour milk*, John thought. Barely able to open his mouth more than a dash, Bellamy drew the liquid through his swollen lips then groaned when he moved to place the mug on the ground.

'This life will be the death of you, Samuel Bellamy,' John said, frowning.

Despite the discomfort it caused, Bellamy attempted a laugh. Unlike the usual rich, sonorous sound that accompanied his amusement, the noise Bellamy emitted now was muffled and choked, evidence of his physical pain.

John looked at him inquiringly.

'You remind me of your mother,' Bellamy articulated with difficulty through his tight lips. John noticed the lightness the memory had aroused in his mentor's eyes but it quickly vanished. The injured man sighed, weary.

Bellamy did not talk of John's mother Tamesine often; John knew the recollection of her made him sad. However, John frequently found himself desperate to say her name out loud and share his thoughts with someone who remembered her too. It seemed to him that this was the only way to hold her in his mind and in his heart.

Most days the image of her eluded him. When he and Bellamy had leapt from the *Whydah* and into the raging sea, it was her image – luminous, intense – that he believed had guided them to the safety of a shallow crevice, only big enough for two, in the cliff face. *How would we have discovered that hollow otherwise?* John often wondered. Now when he closed his eyes, the image of his mother, once so distinct, was a blurred and dusky form. *Memory is like fire*, he thought. *It needs to be managed and nurtured.*

He looked at Bellamy warily, considering the man's words.

'How so?' he asked.

'The truth, but also the contradiction, in what you just uttered ...' He placed his hand on the poultice that surrounded his jaw and shifted it slightly, locating the heat. 'You share a similar way of speaking. She said the same to me in Nassau. Many times.'

'In your pirating days?'

'Aye, John. In my pirating days.'

Nodding seriously, the boy poked the fire with a stick, contemplating his next words carefully. The flames glowed red and orange for an instant, throwing Bellamy's face into sharp relief. Even bruised and swollen, his black eyes were easy to read.

'We have been doing this for two years, Sam. We have money enough to settle somewhere,' John said.

When Bellamy did not protest at the direction the conversation had veered, he continued more forcefully.

'We've ridden from New London to Manchester to Portland and back again. You've not been recognised.'

John paused. Except once, he thought, recalling. He pushed the memory aside in his effort to break down Bellamy's resolve.

'As far as we know, there is no price on your head. To all the world, Black Sam is dead and gone.'

'I know,' Bellamy murmured.

Directing his gaze to the treetops, John went on. 'Why, we could cut down one of these chestnuts right now, if that was our fancy, and start building a cabin tonight.'

Bellamy's mouth curled into a grin. Encouraged, the boy continued.

'Freedom is the only thing that's important in this life. It is what you've always told me. We have that, Sam ... But it seems to me that you're still trapped like a knight on a carousel, going around and around in circles ...'

Judging from Bellamy's silence and the furrowing of his brow, John feared he had gone too far. The boy shrugged as though what he had just expressed meant nothing, made no sense.

'You're right,' Bellamy muttered in a low voice. He picked up the compass and examined it once more. 'It's time to settle down.'

John's heart quickened. 'No more Captain Grand?'

'No more Captain Grand.'

THE WOODCUTTERS ROSE EARLY, before dawn. John's eyes opened and it took a moment for him to remember where they were. He turned his head towards Bellamy. Still asleep. Propping himself on his elbow, John examined Bellamy's injuries. His eyes were as red and shiny as two plump damsons and his mouth was misshapen, his lips purple with bruising.

The night before, man and boy had reached an agreement. Bellamy confirmed that the fight with O'Leary had been his last. His injuries would heal and soon be forgotten. He said he could see the future on the horizon as distinct as a new map. The boy sighed in contentment then rose. He rummaged in his bag for the bar of lye soap he had traded for a tin of snuff neither he nor Bellamy had use for.

Flowing plentifully among the amber forest of leaf fall, the brook invited John to plunge his hands in. When he did, he drew them from the water in shock. Winter was not far off. The sting John experienced made even the thought of washing intolerable.

'Cold, eh?'

John spun on his heels, almost toppling into the icy water. It was O'Leary. He was unbuttoning his shirt, preparing to take the plunge himself. The woodcutter was amazingly stealthy for such a heavy-set man.

'Come on, son, it's only ankle deep. When your feet turn blue, you'll know it's time to get out.' O'Leary had a husky northern accent as thick as porage but, comforted by the merry lilt to his voice, John was encouraged. He began to unlace his shirt.

O'Leary did not appear aggrieved at all by his defeat at the hands of Bellamy. He whistled a cheerful tune as he bathed; a childhood favourite, hedged John. He was not familiar with the melody. Spending most of his youth in Nassau, living among thieves and scoundrels of one kind or another, he did not suppose there was either imperative or necessity for his mother to teach him nursery songs. But he did recall a single lullaby. It was one that his mother had sung to him when he was very young, when they still lived in Mistress Landry's boarding house. John began to hum the melody, hoping the effort in remembering might distract him from the sting of the water.

'You know what's what, don't you?' O'Leary said suddenly, halting John's tuneful ablutions. 'I watched you tending to your father's wounds and collecting his winnings. Serious you are, for such a youngling.' He eyed John's countenance. 'You look like a reader, too. *I* read, you see.' He seemed proud of the accomplishment.

Teeth chattering and with his spindly legs turned purple and prickly with goosebumps, John nodded, barely able to catch his breath. He stepped from the brook and began to dress. Fortunately, he had laid his breeches and shirt over a tree stump positioned in the sun, a trick shown to him by Bellamy. As he tugged the garments onto his limbs, it felt as though he was slipping into a warm bed. He sighed at the memory of such a luxury.

After O'Leary dressed, he produced a newspaper from a leather bag John had seen by his clothes.

'You're welcome to this here. It's old though ...' He held the print close to his eyes. '1717. The fourteenth of September,' he pronounced then handed the publication to John.

The London Gazette.

'Thank you very much,' John said, gazing at the faded

print. He was about to acknowledge the gift once more with an appreciative nod when the front page caught his eye – 'Proclamation for Suppressing of Pirates'.

Without giving O'Leary another thought, he began to read.

2

BOSTON, MASSACHUSETTS

1735

John Kirkcaldie was interrupted in his contemplations when Joshua Williams entered his second-floor room on King Street. He'd heard the familiar sound of the young man's coltish tread on the stairs seconds ago but had been unable to emerge from his thoughts before Joshua had stormed into the room, a grimace darkening his typically happy countenance. Snow dusted his hat and cloak and clutched his boots like a vice. John recognised the document gripped in his friend's hand at once.

'I have just come from the Lion's Head,' Joshua began, referring to his preferred tavern.

John checked his pocket watch pointedly. It was half eight in the morning. Joshua ignored him.

'There I heard from Josiah Heath that you – or should I say *we* – are petitioning the court for "the freeing of a Negro slave and his wife who were unjustly held in bondage".' A small grunt of incredulity escaped his lips. 'Josiah has asked me to talk some sense into you before he presents it to the judge.'

Joshua threw the document, which he had clearly read many times, into the lap of his seated friend as the final punctuation point to his tirade before removing his hat and cloak.

It was the petition that John had delivered to Heath, the clerk of the court, the day before. John placed his timepiece back in his vest pocket then stood and wandered calmly – for John moved with the measured elegance of a cat – to the door which Joshua, in his rage, had flung open. John carefully pushed it closed. The volume of his partner's voice was not compatible with the hour. And, being two months behind with the rent, the young lawyer did not wish to raise the ire of his landlord.

'Would you mind explaining to me how these slaves are planning to pay our fee?' asked Joshua.

'I ... *we* have taken on the case *pro bono*,' said John, drawing his fingers through his thick, chestnut curls.

He lifted the foot of the pallet bed he slept on. Despite his irritation, Joshua helped him secure it flat against the wall with six sturdy fasteners of John's own devising. Following this, John drew across a curtain of dark green calico to conceal the bed.

'*Pro bono*?' Joshua repeated, perplexed, dragging the writing desk away from the wall to the centre of the room.

'It means gratis, free ...' John placed a chair on either side of the desk then opened a cupboard and produced a third with folding legs which he promptly extended out then snapped into place. His father had been a carpenter in another life and had crafted the chair for him following John's design.

'*Voilà*,' John said quietly to himself. From sleeping chamber to lawyer's practice. The transformation never ceased to amaze him.

'I know what "pro bono" means! It's not the Latin that confounds me.' At twenty-three, Joshua was five years the junior of John Kirkcaldie, his friend and partner. He had, however, inherited a shrewd business acumen of his father, Palgrave Williams.

'Your emotions, John, your compassion, rashness and your principles, will see us both in debtor's prison in a very short time indeed.'

'It's a case like this that could make our names,' John responded, eyes bright. 'Do you not see? If we can make an argument that will free slaves ...'

Joshua groaned and slumped into a chair. His blonde hair fell over one eye.

'What's more, this man and his wife were wronged, cruelly so,' continued John. 'We could make our names and play a part in ending one of this society's greatest evils. We both excel at disputation ... we are *made* for this case.'

'That was Harvard, John! There, nothing more was at stake than our pride before our fellow classmates and tutors. Furthermore, neither you nor I are Andrew Hamilton!' cried Joshua, referring to the most renowned lawyer in the colonies. The year before, Hamilton had successfully argued in court that the truth was a defence against libel, freeing the New York publisher John Peter Zenger.

'These are people's lives with which you play,' he continued in frustration.

Joshua walked to the small window that overlooked Long Wharf. He flung it open decisively, allowing entrance to the biting winter wind and the pungent aroma of fish. He turned back to John.

'Do you think I frequent these taverns for the ale and the company? I'm there to seek out clients. Admittedly, their pocketbooks are as meagre as their complaints, but it's these people who keep our practice afloat. We paid our way for three months with the settlement from the Tander case.'

William Tander had been stood down as a lighterman by the Dutch West India Company after he injured his back while operating a barge. Without compensation and the ability to work, the Tander family – Mistress Tander, their five children and William's elderly father – found themselves in dire straits. Joshua came across Tander drowning his sorrows in the Bunch of Grapes one noontide February last and invited conversation. Not long after, armed with only an expertly written letter threatening legal action, the Dutch West India Company paid Tander the handsome sum of 300 pounds – much more than an entire year of his wages.

John sat opposite his partner, thinking. Both men were silent. It was Joshua's tenacity and his powers of persuasion that were keeping their heads above water. But John yearned for a larger case, a spectacle, that would secure their future success and put an end to at least one grim injustice occurring in a colony rife with so many. Fighting injustice, doing what he could to right wrongs, was the reason he became a lawyer.

He had expressed the sentiment to Joshua many times, ever since they had known each other. It was the friendship of their fathers that had originally brought the pair together. John had also been Joshua's tutor at Harvard. At the start, tutor and student had clashed repeatedly. Joshua was hot-headed and often foolish in his displays of haughtiness, a trait he shared with his younger brother and older sister. John had wondered at the time how such sensible and sober parents such as Palgrave and Leah Williams produced such conceited offspring. Joshua was clever – that was a certainty – but he displayed his wits at every opportunity, large and loud like a prize bull. In those first few weeks of University, John had begun to doubt whether there was any substance to the freshman but Kirkcaldie convinced him to persevere.

'It's merely a phase the lad is experiencing. Having been accepted into Harvard he believes all others exist only for his comfort. You were much the same,' explained his mentor.

John had frowned, finding it difficult to recall his own behaviour at that age. In the end, he decided to trust Kirkcaldie's memory; it was far more accurate than his own.

By the time Joshua was a sophomore, the pair were friends. Without knowing how, John had managed to instruct the student in restraint and diffidence, as well as Latin, Logic and Greek. The following year they had grown into confidantes and John trusted Joshua enough to introduce him to his other life at Harvard. Staid, grave tutor by day, John sold rum to his underclassman mates after hours. He had quickly discovered that the young men of Harvard – the men of the future – resented the Puritan restraint that had been the backbone of the college since its founding almost 100 years before.

Gambling too, like liquor, was forbidden at the university. John also organised card and dice games in his study while Joshua acted as his middleman, shrewdly negotiating an extremely generous salary of twenty-five per cent of all takings.

Looking back, John did not know why he risked his place at the university – and Joshua's as well – the way he had. They were two of the only students who paid their term bills, commons and sizings in cash. Most of the students paid in commodities: rye, mutton, apples and even parsnips. But for them, money was never an issue; both their fathers were extremely wealthy.

Despite this, John admitted to himself that he did come from questionable stock. He doubted if any of his fellow students had been raised by a pirate after the murder of their madam mother. In fact, he would wager healthily against it. As a consequence, he had grown to enjoy skirting authority, breaking the rules. There was a freedom he experienced when a sophomore squeezed a pound into his hand for a quart of rum. He was sure this was a trait he had inherited from Bellamy, if that were possible. For the truth was, although Bellamy had raised him, they shared no blood; all they shared was the counterfeit name of 'Kirkcaldie', inspired by a woodsman's compass. He had no 'real' family. He could barely remember his mother, and as for his father … little more than nothing remained.

Joshua pleaded with him again, breaking his reverie.

'So I implore you to burn that petition and come with me to the Marlborough Arms. If you and I work side by side, we might discover a man who has been wronged, and, more importantly, one who is able to pay our fee.'

Contrite, John stood, reached for his coat and slipped his arms into the sleeves.

'Did you remember to collect our calling cards from the printer?' Joshua asked on his way to the door.

'No, I did not,' John replied without excuse.

'Then we shall call in on Wilkins on the way,' Joshua called as he swept through the doorway.

3

When they arrived, the Marlborough Arms was already heaving with dockers and labourers who had just finished their shift at Long Wharf. The tavern was as thick as Boston fog with the stink of fish, rum and tobacco. Scanning the space for a moment, the lawyers broke off in opposite directions and found seats at tables surrounded by broad-shouldered, weary men leant over their mugs as though in solemn prayer.

'Good day to you,' John feigned merriment, taking his seat by a boulder of a man and gesturing to a serving girl. 'How has your day been?'

The man grunted in acknowledgement of the greeting but did not reply to the question. John guessed at the answer based on the man's enervated demeanour and ordered an ale.

As he waited for the girl to return, he racked his mind thinking of where to begin with this hulking, bewhiskered docker. When John was a child, he had the ability to talk to anyone for hours, quizzing them on their livelihoods and interests. He remembered vividly his mother hushing him constantly. Now, although he had excelled in disputation at Harvard, he found it painfully difficult to make 'small talk', as Joshua called it. He had spent too many of his formative years alone with Kirkcaldie, he supposed, a reluctant conversationalist at best. John felt he had lost the knack, perhaps never to regain the childhood confidence that made discourse so simple.

John stared at the man's large hands. They were calloused and knobbly, as though each finger had extra layers of muscle. His eyes moved along the man's arms towards the elbows where John noticed a tattoo of a compass on the underside of one forearm. It was an elaborate design, concentric, more reminiscent of a passionflower than an actual compass. John recalled an Indian in Nassau who had created similar designs on the skin of men using a thin chisel made from turtle shell.

'That's an interesting tattoo you have there,' John remarked. 'My father has a compass that is similar.'

The man raised his head. John read interest in his eyes.

'Is your father a seaman?'

'No, a surveyor.' John had kept Kirkcaldie's secret for nearly twenty years; he was not going to divulge his knowledge of Black Sam now, even if it might mean gaining a client.

When he noticed the man's curiosity waning, he added, 'But I went to Nassau once when I was a boy, with my grandfather who was a merchant. I remember seeing men with similar markings. It's the mark of a pirate, is it not?'

'To whom am I speaking?'

John offered his hand. 'John Kirkcaldie. Lawyer.'

The man's eyes instantly narrowed in suspicion.

'My colleague and I are here to canvass for business of the extremely ordinary variety – wronged workers, slandered neighbours, patients injured by unskilled doctors – but I have a personal interest in pirates, you see, especially those from Nassau. It is purely academic.'

Taking in John's sober clothing and round-rimmed spectacles, the man scoffed.

'Pirates are obsolete. Men like you, with your waistcoat and cravat, study us, passing judgement on our actions, our "crimes", without knowing the grounds on which we made our choices.'

'I apologise, Mister ...'

Remaining suspicious, the man did not offer his name.

'I am not ill informed. Quite the contrary, in fact. As I said, I spent much time in Nassau as a boy and have been among pirates. My position is entirely sympathetic, I can assure you.'

John removed a calling card from his pocket and offered it to the man. It was the first card he'd handed to anyone. Joshua had insisted on printing them, confident the three shillings they had spent in doing so would pay itself off with a steady stream of clients knocking at their door.

The man eyed the card. John looked towards Joshua. His colleague was involved in animated conversation with a docker, his hands wildly gesturing as he explained a point.

'I was pardoned.'

John's head immediately turned back to the pirate.

'A King's Pardon?' John asked. The man nodded.

John's mind flew to the newspaper the woodcutter had given him all those years before. Dated September 14, 1717, the front page had read 'Proclamation for Suppressing of Pirates.' Studying the article, John had discovered that King George I was willing to grant clemency to any pirate who surrendered themselves to a governor of the colonies by September 6, 1718. After that date, any pirate who neglected or failed to surrender was fair game for capture or trial. The Crown offered a reward of between 20 and 100 pounds (depending on the notoriety of the pirate) for the capture – or assistance in the capture – of any pirate after that date. As an added incentive, pirates were offered 200 pounds to turn in their captains.

After reading the article, John had pleaded with Kirk-caldie to surrender. Even though the time had expired, he had been certain the authorities would be lenient. With a pardon, Bellamy's name would have been cleared and the price on his head lifted. They could have lived as themselves, in freedom. Yet, perennially distrustful of the British Crown, Bellamy had refused.

'With whom did you sail?' John asked now.

'Charles Vane, Stede Bonnet for a time. At the end, Benjamin Hornigold.'

John's heart struck up a frantic rhythm and he struggled to remain composed. How he had grown to loathe that name and the man behind it. Kirkcaldie had never divulged the full circumstances surrounding Tamesine's death, but he had heard him discussing the matter with Mister Williams at the time. Even at nine years old, John had been bright enough to realise whose face was the last his mother had ever seen.

'Benjamin Hornigold, you say ...' John's breath was shallow, his head light.

'Aye,' the man replied. 'Hornigold convinced me and a few other in the crew to turn ourselves in. We surrendered together and were issued a pardon by the governor of Jamaica himself, Woodes Rogers. I sailed straight away for New England, hoping my knowledge of the seas would stand me in good stead with shipping companies and the like ...' He gazed into his ale. 'Unfortunately, the company directors did not view my skills in the same light as I. So for the last fifteen or so years I have been a docker, yearning for my life of old, realising it would have been preferable to die by the noose than live by the shackle.'

'And what became of Hornigold?' John asked.

'The bastard turned pirate hunter. He knew our haunts, the hidden bays and firths where our kind took refuge. He claimed a reward for each head he produced.'

John's heart lifted. 'Is he living?' If Hornigold was alive, John could find him and prosecute him for the murder of his mother.

'Nay, his ship was wrecked on a reef somewhere near New Spain.'

The man took a swig of his ale then wiped his mouth with the back of his hand.

'The turd went down with his ship.'

JOHN DEPARTED the tavern without informing Joshua. Wandering along Kilby Street, he was unaware in which direction he was heading. Years ago, before they had departed for Cape Cod, John had begged Bellamy to cease in his reckless pursuit of Hornigold. Finally, Bellamy had acquiesced. After meeting the pirate this evening, however, John wished Bellamy had not. Hornigold had gone down with his ship, an honourable death by a pirate's standards. He was never tried for the crimes he committed, nor for the atrocity of Tamesine's murder.

Watching Captain Grand fight, John had seen the fire of revenge in Bellamy's dark eyes and it had terrified him. But now he felt a stirring in his own belly, one unfamiliar to him. It was an unexpected sensation, not comfortable by any measure. He believed he may be experiencing a similar heat to the one Bellamy had all those years ago. He was unsure of whence the feeling came – but, in truth, he welcomed it.

4

TAMESINE: MADRON CARN

CORNWALL, JUNE 1705

When Tamesine reached the top of the carn, she was breathless. Her chest ached and her face still rippled with the force of her father's slap. Drawing in deep breaths, she wiped the tears and perspiration away with the flat of her hands. She looked at them, noticing a rosy tinge to the palette of her palms. Blood. Sitting on a rock overlooking Penzance and St Michael's Mount, she buried her head in her apron. Although she wanted to, needed to, it was impossible to stem the flow of tears that followed.

Tamesine tolerated the beatings because she had to, because her mother had tolerated them for years. Even at fifteen, she knew her father was not angry with her or her mother. He had been tied to a lugger – never his own – since he was a boy. Other fisherman in Madron loved the sea and life on a boat. Cleaning pilchards at the bay, Tamesine had heard these men regale in the life, sharing tales and memories as they mended driftnets. Her father was never one to join them, preferring to retreat to the alehouse as soon as his work was done. She often wondered what life he had dreamt for when he had been a young, soft-skinned boy.

Now his hands were chafed, his face gnawed to rags by wind, salt and rain.

She tolerated her father's anger because she understood the limits of his life and recognised his frustration – they mirrored her own. And they were choking. Tamesine looked at her blood-tinged hands, her heart saddening at the sight of them; they were already pink and raw from years of hard labour.

Few gifts were in her possession. All the village spoke of her beauty and she knew she was clever, learning numbers and letters at the knee of her granny when not yet five. But unless she married well, which was unlikely due to her humble family, her future was bleak. In her fantasies, Tamesine had been swept off her feet any number of times by the handsome son of the noble family who lived on St Michael's Mount. But these were just imaginings. Coal or fish were her choices. One day, she would be as angry as her father.

After a time, her tears stopped. Rising, she drew a bolstering breath and fixed her shawl around her shoulders. It was June but the wind blowing across the carn from Mount's Bay was as cold as a dog's nose.

She turned in a circle, taking in the bay and the seemingly endless moor, and noticed her sister striding towards her. Eseld's gait was unmistakeable. Not yet ten years old, she was already as tall as her older sister. Tamesine admired her gracefulness and poise. Eseld was the other reason Tamesine tolerated her father's furies; he had never laid a hand on the girl and Tamesine feared if she protested at her own mistreatment, fought back in any way, he might turn to her precious sister.

Eseld said nothing when she approached, but Tamesine

noticed she was holding a cap. Tamesine's hand went to her head. In her bitter sorrow, she had not noticed hers had been lost on her frenzied journey up the carn, probably plucked from her head by the mossy branch of a hawthorn tree. Eseld kept the cap clutched in her reedy fingers and slid her long slender arms around her sister's waist as if they were elegant ribbons. The pair embraced for some time before Eseld passed her the cap. Then she stood back and examined Tamesine's face.

'It's not noticeable,' she said, her voice small against the wind. 'Was there blood?'

'A little.'

Eseld nodded, concerned but unsurprised.

Tamesine's thick auburn hair blew like banners in the wind.

'It is wild,' Eseld laughed at the sight. The sound lifted Tamesine's spirits. 'As wild as the breeze that blows it.'

Tamesine secured her cap then took her sister's hand.

'*Meur ras*,' she said, smiling, wincing. Her lip stung. It was only the fisherman and their families who spoke Cornish now. Even Tamesine and Eseld were speaking it less often to each other.

'You are most welcome, m'lady,' Eseld replied, offering her sister a low, courtly bow. It was a game they often played to cheer their spirits – 'm'lady and m'lord'. Although their father did not approve, they felt there was no harm in pretending.

'I have been sent to seek you out,' Eseld continued in a cultured voice. 'A third rate ship of the line has laid anchor in Penzance harbour. The captain has requested permission to come ashore.'

'Is that so?' Tamesine replied lifting her chin haughtily

and rubbing her hand theatrically across it, contemplating the appeal.

'As high sheriff, you are the only person in the land who can grant his request.'

'Escort me to the ... what is this ship's name, m'lord?' Tamesine inquired, looking down her nose with distaste.

'The *Greyhound*, m'lady,' Eseld answered with a slight bow.

'Then pray escort me to the *Greyhound* ...'

With a small flourish, Eseld offered her arm. Tamesine accepted it with a gracious nod before continuing.

'... and we shall see if this captain is worthy of stepping foot onto our blessed shore.'

Eseld bowed again then the two made their way through the soft, lush heather towards to the harbour.

5
____

AUGUSTA, MAINE

1735

Kirkcaldie gazed at the nine-year-old boy before him by the hearth and attempted to recall John at that age. He had been talkative and excitable, with the gravelly voice of an older man, yet serious at times too, contemplative, as though he understood things more deeply than other children. Through circumstance, Tamesine's boy had become his son and Kirkcaldie thought of him as such, loved him as such. Even though John was now a man of nearly eight and twenty, Kirkcaldie would still lay down his life for him without a second's thought. Familiar with each other's moods and whimsies, they were as close as any father and son could be, without the connection of blood forever bonding them. Kirkcaldie even believed that John had grown to resemble him in appearance in certain ways.

It was only four o'clock by Kirkcaldie's timepiece, but the parlour was already darkening. Candles had not yet been lit and the flames in the hearth shot flickering shadows across the boy's face. Kirkcaldie gazed, lost in his own thoughts, at the heavy snowfall outside.

The boy presented him with a twist of rope. It was a reef knot. He had taught the young lad to tie it on his last visit.

'What do you think, Kirkcaldie?' the child asked, warily.

Kirkcaldie turned and examined the rope seriously for some time before responding.

'Excellent work.' He rubbed the boy's head. His hair was as soft as a bank of moneywort.

'Do it once more so you are sure to remember it, then I will teach you another.'

The boy unknotted the rope then began to tie it again, his pink tongue protruding slightly from the corner of his mouth in concentration.

Kirkcaldie lay back on the rug and considered the boy. Bellamy was the child's name. He had inherited his father's dark features, although his hair was the colour of his mother's. If one looked closely, there was no mistaking him as Kirkcaldie's offspring, although it was never acknowledged or spoken of. And, although never one to stand by tradition, Maria had named the baby after his father. Alike Kirkcaldie in appearance, Bell, however, possessed the identical lightness of spirit and serene curiosity that had drawn Samuel Bellamy to Maria Hallett all those years ago.

Apart from the occasional slip of the tongue by Palgrave, Sam Bellamy had been known as 'Kirkcaldie' for over fifteen years. Even John had come to call him by that name. Always wary, ever watchful and unfailingly distrustful, he still feared his past would return to haunt him. To Bell, he was 'Kirkcaldie' also; a friend of the family who visited three or four times a year when he was travelling through Augusta. The boy did not know of his lineage.

Kirkcaldie was rarely at his own home outside Hallowell. The Crown had ordered the governor to push further west. Because of this, as the governor's surveyor, he was afforded little rest. When, periodically, he did return to the house he had built, it seemed too large for one man alone. He had built it for John, to give him the home that Tamesine had always hoped to provide for her son. Then, once John had moved to Boston only a few years later, he'd had another person in mind with whom to share the space, although he hadn't realised it until it was too late. But it was still his house. He found some comfort in its familiarity, and the bluestone wall he had built by hand had weathered nicely, dotted with velvety moss and lichen as it was.

Bell finished tying the knot and showed it to him.

'Very good,' Kirkcaldie said. 'And do you remember the name of this one?'

'It is called a "reef knot". Right over left then left over right then pull tight.'

Kirkcaldie nodded, smiling. 'Now I will teach you a clove hitch.'

Maria entered the room with a tray holding cups, a teapot and some sort of sweet treat Kirkcaldie could not discern. She wore her hair free, allowing it to flow to her hips in gentle, golden waves. She never wore a cap as was the custom. Although she had grown older, Kirkcaldie considered her more beautiful now than when he first noticed her on the meeting house green in Eastham all those years before. Motherhood suited her. It was as though Maria was now in possession of a quality she had been lacking – contentedness.

As Maria poured tea, Kirkcaldie began to manipulate the rope into a clove hitch.

It had taken him some years to realise that he and Maria had been connected, deeply so, ever since that sweltering noontide on the green, before the sea, before Captain Grand, before everything. Kirkcaldie believed he had loved

Maria then, but what he felt when he looked at her now was a sensation so much deeper and more profound. Since they met again a decade ago, those feelings had resurfaced and had gradually changed, moulded by time and experience. After all, they were entirely different people to those who had met in Eastham nearly twenty years ago. Despite the considerable length of their relationship, they had only laid with each other once, a moment in time that still seemed like a strange dream to Kirkcaldie even now. The result: the handsome child sitting before him.

'Tea is ready,' Maria called. 'There are biscuits too.'

Bell sprang to his feet like an arrow and waited for Kirkcaldie to rise, offering his hand.

Kirkcaldie eyed Maria fleetingly then attempted to rise to his feet with equal vigour, ignoring his son's offer of assistance.

'There are only two cups.' Kirkcaldie noted, disappointed, smoothing his silver-flecked hair. 'Will you not be joining us?'

Bell stood between the adults, gazing at one then the other in quiet fascination.

'Not today. There is a project I must see to before you depart tomorrow.' She looked down and touched her son's cheek then made to leave.

Kirkcaldie grabbed her hand lightly, halting her departure. Her skin was hot from having handled the teapot; Kirkcaldie noted it was also host to a spectacular array of colour.

'A painting?'

Maria nodded, meeting his gaze with a smile before leaving the room.

～

AFTER SUPPER, still feeling slighted and disheartened Maria had not joined them for tea, Kirkcaldie intended to tell his son and Patience a story before they went to sleep to raise his spirits. Drawing on his days of piracy and prize fighting, he could usually embellish an episode from his own life in a convincing manner. The chase and capture of the *Whydah*; the mutiny of Benjamin Hornigold; the felling of the woodcutter Big Jacob O'Leary; each tale featured Black Sam or Captain Grand as the courageous hero.

However, this night the children begged him to read them a book they had recently acquired called *A Description of Three Hundred Animals*. An encyclopaedia of sorts, the heavy tome chronicled all beasts of the earth, from porcupines and bees to griffins and manticores. Both children gathered close to him, examining the richly detailed illustrations as he read. Kirkcaldie enjoyed their soft, sweet breath on his whiskered cheek and the way they gripped his arm when frightened by the artist's depiction of a hideous, mythical creature.

Soon Kirkcaldie found himself enjoying the writing, although he did not appreciate the moralistic tone of the book – man's superiority over beasts and God's dominion over all creatures. He briefly wondered why Leah had purchased it, knowing her scepticism towards the Church.

When he felt Patience's head resting heavily on his shoulder, he closed the book and tucked the children into the bed they shared. It had belonged to Patience's older brother Joseph. The child who had once idolised Samuel Bellamy was now a grown man with a family of his own, a maker of clocks and watches, living in town. Kirkcaldie marvelled at how quickly the years had passed.

Despite Palgrave's hopes for his son, Joseph's temperament had not been suited to the rigidity of Harvard. Anyone could see Joseph was not a scholar, but his father had wanted for his eldest son everything that he himself had been denied as a young man. But to Kirkcaldie's eye, Joseph now made the finest timepieces in the colonies; he had not only inherited his father's stature but his attention to detail as well.

In stockinged feet, Kirkcaldie tiptoed down the stairs and joined Palgrave in his study. On his way, he could hear Leah and Maria in the kitchen discussing, in business-like tones, plans for the morning as Sarah prepared the table for breakfast. The women took turns in schooling the children each day and they took their roles extremely seriously. He enjoyed listening to the melody of their voices, savouring the opportunity to hear Maria speak unobserved.

Palgrave was at his desk when he entered the room, back hunched over a ledger, his quill scratching a lively tempo. Kirkcaldie had forgotten to knock and the oversight troubled him momentarily. Palgrave was not concerned with the liberty, barely even noticing his friend's arrival in the room. It occasionally felt to Kirkcaldie as though Palgrave still viewed him as the captain and himself as the quartermaster. However, the truth was that Palgrave was the absolute master and commander of his domain; Kirkcaldie often felt like a pollywog, floundering his way through life as green as when he first joined the crew of the *Royal Sovereign* when still a boy.

'Sit down,' Palgrave uttered without raising his head from his work. 'I will pour you a drink in a moment.'

'Rum?'

'What else?'

Kirkcaldie laughed quietly but did not sit, instead he took a spot by the window, his gaze drawn to the lights of Palgrave's distillery. It was situated away from the house, closer to the river where the movement of goods and supplies to and from Portland was easier to manage.

Palgrave had fostered many businesses since leaving Cape Cod and moving to Augusta but he seemed especially proud of his distillery, Eight Bells. When he had built the distillery and hired a distiller five years before, he boasted to Kirkcaldie that Eight Bells would be the finest rum in New England, unlike the raw and aggressive liquor colonists typically consumed. Palgrave had sourced the sweetest molasses from Martinique and Trinidad, ordered the barrels from Essex County – each a single-use cask, untainted by the stink of salt cod or nails – and found the distiller, a native of Barbados, who came from a family that had been producing rum for a century.

It had been a costly exercise, he had explained to Kirkcaldie. The distilling shed, the new oak casks and housing the distiller and his family were a great expense. However, the benefits far outweighed his investment. Molasses was cheap, so cheap that, despite the production costs, a handsome profit could be made. Into the bargain, there was a ready market for New England lumber and wheat in the French and Spanish West Indies. Due to his singular devotion to his vision for a quality rum, Palgrave had, over the last five years, created a lucrative trade route for himself.

After a few minutes Palgrave laid down his quill, rubbing his forehead as he stood.

'What troubles you?' Bellamy asked, noticing the leaden gravity of Palgrave's demeanour.

Palgrave sighed and removed his spectacles, pinching the top of his thin nose.

'The duty enforced two years ago by the Molasses Act has gradually eaten away most of the gains I have made from Eight Bells. The tax is grossly unjust and nothing more than a means by which the Crown can control trade in the colonies.'

Palgrave poured two cups of the spirit, offering one to Bellamy.

'What's more,' he continued, 'even the producers of the poorest rum have been forced into absurd price rises, meaning the market for a quality rum such as mine has shrunken to less than a third. Within a fortnight the distillery will be running at a loss.'

'Cut your losses,' Kirkcaldie offered matter-of-factly. 'You can put it down to poor timing.' He took a sip of the rum and smiled. 'Ah, but it would be a great shame. Eight Bells is an exceptionally good drop.'

Palgrave slumped in a chair.

'It's not so easy. I have invested handsomely in the venture. The losses I will suffer – the losses my investors with suffer ... well, it does not bear thinking of, truth be told.'

After refilling their glasses, Kirkcaldie sat down opposite his friend. As they sipped the golden liquid, bright and clean as crystal, they were silent, contemplative, each searching for a solution. Thinking on the situation, Kirkcaldie's ire slowly began to rise. It was a sensation he had not felt for some years, not since Tabby's trial a decade ago. What was happening to Palgrave was a great injustice. Kirkcaldie recognised that the efforts of entrepreneurial and philanthropic colonists like his friend, who had brought employment and prosperity to Massachusetts, who aided those in need, were being unfairly thwarted by an ever-greedy King.

After a moment, Kirkcaldie spoke.

'What happened in the past when trade routes were blocked to ordinary men, when the Crown attempted to control all the wealth in the world at the expense of the common man?'

Palgrave eyes rose from his drink. He looked at his friend dubiously.

'You cannot be serious … Piracy?'

Kirkcaldie lifted an eyebrow. 'Not in so many words …'

Palgrave laughed, a little too much it occurred to Kirkcaldie. It was the laugh of one attempting to talk himself out of a particular notion.

'I'm flattered that you think me capable of turning pirate once more, but I have too much at stake. And, might I remind you, so do you!'

'Not piracy, my dear friend.'

'Then what?'

A smile curled across Kirkcaldie's lips.

'Smuggling.'

6

BOSTON, MASSACHUSETTS

1735

Joshua returned to John's room in the afternoon. He did not scold the elder partner for leaving the Marlborough Arms without a word for he was in good spirits. He was accompanied by the man John had spotted his friend talking to at the tavern, before he had learnt of Hornigold's fate and fled.

The stranger's arm was in a sling, his coat covering only one arm and shoulder. It hung precariously off the other – an unfortunate injury for the season, John thought.

'Go on, Sir. Please tell Mister Kirkcaldie what you told me,' Joshua encouraged, attempting to usher him into the room. Their potential new client was apprehensive and hung in the doorway.

John gestured to a seat by the stove. Finally, the man entered and sat.

His name was Felix Schleck, a German who had a tale to tell that was not dissimilar to William Tander's. Injured at the docks when a hogshead of cacao had dropped on his arm, the company bonesetter had bandaged the arm but did not splint it, advising the suffering patient to drink brandy if the pain became unbearable. That was more than three weeks ago.

Now, with the pain so intense, Schleck spent the good part of every day in a tavern, his funds dwindling fast. The man explained it would not be long before he could not afford the tonic the bonesetter had prescribed, and Mistress Schleck was naturally growing irritable with the situation.

Schleck was a genial man with a smooth, round face and very little hair, making his age difficult to discern. His English was paltry. However, John and Joshua had adequate knowledge of the German language. Andreas Gryphius was a poet much appreciated at Harvard.

John observed Schleck wince each time he shifted in his seat. From the knowledge he had gleaned when ministering to Captain Grand, he knew that if the limb was broken it needed to be splinted.

When Schleck finished, John spoke.

'I see. And this happened more than three weeks ago, you say?'

'*Ja, Dezember dreiundswanzig,*' Schleck replied. 'Two days before Christmas,' he added in English. It was clear he felt the timing of the injury made the situation all the worse.

John rose, pressing his hands firmly in his pockets. It was a gesture with which Joshua was well versed and translated as, 'I have an idea'.

'Mister Williams, would you please run out to the docks and discover the name of the bonesetter used by the Dutch East India Company?'

Joshua nodded in understanding. There were probably other men who had suffered at the hands of this bonesetter – and would likely translate into more clients. He rose.

'In the meantime, I will determine the nature of Mister Schleck's broken arm.'

Schleck looked to Joshua in alarm.

'Do not fear, Mister Schleck. Mister Kirkcaldie has a fair knowledge of medicine, more so, I would wager, than the man who attempted to mend you.'

Joshua tipped his hat to the both of them and departed.

'Please, Mister Schleck,' John said, leaning over the man, indicating that he would like to examine him. Schleck offered his arm immediately, proving himself a far more cooperative patient than Kirkcaldie had ever been.

Slowly, John unwrapped the bandage. With each movement, even the slightest, the poor man winced again in pain. Before the arm had entirely revealed itself, John could already tell by the odour that it had not healed.

'*Der geruch!*' Schleck exclaimed, gasping at the stench.

John explored the arm, lifting it gently.

'*Gangraina*', he murmured in Greek. '"That which eats away."'

The blood drained from Schleck's face. '*Gangrän?*'

John nodded.

A surgeon was called, a classmate from Harvard, Doctor Jonathan Rice. Rice surmised that the ulna had been most likely shattered, the bone fragments causing the putrefaction. It was decided that the arm should be amputated above the elbow immediately. Schleck appeared at peace with the notion; John supposed the poor man was simply eager to be rid of the pain. He had witnessed many men in Nassau make a living and get on in the world quite well without the use of an arm or leg.

Before Rice departed with Schleck, the doctor agreed to testify to the severity of the injury and the shoddy treatment the patient had received by the bonesetter, should the case go before a judge. It was likely, however, that the Dutch East India Company would agree to a settlement.

'I had a quick word to a few men at the docks about this bonesetter,' Joshua said on his return. 'No-one has ever heard a complaint about him, although the three I spoke to agreed that he was an *unusual* type ...'

He handed John a slip of paper. On it was written the name and whereabouts of the man in question.

'Unusual?'

Joshua nodded. 'Outspoken and temperamental was the sense I received of his character.'

Frowning, John pushed the slip of paper into his trouser pocket. Joshua, keen to begin their new case, removed his cloak and coat, then sat at the bureau and began to pen a petition for the court.

THE SURGERY and recovery would be painful, John surmised, but Schleck would live. The Dutch East India Company would pay; Joshua's intimate knowledge of the law and his artful use of language would see to that. However, John could not rid himself of the sense that an enormous moral injustice had been committed by the company's bonesetter. He knew that, while the man might not be a physician, anyone employed by an establishment as reputed as the Dutch East India Company would be expected to be skilled at their profession. *Surely,* John thought, *a bonesetter would not be a quack?* He was perplexed at the notion of why, if setting bones was the man's bread and butter, he had carried out the task so poorly.

Leaving Joshua to his work, John shrugged on his coat

and departed, not sure where he was heading, only knowing for certain that he needed the biting nip of a winter's afternoon to bolster his morale. Pushing his hands in his trouser pockets, his fingers found the slip of paper Joshua had thrust at him earlier.

Henry Bowman
56 Summer Street

Without clear intent, John turned and began walking in the bonesetter's direction.

JOHN KNOCKED at the door and stood waiting, scraping his feet of the snow they had acquired on the short walk from King Street. If and when the door opened, he was not sure what he would say to Bowman – not sure if his spirit required a confrontation or a mere explanation. Either way, Bowman needed to be made aware of the seriousness of the injury caused by his maltreatment.

He was about to knock a second time when a man opened the door. Neatly attired, with a pressed handkerchief in his vest pocket, he stood waiting for John to speak. John noticed that Bowman's moustache and beard were neatly clipped.

'Are you Henry Bowman?' he inquired.

'Indeed.'

'My name is John Kirkcaldie. I am a lawyer and I would like to speak with you about a patient you visited on the 23rd of December last year – Mister Felix Schleck.'

Bowman's eyes showed no recollection of the name.

'A German,' John prompted. 'A docker ... his arm was crushed under a pipe.'

Shuffling uneasily in the doorway, the bonesetter squinted in thought and rubbed his chin. John could see that Bowman now recalled Schleck, but he was attempting (quite inadequately) to conceal the fact. John's experience with liars was vast, especially inept ones. He was extremely fortunate; he had been raised by the best liar of them all.

None of the thieves, adulterers, forgers and fraudsters John came in contact with each day, whether to defend them or prosecute them, possessed skills equal to Kirkcaldie's. When Bellamy had become Kirkcaldie, their lives, their future had depended on that lie. He had devoted much time to contriving an alternate past, a different background for them both. The pair had spent hours, long journeys ensuring the details of their new story was in tune with their old, should they ever be questioned. There could be no missteps, Kirkcaldie had warned, for that would mean certain death.

John remembered questions, followed by answers, followed by more questions. So dedicated was his mentor to the task that John surmised Kirkcaldie had come to believe, to a degree, his own fabrications. He had witnessed Kirkcaldie lie to woodsmen and governors alike without the trace of a tell.

Now, in comparison to Kirkcaldie, Bowman was a rank amateur, a pantomime villain.

'I will have to check my notes,' Bowman declared in a crisp, clean accent suggestive of education and good breeding. But John could tell by the unnatural way Bowman moved his mouth that this accent had been cultivated. Before the man could close the door, John wedged his foot between it and the wall and offered Bowman a reassuring smile.

'May I step inside out of the cold?' John gave a shiver to indicate the chill in the air.

He sensed Bowman brace himself. However, feigning calm, the man allowed him entry. John followed Bowman to the parlour.

As they passed the kitchen, John peered inside, noting only two saucepans hanging above the hearth. There was no homely scent of supper drifting through the hallways, no pot simmering on the fire.

Judging by the ill-matched furniture that graced the parlour and the tallow candles burning on the mantel, Bowman was not well-to-do by any means. There were no paintings or samplers on the walls or embroidered blankets on chairs. Neither books nor adornments graced the table that stood in the centre of the parlour, the surface of which was littered with documents, accounts and reckonings.

If asked, John would wager there was no Mistress Bowman. Still, the terrace dwelling seemed comfortable, if sparse.

The bonesetter sat on a chair and rifled through a green-backed ledger. Loose papers had been crammed between its pages. He carried out this task on his lap, clearly reluctant to disturb the bills on the table. A paper fell to the floor, a pamphlet of some sort. Before John could reach for it, Bowman quickly swiped the document off the floor and scrunched it in his fist. Glancing briefly at John, the man pushed the crumpled ball into his pocket then returned his attention to the ledger.

Eyeing the disarray on the table, John grew curious. *Why is that particular document so offensive?* he wondered. As he considered Bowman's behaviour, he strolled to the window. There was dust on the sill at least a quarter inch thick. *Definitely no Mistress Bowman*, thought John. He turned, returning his gaze to the bonesetter.

After a few minutes, the man's head lifted towards him.

'I have no record of a Mister Schleck and I keep very well-ordered notes of all my patients,' Bowman said.

John lifted an eyebrow. The unruly nature of the ledger suggested otherwise.

'I see,' he replied. 'However, the foreman on duty during Mister Schleck's shift assured my colleague that at the time of the incident – the 23rd of December at nine o'clock in the evening – his records state that it was you who came to the dock to attend to Mister Schleck. In fact, he remembered the evening very well. It seems that after your ministrations were complete, you remained with him until the early hours of the morning. "Chatting", he claims.'

Bowman cleared his throat. Rose. Placed the ledger on the table.

'I assure you, Mister Kirkcaldie, that the foreman must be mistaken. And, if he is the foreman of whom I believe you speak, he is a drunkard, known to drink at least a quart of rum during his shift. His word should not be taken for gospel.'

'You've never shared a drop with him after tending to a patient?'

'I have not touched a drop of liquor in more than twelve years.'

John did not reply. He nodded, thinking. Bowman, for all his faults, had a good point. If the foreman was known for drinking, his word could not be relied upon. Even though John was certain the foreman was telling the truth, a judge would not see it that way. John rocked back on his heels.

'Quite right, Mister Bowman. I'm terribly sorry to have disturbed you,' he said pleasantly. 'The foreman is clearly a drinker. The chances of him being confused are high indeed. Of course, I assume that the East India Company have other bonesetters in their employ?'

Bowman nodded in agreement.

'Then I will be on my way,' John said, turning towards the door. A few feet short of the hallway, he stopped and turned. 'Before I leave, might I trouble you for a cup of cider or ale? I have been traipsing all over the town since midday looking for you.' He laughed good-naturedly. 'I find myself quite parched.'

Clearly willing a hasty exit on the lawyer, Bowman obliged and left the room at a trot. When John was certain his host had reached the kitchen, he made his way quickly to the ledger and flicked through the pages. The date was written on the top right of each page in a mannerly cursive.

December 23, 1734

Lower right arm of immigrant docker, Felix Schleck was injured under the weight of a half-ton pipe. Arm was limp under preliminary examination. When held to the ear, the crepitus indicated a break in several places along the radius and ulna. Patient was in immense pain. Administered laudanum. When patient quieted, arm was bandaged.

John turned the page, hoping for more explanation. Bowman suspected, was certain even, that the arm was broken in more than one place based on the grating sound he noted within the arm, yet no splint was applied. If he thought the arm had been crushed (which he surely did) the arm should have been amputated immediately. More disturbing was the fact that Bowman had kept a record of his maltreatment. John was perplexed by the discovery. He could ascertain no reason as to why the man would allow written evidence of his crime to remain.

Hearing Bowman's footsteps in the hallway, John quickly closed the ledger and returned to his position by the door.

7

TAMESINE: GOLOWAN

CORNWALL, 1705

So desperate were the girls to join the celebrations that Tamesine and Eseld departed the cottage immediately after morning board. Their father had given his permission for them to attend the annual Golowan festivities in Penzance, as long as their chores for that morning were finished (Tamesine and Eseld had sat by candlelight milking Old Wenna and Meraud) and they returned while there was enough daylight to finish the evening round of duties as well.

Fortunately, it was the longest day of the year. *There are so many hours between now and sunset,* thought Tamesine as she strolled arm in arm with Eseld towards Penzance, *that it will be an eternity before we'll need to return home.* Midsummer brought with it glorious long days that stretched out deliciously like warm, soft toffee.

While their father's demands meant they would need to leave before the bonfire was lit and the barrel rolling began, Tamesine accepted her father's unexpected charity without complaint. Their mother had packed them cheese and bread in a basket, along with a beaker of cider made from the season's dufflin apples the girls had picked themselves.

The sun was still low in the sky when they departed. But by the time they were skipping happily northward along the headland, it was as sharp as hot needles. Both girls removed their shawls and pushed them into the basket that held the day's viands. Tamesine rolled up the sleeves of her blouse in order to feel the warmth on her arms. Within a few miles of Penzance, their journey seemed to gather momentum as more and more people joined the route. Appearing from all directions, revellers were drawn into the current heading towards the festivities. The girls looked at each other and smiled as the steady flow quickly became a fast-running stream and the sisters delighted at being carried along by the pulse of the crowd.

Feverish with excitement, Tamesine and Eseld were almost at a sprint as they entered the town through a tumbling cascade of red and blue ribbons. They halted, laughing, clutching at each other. Tamesine's cap had come loose once again; it was forever bothering her. She tore it from her head and stuffed it into the basket, her dark auburn locks falling across her shoulders and down her back.

'Put your cap on, Tamesine,' Eseld advised in a low voice. Tamesine frowned. 'If someone were to see you and tell Mamm ...'

Tamesine rolled her eyes at her sister's prudence but realising it was the correct counsel, reached into her basket and took out her cap. As she did, the wind snatched it from her fingertips and blew it high into the air, the cloth billowing like a sail. The girls watched its woeful flight and subsequent descent at the feet of a naval officer who stood not twenty yards from the pair at a stall that sold hevva cake.

The officer, not more than twenty-one, Tamesine surmised, stared bemusedly at the cap for a time. He looked up into the sky in a confused fashion as though believing the item may have fallen from the heavens. Eventually, he bent to the ground and retrieved it. The Lieutenant looked around and instantly noticed the sisters, staring in dismay at the cap in his hand. It was Tamesine he looked at first, and Tamesine's pretty face he continued to gaze on until the lady at the stall reminded him of the cake he had cupped in his hand.

With some difficulty, encumbered as he was with cap and cake, he hastily placed a coin on the stall then immediately walked towards Tamesine. He removed his cocked hat and slipped it under his arm awkwardly, then offered her a bow.

'Although it will pain me immensely to see your glorious hair reined in, I return this to you as I believe, although I have only been in Cornwall for a matter of weeks, that it is the polite custom of this land for young ladies to don a cap.'

Tamesine reached out and took the offered garment.

'Thank you, Sir,' she replied with a slight curtsey.

The officer was handsome in a quiet way with dark green eyes that smiled at her, belying his seriousness. All the same, he was as bold as the gleaming brass buttons on his royal blue undress coat. His comment about her hair told her that. Tamesine was instantly overcome with a heady mix of excitement and fear.

'My name is Lieutenant John King of Her Majesty's Royal Navy,' he announced. 'Are your mother and father about? It would be fitting that I introduce myself.'

Eseld remained silent. Although she appeared older than her ten years, she was shy towards those she did not know and always looked to her older sister to take the lead.

'My sister and I have come alone from our home in Mousehole to spend the day here,' Tamesine replied, gesturing behind her towards the direction of her village.

'Muzzel?' he responded. 'I have thrice studied all the maps of this area and I have never seen such a name written on any.'

'Englishmen would say "Mousehole" – as in the hole of a mouse,' Tamesine explained in the same accent she used when playing m'lady and m'lord, rounding her vowels appropriately.

'Are you not English?'

'We consider ourselves Cornish.'

'Oh, I see,' he replied, interested. 'That makes sense. Land's End seems a million miles away from the rest of England in custom, language, even frame of mind. Take this celebration for instance.' He looked about him in wonder at the dancers, musicians and the carefree nature of it all. 'It would not be possible where I come from in Surrey. Everyone is too well-bred ...'

'*Dar?!*' Tamesine interrupted, sternly.

King blushed and Tamesine regretted her interjection.

'Although I do not know what that means, I am taking it for a rebuke on my careless turn of phrase. I do apologise.' He bowed again.

'*Gava dhe nebonan,*' she said gently.

King looked at her, confused.

'She forgives you,' Eseld whispered.

'Thank you,' King whispered in response, smiling.

The three stood silently among the crowd for a moment, occasionally jostled and butted. The numbers were growing and the parade would begin soon – it was clearly time to part ways, but it seemed impossible. Finally, King spoke.

'May I act as your escort in Penzance? Two young ladies

on a day of such revelry and carousing should not be alone. If you were to receive a fright or worse ...' He frowned. 'Well, I would not be able to forgive myself.'

Lieutenant John King of Her Majesty's Royal Navy seemed genuinely concerned about them. It struck Tamesine that nobody, apart from Eseld, had ever been overly concerned with her welfare. She was seen as labour by her father and mother who worried more about the work she was capable of achieving than her physical and spiritual comfort. There was very little unsolicited kindness in Tamesine's life.

Tamesine looked at her sister then quickly examined the Lieutenant's flawless white breeches and the brass buttons on his coat glinting in the sunlight. Her fears were immediately allayed.

'Thank you, Sir. Your generosity is most appreciated.'

Lieutenant King nodded. 'May I ask your names?'

'Eseld,' the young girl replied, bobbing into a curtsey.

'Tamesine,' her sister said, offering her hand.

8

———

AUGUSTA, MAINE

As Maria walked towards the stable, she passed her brother on his way back to the house. His expression was queer, it seemed to her – thoughtful with a hint of dread, as though waiting for a storm to pass and wondering at the damage. Palgrave nodded, smiled.

'I'll see you at breakfast, Sister,' he said, distracted.

Maria wondered what had just passed to make her brother appear so at odds.

When she entered the stable, she stood for a moment in the doorway, watching Kirkcaldie prepare his horse for his departure. He was meticulous, taking care to make sure the stirrups, bridle and halter were just to his liking. The snow had ceased sometime during the night, but the morning was overcast and Kirkcaldie had lit a lamp to work by. Maria could smell the burning paraffin, an offensive odour but one she admitted to liking. The lamp cast his face in shadow. *A reflection of his state of mind*, she conjectured. She had observed over the years that Kirkcaldie did not take leaving well. His woe affected her as well, and Bell in turn. He had never voiced it, but Maria knew Kirkcaldie longed to be a father to his son. For her part, this visit she had hoped the snow would not relent and his departure might be delayed for a day or two.

When he was finished, he stroked the beast's muzzle for a time then laughed quietly to himself, quite unexpectedly, slightly embarrassed, as though a private joke had captured his thoughts. Since his 'resurrection', she had noted, Kirkcaldie did not laugh often or even smile very willingly, except for when he was in the company of his son. When she had first met him, Bellamy's smile was always at the ready, like a bird when it spies scattered corn.

'What amuses you so?' Maria asked.

Kirkcaldie turned, surprised by her presence. 'It's nothing.' His mirth disappeared like a daydream. 'Merely something Palgrave suggested. You know how he can be.'

Maria walked further into the stable, wishing to invite conversation. She was carrying a package, wrapped in cloth.

'No, I do not know how he can be. Pray, tell me.'

Kirkcaldie wiped his hands on a rag then hung it over the stall's wall. 'Romantic.'

'How so?'

'It's nothing,' he repeated, walking towards her. 'What do you have there?' he asked, noticing her baggage and clearly wishing to change the subject.

'It's a gift, for you, from Bell and I.'

She handed Kirkcaldie the package and he removed the covering. It was a portrait of Bell. In it, the boy was sitting by the river on a hillock, a length of rope in his hands, his face locked in concentration as he tied a knot. The pink tip of his tongue protruded slightly from his plump, rosy lips. The portrait was unlike her other works and Maria was anxious, awaiting Kirkcaldie's reaction. There were no sweeping swirls of turmoil or swathes of darkness. It was light, the river hued in laurel green, the sky a remarkable shade of blue. The child's face was lifelike, rendered more natural by the detail – the smattering of freckles on his nose and the stubborn curl on the crown of his head that refused to obey and insisted on poking up like a rooster's comb. Bell appeared beatific and true to life all at once. Maria had not painted in such a whimsical style since before it all began.

It seemed to her that Kirkcaldie took an age to react and her heart beat a furious rhythm in her panic. Months it had taken her to perfect the portrait and she wanted him not only to appreciate the image but also the sentiment behind the work.

'You have captured his likeness so well,' Kirkcaldie said eventually. He appeared to speak with some difficulty. 'Thank you.'

It was a favourable response but not the one Maria had been yearning for.

Glancing at her, Kirkcaldie noted the disappointment in her expression.

'I would like to say more, darling Maria, but I fear anything further may be unbefitting our relationship.' He kept his eyes on the portrait. 'Rest assured, however, I will keep this gift close to my heart. Always.' Kirkcaldie cleared his throat and turned back to the stall where his horse awaited its rider.

Maria walked outside, underwhelmed and confused by his response. *Darling Maria? Befitting our relationship?* She frowned, drew her shawl around her and crossed her arms at her breast.

When had she become his 'darling' and why did he assume that he was not hers? These were the questions swirling like a murmuration through her mind. Although they shared a child, she and Kirkcaldie had been nothing more than friends for ten years. He spent a greater amount of time with Palgrave than he did with her when he visited Augusta.

When she had begun the portrait of their son, her motive had not been clear in her own mind. However, as the work progressed and Bell's likeness took shape, Maria came to understand her inspiration fully. She had loved Kirkcaldie for so long. But she was wary, fearing that to open her heart to him once more might mean that the rebuilding of herself she had achieved would be for naught. Now, as she stood in the snow, her feet stinging in the cold, she realised that she was ready. Since Bell's birth, her trust had slowly blossomed like the first crocuses in spring. Maria had hoped the portrait would be a key to reopen a door that had been sealed for an age.

Kirkcaldie departed an hour later following breakfast with the family, during which time he informed them that he was travelling directly to Boston to visit John. He embraced Bell warmly, fixed the portrait securely to his pack, mounted Dobbin then departed at a canter down the long gravel drive.

'It would be quicker by ship, my friend,' Palgrave called, laughing. It was advice he gave his friend each time he departed.

Men find comfort in making light of their deepest fears, thought Maria. She well understood why Kirkcaldie now refused to travel by water. That night on the beach in Wellfleet, during the storm, Maria had felt Bellamy's terror. Hoops of steel had tightened around her body.

Kirkcaldie did not look back, merely held his hand aloft

and within a minute the family lost sight of him. Bell and Patience followed him at a trot down the drive, then Sarah at a measured pace, ensuring her sister and cousin did not come to harm. Kirkcaldie would bid them a final adieu at the gate.

Maria, Leah and Palgrave were left standing outside the house, all three feeling bereft. Kirkcaldie's visits lifted everyone's spirits, even those of Leah who had never approved of the man, although now his presence did not irk her as much as it once had. However, she could easily see how her husband's demeanour brightened whenever his friend was nearby.

Maria sighed. 'I had an unusual conversation with Kirkcaldie this morning.'

Husband and wife glanced at each other.

'Oh, yes,' Leah replied.

'He informed me that you, Palgrave, had made a suggestion ... A "romantic" suggestion. It was clear he did not wish to divulge anything further. I am intrigued, though, for his reaction to your suggestion, whatever that might have been, was interesting.'

Palgrave smiled. 'Yes ... I counselled him to marry you, make a home with you and have more children with you.'

Maria felt a blush quickly rise from her chest, skitter up her neck and settle in her cheeks. *What must Kirkcaldie have thought?* she asked herself. If she partook in magics, she would surely sew up her brother's jabbering mouth that instant using her most secure backstitch.

'Matchmaking?' she cried in consternation.

'Sister, despite your uncommon history,' Leah interrupted, 'you and Kirkcaldie should realise your suitability as a match. What's more, you love each other. Any fool can see it. Even Bell ...'

Maria looked at her sister aghast. 'Has he spoken of it?'

'Not in so many words, but he loves and admires the both of you. It's not unusual for a boy to yearn for a father and to long for his mother's happiness,' Leah explained. 'Bell made the match a long time ago in his imagination.'

Maria's gaze turned to her son. Bell and Patience's journey back to the house was taken at a much slower pace, the cousins stooping to collect pebbles and rocks then hurling them at trees. They would give especially interesting specimens to Sarah for examination. The adults watched them for a moment, all wandering how to proceed. Finally, it was Palgrave who broke the silence.

'Maria, perhaps it is time that you and Kirkcaldie tell one another everything you have not yet shared about your lives. There is much that has been left unspoken between the two of you.'

He looked at his sister gravely.

'Then, and only then, will you be able to make a decision regarding your suitability.'

Leah offered her sister a fleeting, comforting embrace then she and Palgrave entered the house.

As Maria waited for Sarah and the children to reach her, she thought on Palgrave's counsel. Kirkcaldie was aware of some of the trials she had faced in the time he was absent – Silas, her father's downfall and her poor baby – but what had he endured himself? Maria had overheard the stories he told to Bell and Patience involving Black Sam and Captain Grand; by the vividness with which the tales were told she'd surmised they were drawn from real life. And, of course, Leah had informed her of Palgrave's experiences in Nassau.

However, Kirkcaldie had never spoken to her of John's mother or, for that matter, of Tabby. Maria wondered if it would ever be possible to know all that had passed. *Does it even matter now?* she mused. And how could she ever be able to articulate the enormity of her experience, the scope of her sorrow, to Kirkcaldie? There was a period following her imprisonment that she could not even recall. At the time, she had been filled with such impenetrable darkness that she could not see beyond her own leaden mind, as though she had been secured in a cave. In a soundless, sightless, almost airless void, she had been detached and unfastened from the world.

Leah told her later that it was a blessing, that she wished she might be able to similarly forget. There was something to that, Maria supposed.

9

BOSTON, MASSACHUSETTS

By the time John departed Bowman's stone terrace it was dark, and a light flurry of snow dusted his dark brown curls. As he wandered the Boston streets, he considered the scant knowledge he had in his possession and what it might mean. Bowman had lied about attending Schleck, but what had prompted the bonesetter to do so, John could not fathom. Judging from the appearance of Bowman's home, while he was a poor housekeeper and reluctant cook, there were no signs of drinking or illegal activity. However, there was the pamphlet, crushed so hastily.

Although first impressions could never be trusted, Bowman did not appear a callous man, neither was he uneducated, judging from the content of the journal John had so hurriedly read. In gesture and mannerisms, the authority in his tone, Bowman conducted himself like a man well-schooled. *If so, why*, thought John, puzzled, *is he a bonesetter and not a physician or surgeon?*

The visit had seemed to generate more questions than answers. John stopped in his tracks, frustrated. He could not discern what had prompted the bonesetter to intentionally neglect the treatment of Felix Schleck. After a moment, John looked around him, wondering to where he had walked. He stood outside a nameless tavern in Charlestown that he knew to be the haunt of freemasons. Nevertheless, he was cold and irritated, and hesitant to face Joshua and his unfaltering zeal for the law. Venturing inside through the thick oak doors, he found himself a table tucked away in a corner, far from the bar and the crowd of men who hovered around it in a cloud of smoke and lively conference.

As he removed his cloak, he heard a voice behind him call, 'Kirkcaldie! Is it you?'

John turned, disappointed he had been recognised. Boston was not a small society by any means, but John was constantly finding himself in the company of a former client, acquaintance or Harvard classmate, just at the time when he most needed to be alone. However, at the sight of voice's owner, John's heart lifted. It was Ben Franklin, his boyhood friend. Ben was a reminder of a time when life had been simpler.

They had been classmates at the Boston Latin School when they were children. Although Ben had since moved to Philadelphia, the two had remained friends. While there had been immense competition between the two boys in the early days – both had vied for top position in the class during the year Ben attended the school – they had become close and trusted companions. That is, until Ben's father removed him from the school, citing financial hardship. Ben confided later to John that, in truth, his father had had a change of heart regarding the direction of his son's life.

Puckish, curious, sceptical, rebellious and irreverent, Ben Franklin was not a good fit for the Latin School or Harvard University. They were but two steppingstones to one destination – the Church. Franklin's qualities were better suited, or so Josiah Franklin believed, to the world of business. Since that time, Ben had been apprenticed to his father, a candle maker, and his cousin, a cutler, but Ben finally found his niche when he was apprenticed to his older brother James, a printer. Now a resident of Philadelphia, Ben operated his own successful printer's shop and relished the associated occupations – publisher, newspaperman, writer and postmaster. He had found his calling and played a prominent role in the public life of Philadelphia.

The men gripped hands and drew each other into a warm embrace. John clutched his friend slightly longer than was deemed acceptable and, when they parted, Ben looked at John with concern.

'I've never had such a heartfelt greeting in my entire life!'

How could John articulate the all-encompassing comfort and relief he had experienced on sighting Ben Franklin? Sentimental, foolish ... this was how he would appear if he gave voice to his feelings. How could he explain how his heart had welled, almost bringing him to tears? John could not explain it himself, but to say that he was gladdened to see the familiar face of an old and reliable friend was an understatement.

'Why are you here in Boston?' John asked instead. 'You should have written, made me aware of your plans ...'

Ben indicated they should sit then queried in a jovial manner, 'Why? So you could have made room for me on the floor of your dreadful, smoke-filled lodgings, among the detritus of your bootless law practice?'

John laughed.

'A Harvard man, indeed.' Ben slapped John on the back as they sat.

John never resented his friend's good-natured criticism. Ben was predictable in that, if nothing else. It was his way to rebuke authority of every sort, even if that authority was only perceived. Since their schooldays, Ben had been outspoken in his views of formal education, the governor, Harvard and religion, even criticising their headmaster on one occasion regarding the length of his prayers. Even now, despite his position at the top of Philadelphia intelligentsia and society, Ben Franklin considered himself to be an ordinary man.

'If you have concluded your critique of my education and career, perhaps you might deign to answer my question.' John was beginning to regain his composure, finding his usual home in their banter.

Ben smiled and ordered them each an ale before explaining.

'I feel a branch of the Junto Club is warranted here in Boston. The middle class here have grown far beyond that of Philadelphia and I believe likeminded men require a crucible for discussion and debate. I'm here to provide it. There might possibly even be a place among them for a man of law ...' He added with a raised eyebrow.

The Leather Apron Club, or 'Junto' as it was informally called, was an organisation Ben Franklin had founded in Boston to great success. Comprising of local shopkeepers, tradesmen, writers, clerks, and artisans of one kind or another, the club discussed the issues of the day and debated philosophical concepts. Positions in the club were so in demand that the organisation had outgrown all the coffee houses and taverns in Philadelphia, forcing Ben to purchase premises for the sole purpose of hosting their meetings.

'I'm afraid I may not be accepted by your shopkeepers

and tradesmen,' John replied, indicating the group of men at the bar. 'I fear I am too clerkly for your lot.'

'Piffle!"

'And besides, you know I am not a *joiner*. However, I wish you luck with your dreams of expansion.'

Ben laughed. 'Yet you're still handy at the art of word play.'

The pair sat for a time with their ales, discussing the different paths their lives had taken. To John, Ben seemed eminently successful. As Ben enthused about his handsome wife and children and the growth of his businesses, John nodded and *ah-hah*-ed during the brief pauses, all the while privately measuring the similarities and differences between him and his friend. John remained unmarried, unable to win the lasting affections of any young woman, handsome or not. On the subject of romance, Joshua advised he was too serious, that he scared women away. Perhaps it was so. John and Ben were both risk-takers with their careers, but it seemed every venture Ben turned his hand to turned to gold while John, at the same age, was still scraping together a piddling, unsatisfying livelihood chasing clients with worthwhile causes but empty pocketbooks. His time was running out to make his mark in the world. As he pondered on his perceived failings, John's thoughts travelled full circle back to Felix Schleck.

'Tell me, Ben, how did the German newspaper you started fare?'

'The *Philadelphische Zeitung*?' Franklin uttered with perfect German pronunciation.

John nodded.

'It failed on its first birthday. It seems that despite the large number of German immigrants in Philadelphia, the majority of them were the most ignorant and stupid sort of their own nation,' he explained, distastefully. 'Very few were able to read.'

Ben's attitude surprised John. He had always considered his friend to be of the most open mind.

'We are immigrants ourselves,' John countered.

'Speak for yourself. I was born in Boston.'

'But your mother and father ...'

'Why should these colonies, founded by the English, become a colony of aliens, who will shortly be so numerous as to Germanize us instead of we Anglicising them. They will never adopt our language or customs, any more than they can acquire our complexion.'

'But what is our language and our customs? Are we not a nation born of aliens?' John asked, perplexed at his friend's perspective on the matter. 'In the past you have argued that we should not see ourselves as French, Spanish, Dutch, German or English, but as American.'

'But I have discovered that not all immigrants see them-selves as American. They're unwilling and incapable of change,' he said matter-of-factly, finishing his final swig of beer. 'I say, I am not against the admission of Germans in general, for they have their virtues ... Their industry and frugality are exemplary.'

The detour the conversation had taken disturbed John. *And what of the Indians?* he mused. *Are they not the only true Americans?* After hearing Ben's opinions, he expected their country's native inhabitants did not even cross his friend's mind.

Frowning, he considered his own circumstances. Following the wreck of the *Whydah*, Kirkcaldie arrived in Massachusetts a penniless, wanted Englishman. *And I? What had I been then? A foundling, an orphan. I had no nation.* Prize fighting, penny-pinching and Kirkcaldie's unrelenting hard work had seen them realise Tamesine's dream; John had been educated as an equal alongside the cream of the colony and Kirkcaldie had built them a home. *Why shouldn't every man have the same opportunities?* he wondered now. *Even Felix Schleck. Even an Indian.*

'I can discern from your dour countenance that my words are displeasing. But my views are not extreme, I assure you. There is a band of militants right here in Boston that take far greater offence to immigrants than I. They call themselves the "Colonial Vanguard".'

Intrigued, intuiting a connection to his case, John leant closer and related the tale of Felix Schleck to his friend.

'Do you think this bonesetter might have a bias against immigrants?' he asked Ben.

'It is very likely. Do you know this fellow's name?'

'Henry Bowman.'

Ben nodded in recognition. 'It seems you have stumbled upon the founder of the Vanguard. Bowman is a zealous supporter of extreme doctrines. A letter arrived at my office when the first edition of the *Zeitung* was published. It was from Bowman. My enterprise did not sit well with him.'

Being aware now of Ben's prejudices, John could not comprehend how the concept of a foreign-language newspaper had sat comfortably with its publisher. However, John figured that Ben was a businessman first and what he saw when he looked at Germans were not aliens or the uneducated, but a potential market.

'I know it was some time ago, but can you recall the gist of the correspondence?'

'Very well,' said Ben with a strange laugh. 'He threatened to burn down my place of business, the offices of the *Pennsylvania Gazette*, if I were to print a second edition.'

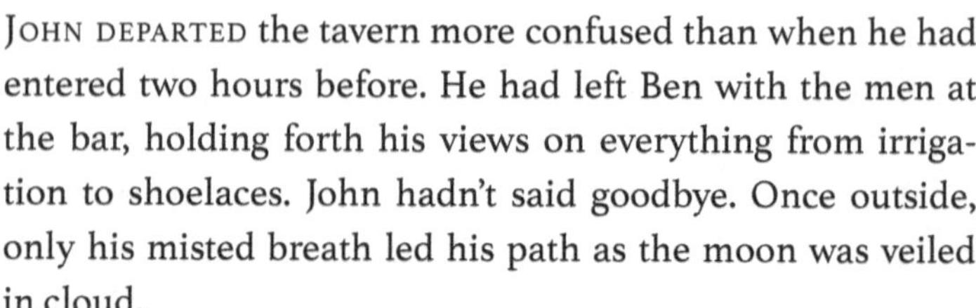

JOHN DEPARTED the tavern more confused than when he had entered two hours before. He had left Ben with the men at the bar, holding forth his views on everything from irrigation to shoelaces. John hadn't said goodbye. Once outside, only his misted breath led his path as the moon was veiled in cloud.

Although his gait was slow, methodical, John's mind raced through possible options. *What am I to do about Henry Bowman?* he wondered. How could he prove that Bowman's actions were intentional? How could he sway the view of an English judge who, in all likelihood, shared similar beliefs to Bowman? John had no evidence of Bowman's proclivity for violence apart from the words of Benjamin Franklin. And would Ben take the stand and swear on the Bible in order to deliver justice to an immigrant?

More importantly, or so John figured Joshua would say, who is to foot the bill? Schleck was penniless. Judging from Bowman's home, the bonesetter himself could not afford costly damages. John's logic darted through his head, struggling to manoeuvre around obstacles. What of the Dutch East India Company? Bowman's employment would likely be terminated but the company could not be held liable for his extreme views. After all, how was it possible to read a man's mind?

John stopped in the cold, empty street and looked into the dark sky, sensing the warmth of his frustration simmering in his chest. Throughout his life, John had solved problems with words, by looking into books; his mother had wanted it that way. When Bellamy had fought for prizes as Captain Grand, John had disapproved at every opportunity, arguing they should settle down and build a home because his mother had wanted it that way. Fighting was not a means of earning a living. Violence was not a means to anything.

John had always wondered about Bellamy, his motives for turning pirate. When asked, he spoke of freedom – it was the only true power a man possessed, he'd say. Bellamy's frustration with the shackles in which authority had bound him had driven him to piracy – to a life of theft and violence. In those days, anger had fuelled him. Angry with all authority for having been driven from Eastham, then angry with himself for not saving Tamesine and allowing Benjamin Hornigold to live ... This rage was expressed with his fists, written on the bodies of his opponents.

John had never understood Bellamy's actions. Later, when Bellamy became Kirkcaldie and his mentor's anger seemed to ebb away, there seemed no need to. But in the last few days – ever since he discovered Hornigold, the man who killed his mother, had died unpunished for his crimes – a new feeling had taken hold of him. Now the realisation that Bowman's actions were malicious, that the man had documented his neglect of Schleck because he was *proud* of his cruelty, brought John to the conclusion that any of his own words and deeds were completely futile against the obvious injustice of the situation. This devastating epiphany struck him like a thunderclap.

John knew that there were no legal means of bringing Bowman to justice. Despite this awareness, without a reckoning he believed his fury would eat him alive.

He turned immediately and began to run.

∼

When he reached Bowman's house, it was just past midnight. His chest heaved in both fear and exhilaration. Removing his hat, he knocked heavily on the door. As he was waiting for the bonesetter to appear, he placed his spectacles in his pocket and tied his scarf around his face, revealing to the world his eyes only. It took some minutes for Bowman to reach the door. It was midnight; the man would be asleep, John wagered. As he waited for Bowman to wake, rub his eyes and slide his feet into his slippers, his rage grew to such a pitch that later he wondered how he had not forced the door open himself.

John glared at the doorknob. He was panting furiously, eager, willing. Ready.

The door opened and John sprang on Bowman like a bobcat, knocking him backwards. His candle fell to the floor. Bowman cried out in terror. Still groggy from his unexpected awakening and stunned by the intruder, in the dark he was unable to defend himself sensibly. John slammed the door shut with his foot, pressing Bowman against the flocked surface of the wall, his forearm wedged against the bonesetter's throat. Positioned so close, John could smell Bowman's fear, salty and acrid. He instantly felt a rush of pleasure spread from his heart into the outer reaches of his body. Bowman struggled for release, but he was a slight man and John stood at least a head taller than him.

John released his grip on Bowman's neck, but his quarry remained pinned to the wall by terror, his eyes wide.

'What do you want?' Bowman asked, his voice raspy.

John did not answer because 'justice' did not seem to encapsulate the immense scope of his desire at that moment. Instead, he began laying his fist into the bonesetter's face, again and again, the mighty weight of his rage behind each swing transforming his arm into a weapon, a blacksmith's hammer. The crunch of Bowman's jaw breaking was a tonic, the wetness of his blood an elixir. Within a minute, Bowman's head slumped but John lifted it, his wrath not yet complete. He seemed to transcend to a different plane; standing outside of himself, he watched the attack as it occurred and relished every brutal blow, every bloody moment. A final strike and the bonesetter fell to the floor, unconscious, his face a red, raw pulp. Jolted back to the world with the solid *thump* of Bowman's body onto the floor, John stepped back, stunned at what he had done, barely able to catch his breath.

He stood staring at Bowman's prostrate form, blood pounding in his ears and sweat dripping from his forehead. Eventually, when his rage receded, John dropped to the floor. He could barely unfurl his tightly clenched fists but he managed to press his fingers (already stinging) against the man's neck. Bowman was still alive. He rose, then stood for a time staring at the body.

What have I done? he thought, as tears rushed to his eyes.

10

AUGUSTA, MAINE

Sarah was the only Williams daughter to resemble Palgrave. Tall, lean and in possession of Palgrave's angular features, she was not born with the comely, soft figure of her mother and older sister Elizabeth. Even Patience, at just ten years old, was beginning to develop the comforting curves of her mother. Yet Sarah's eyes shone with warmth and her smile radiated her open and loving nature.

While Sarah loved her brother Joshua, her twin, it had not been easy growing up by his side. He had always been outspoken, opinionated and flaunted his intellect shamelessly, it seemed to her. They had received the education of equals, even sharing the same tutors once they had moved to Augusta, but Joshua put his wits on constant display, inviting praise and wonder. Sarah kept her opinions in check and was considered reserved and timid by her family. Because of this, she still fondly recalled the morning when Reverend Cotton Mather had visited her grandfather's house in Eastham when she was but five years old. He remarked that twins were 'God's miracle', placing the flat of his hand on her head, as though delivering a blessing. He had not anointed her brother so. It was the only time she had experienced singularity.

There were no likely suitors for Sarah as there had been for Elizabeth. Possessing her mother's dark blue eyes and thick, honey-coloured hair, there had seemed to be a procession of young men hoping to court her elder sister. At three and twenty, Sarah had no such train of gentlemen suitors and she held out little hope that one would materialise. For, although she resembled her father in appearance, she resembled her mother in most other traits. This being so, she was practical, unromantic and rarely dared to dream. However, she did allow herself one realm of reverie.

Benjamin Shute had been a favourite of hers since he had entered the lives of the family more than ten years ago. She had been thirteen when her father had first introduced the doctor to the family at supper one evening. Through her girlish perspective, Doctor Shute was breathtakingly handsome. She couldn't look at him – his amber eyes and the determined set of his jaw – without experiencing a flutter deep down in her belly. Her heart had been stirred equally by his passion for medicine and his desire to do good works in Augusta. Sarah imagined him an excellent match for Elizabeth, but Elizabeth could not see past the admirers who lined the drive, penning her countless missives of romantic love. Benjamin had more serious concerns to deal with.

This is why Sarah was surprised when Tabby Post had garnered his affections so quickly. Sarah would observe Ben observing Tabby and, even to one so young, Sarah could easily see his infatuation. It was strange, she thought at the time, that such a sensible man could be so overcome with ardour. Young Sarah had found herself in a dilemma. She admired Tabby immensely. In fact, Sarah longed to possess the midwife's self-assuredness and candour and, after all, Tabby had saved her mother's life. But when Tabby had disappeared so suddenly, Sarah was secretly grateful. Soon after, when Ben vanished from her life as well, she read the unexpected event as God's punishment for the ill-feelings she had directed at Tabby.

Her family would have said different if they had known her thoughts on the matter. The Williamses did not hold with God. From the time she was five or six years old, Sarah could not remember praying or going to meeting. One day her mother had been devout and the next she was not. Sarah was too young to understand why this change came about. However, during the four years Ben was away fighting in New France for the King, she had prayed every night in the same style as she had when she was a little girl. Kneeling by her bedside, she would bring her hands together at her heart and her mind to the prayers her mother had uttered for her father when he too had disappeared. Perhaps it had been the touch of Reverend Mather all those years ago that had turned her head towards God; she knew not, but she had never told her family of the prayers she said privately by candlelight during the years Ben had been away.

Once Joshua was enrolled at the Boston Latin School and then a few years later at Harvard University, she found herself lost – educated but lacking a vocation or a calling. She did not paint like her aunt, nor did she possess a family to care for like her mother. Sarah knew not whether it was her mother's insight into her daughter's character or her desire to see her married that had prompted her to suggest she offer her time at the hospital. Sarah had agreed, possessing the disposition of one who enjoyed occupation.

The notion of working by Ben's side only sweetened the suggestion.

These were the thoughts running through Sarah's mind as she attended to her patient, a young man she knew from the town. He helped her mother's friend Riyogi at the Green Dragon – chopping wood, carrying out repairs, fixing loose shingles and the like. He had been a roamer whom Riyogi had found on the banks of the river during the summer, beaten and stabbed, left for dead. His name was Charlie Purse.

Under Ben's care, then Riyogi's, Charlie had taken months to recover from his broken bones and wounds. Now he suffered from a different ailment – a brutal fever and a dry hacking cough. The sound of it reminded Sarah of an old dog attempting to bark. Ben assured her it was not consumption, for if he even suspected that disease, the patient would be isolated and Sarah would not be permitted to step within even six yards of the room. Sarah hoped Ben's concern sprang from a modicum of affection for her rather than a desire to keep his best friend's daughter safe from harm.

Charlie gazed at her as she dabbed his sweaty forehead gently with a cool, damp cloth. His eyes were misty but his gaze was intense. Sarah felt herself blush.

'What's wrong with me, Mistress, that I invite so much illness into my life?' he murmured.

Sarah dropped the clout into the dish that rested on her lap and took his hand.

'There is nothing wrong with you, Charlie,' she replied. 'None of this is your fault. We all have times when events do not run in our favour. You should be grateful that your time is now, when you're young and in good kilter. Doctor Shute believes you'll recover quickly.'

His mouth quirked into a smile.

'You are well-versed in the language of comfort. For that I am grateful.'

He closed his eyes then, but his hand found hers. Sarah remained by his bedside until he drifted into a peaceful sleep.

11

BOSTON, MASSACHUSETTS

Kirkcaldie arrived in Boston in the early hours of the morning. He had stopped in West Hoosuck the night before but had risen early, eager to see his eldest son. Besides, he had business to attend to. Palgrave had at last responded favourably to the idea of smuggling molasses into the colony, realising it was the only means of continuing his manufacture of Eight Bells.

'The risk ...' Palgrave had uttered, weighing up the scheme on the morning Kirkcaldie had departed. 'I must admit, my friend, that I am at once petrified and exhilarated by the notion.'

'It is your risk to take,' Kirkcaldie replied as he brushed his horse in long, straight strokes. 'You have been trapped by the Molasses Act. I am merely offering you an escape.'

Palgrave nodded. 'I understand you want to help me and I'm grateful for it, but why would you consider taking to the sea again after what you've been through?'

Kirkcaldie shrugged. 'I cannot say. Yesterday, when you were describing your predicament, the injustice of the tax, I felt something in me stir, a desire I cannot explain fully. An old friend ... or perhaps an undefeated foe.'

'And if we are captured?' Palgrave asked. 'What of our families?'

'You have more to lose than me in that regard,' Kirkcaldie said, lifting the saddle onto the beast's back. 'Maria does not want me and I fear she never will.'

'You cannot know that. I see the way she looks at you, even if you don't. Have you asked her directly about her feelings in the matter? Samuel Bellamy did all those years ago. A more direct man I never knew. He confronted her father, I seem to recall, to plead his case. He even won old Joseph Hallett over, which is more than I was ever able to achieve.'

Kirkcaldie's eyes narrowed. 'And look how that turned out.'

Palgrave sighed. 'You are the same man, a little older, greyer perhaps, but the same man.'

Am I the same man? Kirkcaldie pondered now as he rode through the deserted streets of Boston. It would be twenty years in July since he had first noticed Maria Hallett on the green in Eastham shaded by an enormous oak. In the time between then and now, he had earnestly endeavoured to become a different man; his life and John's had depended upon it.

The heavy tread of a watchman drew his attention. Kirkcaldie tipped his hat and continued on his way.

KIRKCALDIE HOPED to find a crew while he was in the city. Just a small one – three or four men, including himself – for the boat would need to be small, a ketch would be the most likely choice, he had decided. Of course, it would mean taking to the sea once more. The problem of whether he would be able to overcome his fear, his memories of the wreck, he had not yet wholly considered.

As he travelled slowly though the quiet dawn towards Long Harbour, he mulled over these questions and the unexpected direction in which his fortunes had turned. He passed the courthouse. Stopping at the laneway where he had last seen Tabby, he thought on their final meeting. *To where did she disappear?* he wondered. *Nowhere with Benjamin Shute, that is certain.*

Palgrave had informed Kirkcaldie when he returned to Augusta that Shute had joined the military to serve in New France. An odd choice for a young doctor, but not surprising considering his lineage. Moosehead Lake? Kirkcaldie had travelled there too. Her wigwam was empty when he arrived and her friend Mongwau had not seen her since she had returned to bury Edie.

Ten years on and Palgrave still acted as her banker, investing her money in property and trade. He had even established a charity hospital in her name, by Leah's urging, Kirkcaldie guessed, which Ben Shute now headed.

'Tabby Post is a very wealthy woman,' Palgrave had informed him on his recent visit. 'And she would not even know it.'

The memory of her unusual ways and the lemony scent of her, her skills as a healer and as a huntress, suddenly filled Bellamy with sadness. He alighted Dobbin and walked to the spot where he had last seen her. He had left to fetch the carriage from a blacksmith around the corner. When he'd returned, she was gone. Standing on this spot from the past, he hoped to gain an insight into her whereabouts now.

Kirkcaldie took his compass from his pocket and flicked it open. A smile crept upon his lips. He gave silent thanks to Tabby as he waited for the needle to still. Despite everything that happened on that terrible afternoon at Harper's Creek, despite her grief at losing her best friend, Tabby, with the help of Palgrave, had managed to retrieve the compass Jeremy Cool had stolen from him. He took it as a sign that perhaps he meant something to her once after all.

Kirkcaldie sighed. It had been a decade ago since he last saw Tabby. Would he recognise her now? Of course he would. Her striking red hair was unforgettable. Had he loved her? His willingness to sacrifice his freedom to secure her safety indicated as much. But that time seemed so long ago. He could barely recall his exact feelings for her, yet the memory of her clung to his thoughts like ivy. Tabby was gone, never to return – he was certain of that – and it gave him no happiness to dwell on her. He closed the compass with a sharp *click*.

As he made his way back to Dobbin, Kirkcaldie shifted his thoughts to Maria again. It was with her and his youngest son where his future lay, he was sure of it. However, it didn't seem possible to him that Maria could forget the past. The pain that his arrival in Eastham had precipitated all those years ago had made an indelible mark on her. He knew it the moment he came across her in the glade.

That night, it was as if he had been summoned to leave his bed. He had believed he was riding towards Tabby; the awareness that she needed him urgently overrode his good sense and he had saddled his horse immediately. In retrospect, he realised it *had* been a summoning but, instead of Tabby, he had found Maria waiting for him.

The discovery of her in the moonlight, her strange beauty radiating into the darkness, had mesmerised him.

When she, unsurprised by his presence in the forest, beckoned to him, he could do nothing but obey.

'Maria ...'

'I was on the beach at Wellfleet the night of the storm. I sensed you were out there among the turmoil and the noise ...' she whispered. 'Then I saw you in my mind's eye, so clearly. I closed my eyes, hoping to reach you, to raise you out of that terrible scene.'

Kirkcaldie frowned at the memory. He could still recall the wave cupping him and John like a palm. But to have command of the sea was impossible. In the glade, he had not wanted to tell her that his survival had been a mere coincidence. Now he was no longer sure. She had appeared so ethereal then, dispossessed – much changed from the girl he had known in Eastham. But she was just as lovely, perhaps more so.

'You refused to lie with me once. Do you recall, Samuel Bellamy?' she said, moonlight and candlelight braiding together, stroking her pale skin.

Her words startled him. Kirkcaldie nodded, concerned. He thought of Tabby and, of course, Tamesine, leading him to contemplate his failings as a man.

'I do. But Maria, the feelings we once shared ... there has been so much ...'

'The day you left Eastham, Silas – my friend, the man who professed to love me – raped me by the willow. He had grown to hate me. It was hatred that drove him to it, but he thought it was love.'

Kirkcaldie took a sharp breath, shocked at what his actions had precipitated.

'It was why I could not marry him, even though I carried his child. Do you understand?'

'Of course.'

'The child was a boy. He was born dead.'

'Oh, Maria ...' her words tore at Kirkcaldie's heart. Regret and sadness washed over him.

'There is much that I have lost, Sam. But I knew you would return. I knew that I had not lost you.'

She took a step closer to him.

'That child should have been yours, Samuel Bellamy. So lie with me now. Give me what is owed – a baby born of love. For I still love you and I saved your life.'

Before Kirkcaldie could give voice to the pain he had caused, the promises he had broken, she had walked to him, kissed him and drawn him to the ground.

Despite his feelings for Tabby, he had been powerless to resist.

Over the years, as he watched Maria with Bell, as he slowly took the measure of her, his love and desire for the woman she had become stole upon him, stealthy and constant. Now the memory of that night, the feeling of her, played on his mind ever more frequently.

If Maria would accept him then they, together with Bell, might be a family. He reached behind and touched the portrait of Bell that was wrapped in cloth and secured to his saddlebags, ensuring its safety. He had been overwhelmed by the gift; had he revealed his true emotions to Maria when she had given it to him, perhaps things might already be different ... But fear had held him back.

After that night in the glade, he immersed himself once more in Tabby and her trial. When she disappeared, he spent months, years searching for her. In doing so, he realised later, he abandoned Maria a second time. It was only thanks to Palgrave and Leah that he had been able to build a friendship with her, slowly, tentatively. And he was humbled and grateful when, despite everything, she asked him to be part of Bell's life.

The image of Bell drew his thoughts back to Maria's painting. *Could it be an olive branch?* he mused, hope glimmering in his heart.

His contemplations were interrupted by a familiar odour. Wafts of brine and fish gut lifted to him in the air, becoming stronger and more repugnant, indicating that he was drawing near King Street, near Long Wharf. When he dismounted Dobbin again, he was outside the rooms of his son.

Kirkcaldie gazed up towards the window he knew to be John's. The curtains were still closed but he entered the building anyway and began to make his way up the stairs. He tried the door handle. Finding it unlocked, he entered the darkened room as quietly as he was able while carrying saddlebags and the portrait. John was asleep on his pallet. The room was deathly cold and no embers burned in the meagre hearth for Kirkcaldie to rekindle.

Why would John not light a fire? Kirkcaldie wondered. It was the middle of winter. Bellamy rested his belongings on the ground then examined the hearth more closely. The fire had been doused, the ashes still damp. Digging through them with a poker, he found a button, slightly blackened but still intact. Snatching it from the ashes, he rubbed it on his breeches. It was the button Tamesine had given John the night he had joined Kirkcaldie on the *Whydah*. 'A Lieutenant's button', she had called it before kissing her son and bidding him farewell. It was the last time John had seen his mother.

Kirkcaldie polished it now as best as he could then placed it on John's writing desk. He went to his son and looked down on him, remembering him as the boy he was then. Even while slumbering, John always appeared concerned. As a child, his brow had been knotted into a permanent frown. Kirkcaldie had first noticed this peculiarity the night after Tamesine's murder. Finally asleep aboard the *Whydah*, John's smooth brow had crinkled into a frown and that was how his forehead was to remain. The boy never seemed to be entirely at rest.

John rolled over, revealing his hands as he attempted to draw his blankets over his bare shoulders. However, the bandages that encased them prevented this. Concern flooded Kirkcaldie's face. What he saw reminded him of the period when he had masqueraded as Captain Grand. After a particularly hard-won fight, John would anoint Kirkcaldie's bruised knuckles with barbary then wrap them tightly in cloths to ease the swelling. *But John does not fight*, thought Kirkcaldie. His son solved arguments through rhetoric and reason. Although he had instructed him in the pugilistic arts, he was certain John, always rational and calm, had never called on those skills.

In the depths of sleep, John again struggled to grip his covers. Kirkcaldie reached down and pulled them over his son's naked torso then sat by the pallet with his back against the wall, wondering in what John might have become involved.

Within the hour, John opened his eyes. On seeing Kirkcaldie by his side, a small smile formed on his lips.

'Kirkcaldie, I was not expecting you.'

His voice was hoarse. Kirkcaldie reached into his saddlebags and produced a flask, offering it to John.

'Whiskey?' John croaked with a look of distaste.

'Water,' Bellamy replied. 'From the Kennebec. I have been staying with Palgrave and Leah for a time.'

John nodded in understanding.

Kirkcaldie unscrewed the lid and held the flask to John's lips. He watched his son drink greedily. Kirkcaldie recalled his thirst during and after a fight, gulping water hungrily from a bag between rounds to replenish all that he had expended. It was not only the physical effort involved in fighting a man, but the emotional too; it took some mettle to battle it out bare-fisted with another. The weight of it was exhausting.

'Have you used barbary on those hands?'

'I have none.'

Kirkcaldie reached once more into his possessions and held up a small jar of ointment.

'Have you been fighting?'

John cleared his throat. Stalling, Kirkcaldie could see. John was never lost for words.

'I joined my friend Ben Franklin at a tavern last night. Do you remember him?'

Kirkcaldie nodded.

'Well, you probably also remember how outspoken he can be, how he can raise the ire of those who are unfamiliar with his manner ...'

John straightened in the bed, wincing when he tried to use his hands as support. Kirkcaldie placed a pillow behind his back.

'Ben was accompanied by a group of similarly-minded men who were discussing British taxes and the like. Before long, a considerable amounts of ale was imbibed. Ben went too far, as is his want, calling the King and all who serve him "grabby" or something similar ... I cannot recall his actual turn of phrase. Before we knew it, a group of four or five men had risen to defend the King's honour. Ben refused to submit and apologise, so a fight erupted.'

'Benjamin Franklin in a fight?' Kirkcaldie questioned

sceptically of the bespectacled, pasty-skinned youth he remembered.

'I am not suggesting he's handy with his fists ...'

'And your role in this ruckus?'

'I was defending my friend. He would have been pummelled to a pulp if I had not intervened.'

Kirkcaldie nodded in the darkness, disbelieving. He was certain John was lying, although he did not know why. He decided not to press the issue. John would confide in him when he was ready.

12

TAMESINE: THE QUAY

CORNWALL, 1705

Tamesine stopped and turned towards the ocean. She could see the bonfire embers glowing like rubies below her in Penzance, thin coils of smoke curling into the brightening sky. To her right was Mousehole, the harbour and the crooked little stone cottage where she lived. The air around the carn was misted with smoke; Tamesine took in a bolstering breath of the homely scent before she spoke.

'You cannot come with me any further,' she said.

'I will speak with your father. Explain ...'

'He will kill you.'

'An officer of the Royal Navy?'

'He wouldn't be concerned.'

When the hour arrived for the sisters to depart Penzance and the festivities, Tamesine found she could not. The idea of leaving John was unthinkable. The day had been perfect, the most perfect day of her life. She could live on this one day forever, she believed, but she had not been able to let it end so soon.

She looked out at the first light of midsummer, the day

just beginning. During their time together, John had been gentlemanly and generous; he had flattered her and Eseld and, most importantly, he listened when Tamesine spoke. Consequently, she had sent her sister back to Mousehole alone.

At first, the girl had vehemently refused. Tamesine admired Eseld's loyalty and courage but she had eventually convinced her faithful sister to turn for home. She had concluded that there was no point in both of them being punished, beaten probably, when only one of them was in love.

Once the sun had set and Tamesine and John were alone together, they had lit torches and added their flames to the burgeoning bonfire that was alight by the harbour. Then they had sat together in the flickering shadows touching hands. John told her of his life in Surrey and of his mother. She had doted on him, he said, her youngest child, since his father died.

When he told her of his life as an officer in the Royal Navy, sent to Cornwall to capture smugglers, Tamesine bit her tongue. Fishing was seasonal at best; if smuggling French brandy from the Scilly Isles fed a man's family, then why did the Crown object to it? Reluctant to tell this Englishman that every man in Mousehole engaged in smuggling at one time or another, Tamesine instead spoke to him of the giants and mermaids that inhabited Cornwall, and of the miracles of Saint Madron.

Transfixed and intoxicated by the magic of midsummer, in the early hours of the morning they had joined hands and danced in a long line from the quay, looping and twisting through the streets, through the embers of the torches and fires.

'An eye, an eye,' they chanted to the moon.

Then it ended.

Their hands fell.

They kissed.

'*Dyw genes*,' Tamesine said now, turning towards Mouse-hole. Her home was visible in the distance.

'If that means goodbye, I do not wish to hear it.' He took her elbow and gently turned her to face him.

'Thank you for this day, Lieutenant John King,' whispered Tamesine. 'It will live in my heart always.'

He looked down at her. His eyes were shining.

'I love you, Tamesine Rosevear, and I will not rest until I am your heart.'

Tamesine smiled, shaking her head at his naivety.

'What will your *maah maah* think of this fisherwoman from "Muzzle"?'

She twirled around like a fine lady, showing off her simple pinafore, mended countless times.

'Fisherwoman?'

'That is what I am. I clean fish for a shilling a bucket.'

As she began to feel the first spring of disappointment rising in her belly, her voice grew louder.

'I reek of salt and the inmeat of pilchards!'

Tamesine had not wanted to shout at him. But if John departed now, immediately, she thought she might just be able to bear it. She was sure that the longer their parting took, the more painful it would be.

John did not flinch at her anger.

'Then I shall be the Fisher King and you my queen,' he said quietly. 'And we shall drink from the grail together.'

Tamesine smiled ruefully, astounded by his idealism. She stepped closer to him, clutched his face and kissed him hard on the lips, then turned and strode downhill towards the crooked little cottage alone.

Tamesine yawned, making her jaw ache. She knew it would, but she could not stifle her weariness any longer. Her eye was blackened but her teeth were intact. A small blessing, she supposed. Sensing her sister tense with pain, Eseld patted her hand. *The girl is more mother to me than sister,* thought Tamesine. She hoped she gave her similar comfort.

The sisters sat by the harbour mending nets with their friends, the other girls chatting merrily beside them. Tamesine, however, could not join them in their cheerfulness as she usually would for she refused to feign happiness any longer. Her mother was present by the quay, sitting apart from her with the older women. Tamesine knew she would be shunned for a time for her errant behaviour but it was a small price to pay.

Then the banter ceased.

The fishing boats must be coming in, thought Tamesine absently, looking up from her work. Eseld tapped her arm and pointed to the quay. It was not the sea that had silenced the chatter and drawn the girls' eyes. It was the figure of a man.

Lieutenant John King strode purposefully along the quay towards the group of girls. The older women, including Tamesine's mother, had not yet noticed the handsome young officer coming their way. Nervously, Tamesine rose and glanced out to sea. Her father was due back soon. After the greeting Tamesine received when she had attempted to steal through the door that morning, she was concerned for John's safety.

'*Hora!*' her father had shouted, again and again.

'*Rag meth!*' her mother had cried, clutching a kerchief to her mouth.

Her father had hit her only once but it was with such ferocity that she had fallen, knocking her head on the stone hearth. When she awoke, she was still on the floor. Eseld was kneeling by her side dabbing Tamesine's wounds with a dampened cloth. Neither her mother nor father were there; they had already departed for the quay.

Tamesine rushed towards John, hoping she might persuade him to turn back before her mother spied him. When he saw her face, he seemed stricken, as though he was the one who had been beaten. His bronzed complexion turned to ash.

'My darling,' he said, gently taking her head in his hands in order to examine her injuries. His green eyes, soothing and kind, traversed her face.

So touched was Tamesine by the warmth of his gaze, she hesitated in sending him back to Penzance where his ship, the *Greyhound*, was anchored. A moment later, she heard her mother screaming at her from behind.

'*Ke dhe-vas!*' she cried at John. 'Go away!'

An instant later her mother was there, clutching Tamesine's shoulders, attempting to pull her away from John, but he would not let her go.

Tamesine could not respond. Questions raced through her mind. *I cannot return to my father's house ... But how can I leave with John? Is he here for me?* Although she had fantasies of marrying a man who could pluck her from her wretchedness, she was not fool enough to place stock in them.

As she deliberated, neighbours and fisherman collected around the scene like barnacles, standing stock-still, staring.

Ignoring all those who gathered, John looked only at her.

'*Ow melder,*' he said. '*My a'th kar.*'

My darling, I love you.

A murmur went through the crowd. All were stunned by what they had just heard. The chaos inside Tamesine fell away and her eyes filled with tears. She realised John must have learnt the words for her.

Tamesine, her eyes locked with John's, his hands still cupping her face, felt her mother's grip on her arms slacken.

'*My a'th kar,*' Tamesine whispered in reply.

John nodded, a slight smile forming on his lips. He released Tamesine then stepped between her and her mother. The expression on his face was coloured with such venom that the woman took a hurried step back.

Then, without speaking, John took Tamesine's arm and led her along the quay towards Penzance.

13

AUGUSTA, MAINE

Leah dressed hastily in the morning, hoping for a head start on the day. She had promised Ben Shute she would help at the hospital but first there were vegetables to tend to in the new greenhouse.

Palgrave had designed it for her last winter. The idea had come from her father who had utilised a small cold frame to harden off his seedlings. His had sat low to the ground against the southern wall of their barn in Eastham, capturing even the most meagre winterly sun. Palgrave's structure was much grander (of course) and was heated by a small stove. Some months ago, Leah had stood mesmerised on the riverbank as a large raft carrying thin sheets of glass moved along the Kennebec towards her. The sun casting off the sheer panes hurt her eyes. Squinting, she had turned her head. She would have been content with a cold frame like her father's, but she didn't tell her husband this. The greenhouse had taken a week and five men to erect. Although glad for the fresh produce in winter, today Leah considered working in it a chore, one to dispense with prior to her visit to Ben.

Sarah was likely at the hospital already, working by the doctor's side. Her middle daughter was the only one of Leah's children about whom she occasionally worried. Elizabeth had always been outspoken in regard to her feelings – which suitor was currently in favour and the like – but Sarah was so reserved that Leah realised she knew very little about the workings of her mind. She hoped Ben might one day return Sarah's affections. Although there was an age difference, to Leah's mind they made an extremely good match.

Leah enjoyed helping Ben. He was always understaffed and overworked. Tabby's influence had endured and she had witnessed him give each patient the care and time they required, often chatting with the elderly or amusing a child for much longer than his duties permitted. Tabby had shown him that healing was equal parts body and spirit. Ben worked tirelessly in her honour, 'taking in strays' as Palgrave liked to refer to the man's mission of ministering to one and all. The hospital, his work – they were all offerings to the woman he loved but would never have. Unmarried at thirty-two, Ben still held Tabby in his heart.

While Leah admired his forbearance, she wished he might notice Sarah, a young woman he could (and would) have if he'd only take notice.

Although in a rush, Leah took time to gaze at herself naked in the mirror in the morning light. Nothing was hidden – not the flaws that came with age and motherhood nor the scars of disease and punishment. This showing had become a morning ritual and one Leah relished as she had once relished prayer. It reminded her of all she had gained since Tabby had removed her breast. The notion never failed to strike her as exceedingly strange, but it was true; her life was more complete now than it had ever been.

When the cancer had threatened to take her, all the lies and concealment that typified the early days of her marriage to Palgrave had given way to a new era of openness. Examining her hollow chest carefully, touching the scars, Leah was thankful every day for Tabby Post and the miracle she had performed. That woman had more goodness in her than all the ministers Leah had met in her entire life put together.

Stepping into her skirt and securing the ties, Leah then slipped her arms through her stay and began on the laces. This one was her favourite, one that Maria had embroidered for her. It was decorated in yellow and green with a daisy chain that looped around her breasts and waist.

The women had crafted many stays together since the amputation of Leah's breast. Just like the cloth cupboard that Maria had decorated so painstakingly was a part of her, Leah's stays were a symbol of who she had proudly transformed into.

Both Leah and Maria were gifted seamstresses but the design for the perfect stay had eluded them for many months following Leah's lengthy recovery. Padding a pocket Leah had sown into one side of a stay with various materials and testing their suitability became a maddening, almost obsessive occupation. All sorts of cloth were tried in their quest to discover the most life-like substance, as was straw and river sand. But all the materials tested were either too firm, made Leah's skin itch and perspire, or were too heavy and hung too low.

One day, at the peak of their frustration, the sisters ventured into the barn where Palgrave housed stock for his clients. Prodding and poking bags of tobacco leaf, coffee and wheat seed, Leah spied a tightly stitched hessian bag standing in a darkened corner all by itself – an outlier. She approached warily, almost fearing to touch it. When she did, she was immediately heartened by the soft, yielding texture of the contents. Pressing the bag more firmly, squeezing the corner of it in her palm, her face brightened.

'This feels like what we are looking for!' she cried to Maria who was lost among the rows of flax bales.

Maria came to her at once, produced her scissors from her pocket and stuck them firmly into the bag, tearing it open with her fingers.

'Cotton bolls,' she said in wonder. 'Of course, why hadn't we thought of that sooner?'

Leah eyed the bag. 'I suppose because cotton in this form is not readily available to us this far north. This freight has come from Virginia.'

'Then it is ours and we shall make good use of it.'

From then on, they had used the bolls in every stay the pair crafted.

Leah finished buttoning her bodice, placed an apron over her head then ventured downstairs. Palgrave was already awake and in his study, working. The door was ajar. She inched it open slowly then tiptoed towards her husband, who was sitting at his desk in deep concentration. He had not heard her enter. As she approached, she realised he was examining a map. Palgrave held an instrument in his hand that she had never seen before.

'What is that?' she asked, peering over his shoulder.

Palgrave started. Leah noticed his cheeks flush and it took a moment for him to compose himself. He coughed a little before he began.

His unusual behaviour made her stomach clench. *What are you hiding from me?* she wondered.

'This instrument is called a calliper. Come. Look.'

Now calm, he turned sideways on his chair and patted his knee. Leah sat.

'It's a tool used to measure the distance between two points on a map. It's very simple, really.' Palgrave demonstrated. 'You see, if you wish to travel from Boston to say ...' he scanned the map, 'Nuevitas on the island of Cuba, you separate the callipers according to ten miles on the latitude scale here.' He indicated the scale to the right of the map. 'Then you walk the instrument from Boston across the sea to Nuevitas, marking off each ten miles. The sharp points of the device prevent it from slipping.'

Palgrave showed her what he meant, skilfully manipulating the callipers as though they were an extension of his own hand – twisting this way then that, his fingers moving in an elegant dance.

'But the callipers at ten miles do not reach Nuevitas,' Leah observed.

'True. So we must mark the spot they do reach with an "X" then measure the distance remaining using a spot on the scale closest to Nuevitas.' He handed the tool to Leah. Rotating the tiny brass knob at the top of the instrument, she measured the short distance then held it against the latitude scale, carrying out her husband's instructions expertly.

'The distance measures four,' she said.

'Correct. Four nautical miles.'

'Then the distance between Boston and Nuevitas is,' she counted the markings made by Palgrave on the map, 'thirty-four nautical miles.'

'Excellent!' He hugged his wife around the waist. 'We shall make a sailor of you yet.'

'Hmmm,' she muttered, rising, still clutching the callipers. She examined them closely, tapping the tip of her index finger softly against the tool's sharp points.

'I have never seen you use these before. When did you get them?'

'When I was in Nassau.'

'And you were instructed in their use by Bellamy?'

Palgrave nodded. 'Kirkcaldie. Among others.'

Then Leah spied a leather bag under her husband's desk.

'What is that there?' she asked, gesturing towards the bag.

Palgrave retrieved the item with what seemed like reluctance. To Leah's eye, it was very similar to a doctor's case.

'These are ... were ... my navigational instruments,' he said, opening the bag.

Palgrave named each tool as he lifted it from its resting place. 'Compass, of course, chip log, astrolabe, telescope. And my charts.'

In the many years Palgrave had been home, Leah had never seen this bag, let alone the instruments contained within.

'I see.' She scanned the tools from afar, not wanting to touch them. 'Are you merely reminiscing, husband, or should I be concerned?'

It took a minute for Palgrave to respond and in that time Leah's heart took up such a thunderous beat, she thought she might be ill. He looked at her gravely.

'Merely reminiscing,' he remarked, meeting her gaze. 'You know how Kirkcaldie's visits make me sentimental.'

Leah looked down at the callipers still in her hand. The tip of her index finger was bleeding. She moved towards her husband and handed him the instrument.

She nodded. 'I must get on with my day,' she replied before leaving the room.

14

BOSTON, MASSACHUSETTS

John had fallen asleep with Kirkcaldie sitting by his side. When he woke, he checked the timepiece that lay on the nightstand. It was eleven o'clock in the morning. He scanned the room. Kirkcaldie was absent. It took him a moment to get his bearings. *Where was Joshua?* he wondered.

John noticed that the bedsheets were damp with perspiration and his head bore the shadow of a headache. He closed his eyes again, wondering if he had not dreamt his father's presence in the room. It was Saturday, he remembered, which explained Joshua's absence. He rose and placed his feet on the floor and noticed Kirkcaldie's saddle bags opposite the bed. *Not a dream.* Taking a deep breath, he began to recall their conversation about the brawl.

It took some time for the heavy fog in his head to clear. The recollection of the true events blew into his mind with the force of a hurricane. There had been no tavern brawl. When he recalled the image of Henry Bowman's bloody form slumped against the wall, the bile rose in his throat. He reached for his chamber pot and vomited violently into its pewter depths, hoping to purge himself of the memory. Wiping his mouth with his bandaged hand, he struggled to take stock of his emotions. He was heartsick, both in dismay at his unprecedented actions and in fear – fear at the realisation that he had enjoyed hurting another man. For after the initial shock of what he had done had receded, he realised as he stood over Bowman's body that he did not care about the man at all, or about the damage he had rained down upon him. It had felt good to mete out his own justice on a man like that.

What am I turning into? he asked himself. *What have I already become?*

John unwrapped the bandages on his hands and examined his injuries. The fingers were bruised and swollen but he remembered that Kirkcaldie had suffered much worse and had always recovered, although his knuckles now ached in the cold. John dabbed the barbary ointment Kirkcaldie had left on the nightstand onto his swellings then decided to dress.

Rising from his bed, he discovered he was naked. Typically, in the evening he would undress and lay his clothes on a chair, ready for the next day. However, this morning they did not rest in their usual place. John shut his eyes tight, struggling to remember the whereabouts of his clothes. Then he turned to the hearth where a fire was burning.

He realised then that he had destroyed his clothes. They had been so monstrously splattered with Bowman's blood that he had ripped them off in a frenzy and burned them. When they were ashes, he had tipped the contents of his ewer onto the hearth, as if to erase the event entirely. Kirkcaldie must have built another fire to heat the room.

John rummaged in a rickety chest and produced a second set of clothes. As he was pulling on a boot, he raised his head, as if remembering a task he had forgotten. He looked around the room urgently, on the floor and under his bed then towards the hearth. His heart plummeted in his chest and his eyes instantly filled with tears.

It cannot be, he thought. *Even in my madness last night, I would not have burned it.*

He spun on his heels in panic and then his eyes alighted upon what he yearned for, sitting in the middle of his desk. He lunged for it, grabbing the button as though it might vanish in an instant. It was slightly tarnished, but could be polished to its original shine, he reasoned. Kirkcaldie had saved it from the ashes. Closing his eyes with the button clutched tight in his palm, he attempted to compose himself, still his breath and quiet his thoughts. Every part of his being – mind and body – was howling like a dervish. Now he was dressed he did not know to what purpose.

Bowman had been alive when John had departed. Yet thinking on it now, John concluded that the injuries he inflicted on the man were so severe that in all likelihood Bowman may have died during the night. John had wanted to punish him for the cruelty he had dispensed to Felix Schleck, but did he want him dead? No. Bowman was a fiend and John had wanted the man to suffer just as Schleck had done, but in doing so John had lost all control of himself. He had become a man no better than Bowman.

John squeezed his swollen hands into his gloves, searching momentarily for his spectacles without success, then departed his room. He needed to know if Henry Bowman was living or dead.

~

ONCE HER FATHER had fallen asleep it was almost noontide. Eliza stood staring at him, taking in his injuries. His face was swollen and stained purple as though by wine. As she scanned his face, she noticed a small pale, puckering of flesh on his neck, an old scar. She gazed on it for some time, wanting to touch it, certain she should know how he came by the wound that made it. Closing her eyes in an attempt to remember, she heard the distant sound of frantic screams. Bowman stirred and her eyes shot open.

I could kill him now if I chose to, she thought. She was certain she could inform the authorities he died from his injuries and be believed.

Eliza quietly left his chamber carrying the bowl of warm water and blood-soaked clouts she had used to tend his injuries. She had watched her father stitch a wound many times before. Using her father's own equipment, she had stitched his brow and chin, although the idea of touching him had made her feel queasy.

Stupid, stubborn man, she thought. A teetotaller for twelve years, he had repeatedly refused the whiskey she had offered. Instead, he had born each stitch stoically, if not a little dramatically, wincing at her slightest touch. While she worked, she had remembered how her mother had begged him to give up the drink many times but he had always refused. It was only when the Vanguard was formed that he stopped, overnight it seemed. He sacrificed that weakness for a much greater one.

Eliza would not have normally come when summoned by her father. She had not spoken with him for four years, although she had seen him in the street. On each occasion, her stomach had rolled into a tight scroll. However, when his neighbour Mister Hardcourt had almost banged down her door at four in the morning, she could not refuse. An unwelcome sense of duty or responsibility took hold. What's more, how could she tell Mister Hardcourt that she refused to come to her father's aid? She did not want to be thought of as a monster. Fortunately, Eliza had learnt to master her emotions when she was a child. She was able to mask her inner feelings, like a watch face concealed the complex works beneath.

After the attack, her father had managed to crawl out his front door and drag himself along the cobbles the few yards to Hardcourt's door. Although she possessed no kindly thoughts for her father, Eliza was forced to admire his fortitude and determination. Most men would be dead after such a fierce beating.

She had tended to him as best as she could. Once the sun had risen, Eliza had sent a message via Hardcourt to the school where she taught. The headmaster would not be pleased by her absence but there was little else she could do. Anyhow, it was Saturday and the students would be dismissed at noon.

Scrubbing her hands of her father's blood, she heard a knock at the door. She *tsk*-ed, annoyed at the intrusion. She had hoped to rest once her father was asleep. She wiped her hands on her apron and went to the door.

When she opened it, she could see the visitor was taken aback by her presence. He was a striking man. Tall, lean and with a serious gaze, as though without even knowing her he was concerned for her wellbeing.

'Can I help you?'

'Mistress Bowman?'

She nodded. He seemed puzzled as though he had knocked at the wrong door.

'I was wondering if your husband was in?'

'My husband!' she repeated, alarmed. 'If you are

searching for Henry Bowman, he is indisposed. Furthermore, he is not my husband but my father.'

The man's confusion fell away.

'My apologies. I did not realise he had a daughter.'

'I do not live here.'

Raising her chin, she waited for him to speak. Unconcerned with the time it took him to do so, his eyes drifted over her form to her bloodied apron then beyond her and into the hallway and towards the ground, fixing his gaze on the blood on the wall and floor that she had not yet cleaned away. His expression grew pale.

'Has your father come to harm?' he inquired.

'Who are you, Sir?'

The visitor then seemed to shift gears entirely. He removed his hat, offering her a slight bow.

'Forgive me,' he replied. 'I am John Kirkcaldie, a lawyer. I met with your father yesterday on a matter of some urgency. I've a few more questions I was hoping he might answer in regard to a former patient.'

Did she trust this man? Eliza was not certain. His solemn grey eyes were tinged with green, the colour of buckwheat honey. She had always favoured buckwheat honey. From his voice and manner, he was a learned man. Yet he dressed in the strangest way, like a gypsy. His breeches and coat were ill-matched and he wore no cloak despite the cold. Snow dusted his dark mahogany curls making them glisten in the drab light.

And his hands were gloved, a detail that struck Eliza as odd considering he had forgotten his cloak.

'Have you a calling card? I could give it to my father when he wakes.'

He checked his pockets for a card then sighed as though remembering an oversight.

'Unfortunately, I do not. They are in my other coat, or perhaps my cloak ...'

He smiled wearily then turned to leave, appearing to give up on his mission. It was his resigned smile that finally made her trust him. He seemed lost, separated from himself somehow, and she wanted nothing more at that moment than to be able to help him.

'Please, come in, Mister Kirkcaldie.' She opened the door wider and stepped back. 'Perhaps I can assist you with your inquiries.'

He turned to her with a look of vague surprise. After a moment's hesitation, he nodded. Eliza suggested tea but he refused. Instead, he examined the blood and the splintered bannister.

'What happened here?'

'I'm not entirely certain for my father cannot speak. His jaw is severely swollen, most likely broken. I will say, however, that I do not think he is in his right mind at present for I offered him paper and quill on which he might tell his story and he brushed both aside. My father is not one to snub the opportunity to express himself. Perhaps in a few days time ... What I can gather, it seems there was an intruder who beat him rather brutally.'

'A thief?'

She shrugged. 'Although my father has little by way of worldly possessions, nothing seems to be missing. A robbery seems unlikely. Would a thief knock at the door?' she asked rhetorically, frowning. 'To my eye, it seems my father came down the stairs, opened the door and was attacked. Right here. No other room has been disturbed.'

John stared at the scene, his expression darkening.

'But it is all conjecture at this point,' she went on, observing him, wondering what might have caused the shadow she discerned on his features. 'As I said, I do not live here, and my father cannot speak yet of what happened. The only thing I know is that he did not recognise the man – he shook his head when I asked him.'

John glanced at her briefly before continuing his examination of the room.

'How did you hear of your father's predicament?' he asked.

'A neighbour collected me in the early hours of the morning – by which time the blood was already drying on the floor.' She gestured towards the red smears on the ground. 'I will get to that shortly,' she stated in a matter-of-fact way.

'Have you informed the authorities?' John asked.

She shook her head. 'And I don't intend to. It is enough that I am here. I refuse to do anything more for the man.'

Eliza walked into the parlour without elaborating further and took up a pear-shaped drawstring bag that rested on the floor. Tiredness washed over her in a sudden swell and she thought she might collapse if she did not sit immediately. She sat heavily on a chair, the same chair, John noted, where her father had sat the night before. John followed and took a seat opposite her.

Rummaging in her bag, she produced a silver flask, unscrewed the lid and took a deep drink. She offered the flask to John, who appeared equally exhausted. She sensed it had been a long day already for the lawyer too.

Showing no surprise, John accepted the flask and held it to his lips before returning it to her.

'You are not a teetotaller like your father?' he asked, wiping his mouth.

Eliza rolled her eyes. 'My father's extremes ...' she shook her head, sighing. 'They cannot be maintained. He has fallen off the wagon any number of times but he always climbs back on, more sanctimonious than ever.'

She took another swig from her flask. Temporarily revived, Eliza explained.

'If I sound callous or indecorous, I do not apologise. My father has many enemies. In all honesty, this attack does not surprise me. His views, which are not my own, are fanatical and he expresses them publicly. I have not lived with my father for some years. He offends my sensibilities and my good reason. I warrant there are a hundred men in Boston who feel the same.'

John nodded, staring at her gravely. Suddenly self-conscious, she pushed her errant locks behind her ear, realising she must appear a washer woman, her hair frizzed by steam, her sleeves rolled to her elbows and her apron stained copper. She looked as though she had just stepped from the field of battle.

They were silent for a time, passing the small flask back and forth, sipping as they pondered their very separate but connected thoughts.

'What is your name?' John asked finally.

'Eliza Bowman.'

JOHN LEFT SOON AFTER, reassured that Henry Bowman, although severely injured, was still alive. It was a small relief made greater by the knowledge that he had not been recognised by the man. As he made his way towards Long Wharf, he silently vowed to keep his anger in check, for he came to understand that it was a great and terrible rage that had spurred his violent actions of the night before. He had never been an angry person, rarely even raising his voice; these concerning new feelings confused him.

John shivered. The snow was falling heavier now and he longed for his cloak.

His cloak?

He hadn't been wearing it when he had attacked Bowman. Of that he was certain. He stopped in his path and thought hard for a moment, struggling to recall. The events of the night before were so obscure, they were fading further away each second. Had he removed his cloak and spectacles outside Bowman's house? Had he been wearing the cloak and subsequently burnt it, too? If he had left it carelessly in the gap between houses on Summer Street, it would eventually be found. And his calling cards, those damn calling cards that Joshua had insisted on being printed, were in the pocket. Most likely his spectacles, too.

John turned immediately and ran back towards Bowman's home.

Eliza did not notice John Kirkcaldie searching Summer Street for his cloak for she was standing over her sleeping father, considering her position. Practical to her core, Eliza realised she would have to stay in his house until her father had recuperated. This pained her greatly but, despite her deep loathing of Henry Bowman, she could not seem to silence her sense of duty and responsibility. They cried out like sirens. She was like her father in that respect, she supposed, although his sense of duty was profoundly skewed. The thought of smothering him with the pillow that he rested on flickered across her mind again. It was she who was in possession of the power now; he was at her mercy.

Gathering herself, she resolved to send a message to her landlady immediately explaining her absence. In it, she would include a shilling – her forthcoming rent. And her work? She would have to manage the best she could. The school was not far. If she was organised (which she was, staunchly so) she could hurry back to Summer Street at mealtime, see to her father's dinner, then be back at the South Writing School for the afternoon session. She could not afford to lose her position; her finances and her sanity depended upon it. Besides, it would not be more than a week. Unfortunately, her father had the strength of Samson.

With that sorted she turned her thoughts to Mister Kirkcaldie the lawyer. Considering herself an excellent judge of character, she believed him to be an honest man but there was something out of kilter about him. It was this attribute (as well as those buckwheat eyes) that had charmed her. As she made her way downstairs to pen the message to her landlady, she wondered what he had thought of her.

15

After scouring Summer Street for his cloak, John arrived at his rooms empty handed. He could only hope he had either burnt it or misplaced it somewhere other than the vicinity of Bowman's home. When he opened the door, his concerns were instantly alleviated. On his bed lay his cloak.

'Your friend Mister Franklin recovered it from the tavern,' Kirkcaldie said.

Startled by the voice, John turned.

'He said, "You drifted out of the tavern like an unsteered log" and forgot the thing.' He rose from his seat in the corner. 'Ben looked in remarkably good shape considering the fistfight you described.'

John removed his gloves gingerly and placed them alongside his cloak. He checked the pockets, his fingers finding his calling cards but nothing else. The cloak was found, but where were his spectacles? He had searched every nook, cranny and loose cobblestone on Summer Street and had walked away empty handed.

Frowning, he examined his damaged hands. John still felt sick with guilt. An image then came into his mind of Eliza, her father's blood staining the crevices around each delicate fingernail.

'I took to a man myself, in his house.'

Kirkcaldie did not speak for a moment. John could see him weighing the admission in his mind, considering the wisest counsel.

When Kirkcaldie eventually spoke, his voice caught in his throat.

'For what reason?'

'I was angry. I was so angry that I could not contain my rage any longer, so I hit out at this man.'

'An innocent man?'

John shook his head.

'Not by any means. But within the bounds of the law, the man he wronged will never see justice done.'

Kirkcaldie walked to John and lifted his son's hands, examining the cut and bruised knuckles. For a large, physical man Kirkcaldie had a gentle touch. Surveying required precision of both eye and hand.

'You despised me fighting when you were a boy – your looks of disapproval shot at me like arrows from the crowd ... They were withering because, even as a child, you knew why I was fighting. Of course, Captain Grand earned us good coin, enough to build our home.'

He paused and walked to the window, gazing out on the street below. He longed to be back in Augusta.

'But there has always been something more to fighting for me than coin and I know you recognised that.'

Kirkcaldie readied himself before saying the words he had never expressed.

'I didn't fight because I needed to. I fought because I enjoyed it. Each time I laid my fist into another man's flesh, the madman, the creature inside me was appeased for a time and I was calm.'

John nodded in understanding. 'I fear I have been possessed by similar desires.'

'Many men are, I expect,' Kirkcaldie responded, thoughtfully. 'The way a man controls them will determine the sort of man he is.'

'How do you appease this ... *beast* for good?' John asked quietly, concerned that in his case it might not be possible.

'I'm not certain. Perhaps mine is merely resting,' Kirkcaldie smiled ruefully, remembering the fire that had stirred in his belly when Palgrave had described the injustice of the Molasses Act. 'But for me, it was you. I realised that the only way I could honour your mother was to love you and shape you into the man she wanted you to become. I could not do that as Captain Grand. Now it is Bell. Even though I cannot be a complete father to him, I will do my best to set the finest example of fatherhood.'

He paused, considering his words.

'And Maria ... I admit that my affection for her, my love has grown. It is more powerful now than when I first met her. I want to be the best father, the best man I can be, for her.' Kirkcaldie's face clouded. 'However, although I know she cares for me in her own way, I fear she will never forgive me for my wrongs.'

John sighed. Poor Kirkcaldie. Burdened with the love and care of a child not his own then hampered with restrictions that forbid him to be a father to his actual child ... *Ill-fortuned in love as well*, thought John. Chased from Eastham, forced to sever ties with Maria, suffering the untimely death of Tamesine ... all had been cruel twists of fate. It occurred to John that Kirkcaldie had been a victim of divine injustice: the man had spent his life desperately pursuing freedom, yet still he was not truly free to live as he would. *It's a miracle the darkness in him rests at all*, he marvelled.

A thought struck him. 'Kirkcaldie,' John began. 'Do not allow me or the love you had for my mother stop you from loving Maria and Bell now.'

Surprised by his son's concern, Kirkcaldie gently gripped the young man's shoulder.

'I will always love Tamesine just as you will. However, I do not grieve as I once did. As far as Maria goes ... I can honestly say, perhaps for the first time in all these years, that it may not be only me that is keeping us apart. I fear the problem may lie with her inability to trust me a second time,' he said, ending with a sigh.

'Regardless of her feelings for me, I am grateful for the friendship. The bond between Bell and I ...' Kirkcaldie frowned, unable to describe the connection. 'Teaching him to use a rifle and tie knots has given me as much pleasure as these simple tasks did when I taught them to you.'

John looked at him in confusion. Kirkcaldie tried to clarify his words.

'This was surprising to me, you see, because the bond you and I share was born from hardship and struggle and the immense hours we spent in each other's company. It was born from our complete and utter reliance on one another. Bell and I ... well, we hardly know each other.'

Understanding, John nodded. There was not a soul on earth he knew better than Kirkcaldie. There was not a man or woman alive in whom he had greater trust. Growing pensive, he wondered who would be his Bell or Maria. Who could he temper his rage for? Perhaps it could be Kirkcaldie, the person he most trusted, the only father he'd ever known. Or perhaps it would be someone else …

As a child John had wanted to go to sea, like his father. The Lieutenant's button was a sign of his future, he was positive. But those childhood desires and dreams were quickly lost in the reality of his mother's death and his life in the care of a fugitive.

Looking back on those days, he could see that the beast inside Kirkcaldie had wanted revenge, while John had only wanted justice – he yearned for justice still. Why were women beaten and murdered without consequence? Why were Negroes enslaved? Why were poor immigrants maimed by men begrudging their very existence? John had no answers to these questions but there was a time when he thought he could be an advocate for these people.

However, now he saw that judges were biased, juries were easily swayed, and power and wealth were the jurisdiction of a few. Could this be the cause of his anger?

'What was my mother like, Sam?' he asked then, suspecting that he might have been a different man had she not died. 'I can barely remember her. During spring, there is often a scent that brings her to mind. Honeysuckle, I believe. Did she smell of honeysuckle?'

Kirkcaldie faced his son. It had been an age since John had called him 'Sam'.

He nodded.

'Tamesine was just as sweet in so many ways,' Kirkcaldie said, 'and a great beauty as well. Her hair was a similar colour to your own and as soft as silk. And her voice … when she spoke, each word was a perfectly formed note. Her West Country accent was stronger than mine and far more musical – she had the voice of a lark. Your mother was clever and shrewd, courageous too, but she had a stubborn streak. As stubborn as stone.' He laughed softly as though lost in a memory. 'But she was gentle and kind and showed concern and sympathy for people, just as you do.'

John wondered what his mother would make of her son if Benjamin Hornigold had not cut short her life. He longed to be the man his mother had hoped but he feared that whatever stirred inside him, so recently awakened, would not rest easy.

FOR AN INSTANT, Kirkcaldie had considered telling John of his plans to smuggle Palgrave's molasses into the colonies. Violence was not the only means of seeing justice done. However, Kirkcaldie fast realised that there was no good end that could come from John knowing of his and Palgrave's plan. He would either disapprove and volley another barrage of withering glares Kirkcaldie's way or he would want to be involved. Kirkcaldie could tolerate neither outcome. As a consequence, when he departed John's company in the early evening, he explained he was meeting an associate of his friend, a gentleman who wished to purchase a large supply of rum.

'Palgrave asked if I might act as middleman on this occasion,' he remarked to John, offhandedly. 'He had planned to come to Boston himself but there are equally important matters he must attend to in Augusta.'

It was a lie – but only a white lie, Kirkcaldie told himself.

In truth, he was meeting with a man he had conversed with earlier that day at Long Wharf. After some conversation and monetary coercion, the man – a docker named 'Smith' – had professed a willingness to return to the sea. He had been a pirate once and had sailed with Jack Rackham, a captain in the same style as Bellamy. Smith had been one of the lucky ones who had been granted a King's pardon.

Always cautious, Kirkcaldie would only say that he had some dealings in Nassau at one time. By the close of the conversation, the docker, a wizened Scotsman whose forthright manner Kirkcaldie admired, committed to assembling a crew for the smuggling expedition.

Smith also vouched for the three likely candidates they now sat with at the Poseidon's Trident. The trio had smuggled before and seemed adept at the art, matter-of-factly explaining the intricacies of the profession in an animated manner that proved to Kirkcaldie their enthusiasm and suitability for the venture. The environment created by the Navigation Acts and the Molasses Act was fertile ground for smugglers. What's more, Smith explained, it was cheaper for the Crown to turn a blind eye to the smuggling than to send more Red Coats to enforce the law.

'Tha's not to say that it will be a simple matter,' Smith went on. 'But as long as we dinna announce our arrival in Boston Harbour to the customs official, there is verra little chance of us being hampered in our cause. And you, Sir, have you sailed in the past? The Atlantic can get squally this time of year.'

'I have,' Kirkcaldie said in a low voice, attempting to conceal the fear that suddenly rose in his belly.

'And Mister Williams?'

Kirkcaldie nodded, giving no hint as to the degree of his and Palgrave's experience on the sea.

The men parted ways with a plan to meet in Portland on the third of the following month. Bellamy handed Smith a purse of coin.

'For the ketch and supplies. You and the crew will receive your payment when we return to Portland.'

Smith nodded, content with the arrangements.

'And who should be captain?' Smith asked. 'There needs to be a sole man in charge.'

'I will,' said Kirkcaldie.

He departed the tavern feeling quite enlivened by anticipation and fear in equal measure, more so than he had in many years.

16

TAMESINE: BOSWARTHEN CHAPEL
CORNWALL, 1705

Tamesine walked in the direction of Madron Well along a rough, muddy track lined with blackthorn and hawthorn, uncertain why she was heading to the ancient holy site; she only knew she must go there. Having walked the path hundreds of times, her steps were sure and certain. She was familiar with every root, rock and hollow.

Unacquainted with the area, John followed close behind, ignorant of Tamesine's destination. Against her mother's wishes, she had departed the quay with John. If she returned home, she would surely be beaten again then banished. *Were John's words at the quay heartfelt?* she worried now. Trusting others did not come as easily to Tamesine as it did Eseld. Doubt sat as heavy as a headstone in her chest.

A short way from the well, the path was blocked by a large puddle. It had not rained for some time, so while the puddle was wide and deep it was also swampy, smelling marshy and fetid. It had been shielded from the sun by the overhanging branches of the birch trees. Tamesine, used to doing for herself, hitched her skirt knee-high, revealing her stockings and slippers, and readied to step into the mire.

'Wait!' John cried, moving closer to her. In one swift movement, he lifted her into his arms.

Their faces were so close, almost touching. She could feel his breath against her lips and his arms against her legs and waist. They smiled nervously before John stepped through the puddle, placing Tamesine gently on her feet on dry ground.

'Thank you,' she uttered softly.

'My boots are made from calfskin,' he explained. 'They are quite water-proof.'

Tamesine could sense his uncertainty, too. They were suddenly awkward, when just that morning they both had been entirely eclipsed by love. From where did this agitation spring? Was he troubled by his decision to save her, now only realising what his hasty actions and words meant? Hampered with a wife from the most common of stock until his dying day? However, his gallant gesture spoke otherwise and it heartened her.

They reached the well by midday. The high sun filtered through the mossy branches overhanging the spring, illuminating the colourful clouties tied among the leaves. John stared up at them in wonder.

'They are offerings,' Tamesine explained. 'This is a holy well. Those who bathe in the spring are healed.'

She knelt on the muddy bank and lowered her hand into the water. Cupping it, she raised it to her mouth and drank deeply.

'Come,' she said, water trickling down her chin. 'Even if you don't believe in the magic, the spring will certainly do a fine job of curbing your thirst on this hot day. Your chacking for water must be as great as mine.'

John joined her by the bank and they drank together. When he rose, he took in the unfamiliar scene. His sharp emerald eyes, made keener from three years at sea, caught on something further along the path.

'What is that?' he asked, pointing.

Tamesine did not need to look.

'Boswarthen Chapel.'

Sensing that the waters had worked their magic, Tamesine was feeling more settled, happier with the choice she had made. She took his hand and led the way to a space surrounded by four low stone walls, about chest height, that were covered in lichen and moss. John ventured warily inside the ruins as though frightened of what he might find. He touched the sturdy granite altar stone, rubbing his hand across its surface in amazement. Unlike the walls, the altar and rugged stone pews were absent of moss.

'Are services still held here?' he asked.

Tamesine nodded.

'It's a *teg* place for Mass,' she murmured, reverently. 'Without a roof, walls or a door surrounding me, I feel as though I'm closer to God somehow ... As though He's all around me.' She breathed in the air, as if breathing in the Holy Spirit. 'Foolish, I know,' she added, embarrassed by her admission.

'Not at all.' He walked to her and raised her chin with a fingertip. 'A "*teg*" place to be wed?'

Before she could respond, Tamesine grew distracted by his clear green eyes. Taking her silence for doubt, he went on.

'I love you, Tamesine. I believe I fell in love with you the moment I saw you in Penzance. I do not understand why the fates have chosen to bring us together, but they have, and I love you.'

'The fates?'

'Indeed. Surely it was the fates that instructed the wind that day to blow your cap to me in the breeze.'

He untied her cap and removed it, touching her dark amber curls where they fell against her shoulder.

'My love, I am being reassigned to Nassau on New Providence Island.'

Tamesine felt the panic rise in her chest. Seeing her expression, John hurriedly sought to explain.

'In my time here, I have established a reliable system to root out smugglers. New Providence has, in recent years, become a pirate haven, the scourge of the Crown. I am to go to the island to assist in finding and punishing these wicked men. I take a personal interest in this undertaking as well. You see, my mother has business interests in the Caribbean.'

His earnest green eyes searched her own.

'I leave in two days' time. Tamesine, there is a captain aboard the *Greyhound* who will see us betrothed by supper. I would have you follow me to Nassau and there we will begin a life together.'

Although John spoke with a determination and purpose that was difficult to resist, a million fears and dreams surged through her mind like hope upon a deathbed. They centred on the world into which she might be stepping with a man she barely knew. In her life, she had never ventured further than Penzance; how could she trust John King when she trusted no-one? How could she leave Eseld, the only person she did trust?

Then Tamesine remembered her father and her future flashed before her in an instant. Among the sea of images that rushed over her consciousness she could not discern a spark, a hint of a life where she might be happy. *A life without hope is not a life worth living*, she decreed unto herself at that moment.

But Tamesine would not be wed by an English captain on board an English ship.

Having decided her fate, Tamesine slowly unwound the cravat from around John's neck. She took his hands, loosely tied the fabric around them and finally slipped her own hands through the unsecured fabric. Then she pulled the knot tight with her teeth. John seemed wary. Before she spoke, she offered him a reassuring smile.

'Repeat after me if you feel the same,' she whispered. 'But I warn you – do not utter anything you do not believe.'

Tamesine gathered her thoughts, taking comfort from the ruins around her. Boswarthen Chapel was her place; she and Eseld had played here as children. She had prayed here too. The surrounds were as familiar as her own skin. There was no reason to feel uncertain.

She began.

'You cannot possess me for I belong to myself, but while we both wish it, I give you that which is mine to give. You cannot command me for I am a free person, but I shall serve you in the ways you require, and the honeycomb will taste sweeter coming from my hand.'

She paused for a moment, as John repeated what she had just uttered, and thought of her next words. While she had witnessed three handfasting ceremonies, she had not committed the words to heart; the vows were different each time and depended on the couple.

'I pledge to you that yours will be the name I cry aloud in the night and the eyes into which I smile in the morning. I pledge to you the first bite from my bread and the first swallow from my cup. I pledge to you my living and my dying each equally in your care. I shall be a shield for your back and you for mine. I commit myself to your path in life. Your happiness is my happiness. Your troubles are mine also.'

She listened as John repeated her words. There was but one more oath to make.

'This is my handfasting vow to you, to be held in a partnership of equals forever.'

'This is my handfasting vow to you, to be held in a partnership of equals forever,' John echoed.

Tamesine pulled at the knot with her teeth once more and the pair unravelled the fabric together.

John looked at her, a smile on his lips.

'Then we are betrothed.'

'Handfast,' Tamesine corrected. 'In Cornwall, they are one and the same.'

'Wedding bands?' John asked, looking about him as though two golden rings might appear among the rocks and moss of Boswarthen Chapel.

Tamesine shook her head.

'We have drunk from the same cup, as is custom,' she pointed, indicating the stream, 'But we *should* exchange gifts, a token that's close to our hearts.' She frowned. 'I have nothing to give you.'

If gifts could not be exchanged, then the handfast could not be made sacred. She began to panic.

Sensing her alarm, John lost himself in a moment of serious contemplation, then removed a jackknife from the pocket of his breeches.

'May I remove a lock of your hair from the strand that hangs over your heart?'

She nodded, proud of his resourcefulness.

As his hands moved cautiously towards her breast, Tamesine's heart began to flutter like the wings of a lark. He cut through a strand of hair delicately. Once the lock was in his hand, he wrapped it in his handkerchief and placed it gently in his pocket.

'Now that's done, I fear I have nothing to offer *you*,' he said, tilting his head.

Tamesine looked about his person, determined to complete the final part of the custom. Then she hit on the solution.

'One of your brass buttons ... that one,' she pointed, 'the one on your breast pocket.'

John promptly cut through the stitches and handed her the object.

'*Now* we are handfast,' Tamesine confirmed.

TAMESINE LED John to a grassy hillock not far from the chapel.

'The is St Maderne's bed,' she explained as she sat on the velvety moneywort.

She waited for her husband to join her before she went on.

'A poor crippled man came to the well near seventy year ago. He bathed in the spring then came here and slept. When he woke, he was healed.' A smile crossed her lips. 'I don't know if the tale is true or merely folklore like the tales of mermaids and piskies, but I like to believe it happened. It gives me hope that wounds can heal.'

John took her hand and examined it. He stroked each finger gently. Tamesine was ashamed of her coarse, weathered skin and she tried to pull her hand away.

'This will heal, too,' John murmured, kissing each fingertip softly.

Tamesine's heart lifted with both longing and trepidation. She had heard the women at the quay speak about what went on in their beds at night. They spoke crudely – of poking and pounding, burdens and babes – laughing in resignation at the wretched hand they had been dealt. To Tamesine, the act – whatever it was – sounded unspeakable. But Tamesine knew it was what couples did once they were handfast, sometimes even before. When she looked at John now, pleasuring at the gentle touch of his lips against her fingers, she could not imagine it being as the women described.

'There's a ceremony the girls in Cornwall perform on May Day every year,' she said nervously. 'They come here to St Maderne's bed and fasten two stems of grass around a pin. They drop it in the water and as it sinks, they count the bubbles that rise.'

'Why?'

'To be certain of the number of years they have left of waiting to be wed. People like me – boys, girls, men and women alike – live on hope. It's all we have.'

'Have you ever taken part in this custom on May Day?'

'Never,' Tamesine answered.

John drew her to him and kissed her gently on her lips.

'Shall this be our marriage bed?' he asked

Tamesine nodded, then lay her back against the cool, silken heather.

AUGUSTA, MAINE

Palgrave nodded gravely and without enthusiasm as Kirkcaldie outlined the arrangements he had organised with Smith.

'Are you losing interest in the venture?' Kirkcaldie asked, concerned by his friend's reticence. 'You seem displeased.'

'No, no ... Everything you have told me has eased my mind considerably of any concerns I may have had. Smith seems like a trustworthy sort – the Scots we had on the *Whydah* were hard-working, honest types – and the risks involved are low, medium at worst. I was merely cataloguing the tasks I must complete before the morning of the third ... I must notify my suppliers in Trinidad and Martinique, and there are still some calculations to set my thoughts to ... I will not bore you with the details.'

'There's no need for you to sail with us,' Kirkcaldie put in, 'if, as you said, the stakes are too high.'

Palgrave laughed. 'Who, then, would manage you and your worriment? This enterprise shall have a captain who is petrified of the sea.'

Kirkcaldie shrugged as though his decision to captain

the ship had not been his choice. Absently, he walked to Palgrave's well-stocked bookshelves and gazed at the rows of leather-bound tomes.

'I was a good captain, I believe.'

Palgrave nodded heartedly in agreement.

'But I have lived with this fear since the *Whydah* was wrecked.' He turned to face his friend. 'In truth, I have missed the sea and the life that came with it. Surveying with a crew has shown me a few of the same joys, but there's no hunt, the risks are fewer and the quarry not as great. Besides, every inch of land I survey is at the behest of the governor.' He gave a wry smile. 'And you know how bothersome I find authority. Thinking back on the hardships I've overcome before, I believe I can overcome my fears now.'

Kirkcaldie never ceased to amaze Palgrave. Here was a man willing to face his greatest fear in the pursuit of something even greater. In contrast, Palgrave shied away from his own fear, allowing it to chase him around corners and into hiding holes, worrying excessively day and night. The thought of what he would lose if Leah discovered their scheme circled in his mind constantly. However, if he did not embark on this venture, they would lose everything gained since his return nearly fifteen years ago.

'What are you planning to tell Leah of our intentions?' Kirkcaldie asked, as though reading his mind.

Palgrave rose and moved to the piecrust table on which stood two bottles of Eight Bells rum and four cut crystal glasses. He poured them each a drink then brought his glass to his lips.

'I do not know,' he said, suddenly tired. 'In all honesty, I do not know.'

～

THAT NIGHT, Kirkcaldie's sleep came in fits and starts. Concerned for John and Palgrave, he was uncertain how to advise either of them. He had departed Boston with John's promise that he would seek Kirkcaldie out if he sensed the desire for violence surge in him again. As for Palgrave, if he confided in Leah, their plans would surely be scuttled.

Eventually, as the lantern clock on the landing chimed one, Kirkcaldie resolved that his son and his closest friend were both grown men, possessing wits far greater than his own. He turned his mind to the upcoming enterprise and was made excited and anxious all at once and, like Palgrave had earlier, he began to inventory what must be done before the day of their departure. When sleep finally came, it was as deep and as fathomless as death.

Then he woke, dragged from the depths, gasping for air. Maria was by his bedside. Her face was cast in darkness but her body seemed to glow, as though her veins ran with lightning; it was as if she were a ghost.

'What are you doing here?' he said groggily. She touched him, laying her hand on his chest. He did not move.

'You were dreaming of the wreck,' she whispered.

Her presence and the touch of her hand were calming. He often dreamt of the *Whydah*, of the sensation of drowning. Of gripping John in his arms, desperately hoping to save the boy. *How had she known?* he thought, still a little stupefied by sleep.

He put his hands on hers and his breathing began to ease.

'Thank you. I thought you were a ghost ... but instead you are an angel come to my rescue.'

Maria twined her fingers in his.

'I will always save you, Samuel Bellamy, as I did on the night of the wreck, and as I will continue to in the future.'

He marvelled at her – her words, her body; she radiated heat. He was growing warmer, sensing his blood surging through him. *Is it possible she cares for me?* he wondered, a glimmer of hope fuelling his desire further. Her eyes were fixed on his. He could not look away.

'What do you wish for, Samuel Bellamy?' she said.

She was filled with a fire, a vital energy so strong that if he wished for riches, for the world, he was certain she could grant them both to him in this moment. But instead, he asked for his innermost desire.

'You.' It was the truth. He loved her, solely her.

A soft smile glanced across her lips.

'How?' she asked, slipping under the blanket, pressing her body against his. Despite the heat of their bodies together, her breath was cool on his face.

'In every way.'

The rise and fall of her chest fell into rhythm with his own, as if it had always been so. Wrapping his arms around her, he drew her even closer until any space between them closed. He could see her eyes now, wide open, blue and tender, searching his face, as though she could see more than other people. If he were denied her now, his body and soul would fracture into a thousand pieces.

Finally, their lips met and he fell into her entirely.

IN THE MORNING, she was still by his side. He gently brushed her hair from her face to take in her beauty in dawn's first light. *I was right, she is an angel*, he thought. *My angel.* Yet the energy he felt in her last night was not pure by any means. She had wanted to consume him ... and he had let her.

Last night had been unexpected. He had assumed that

the portrait of Bell she had painted for him had meant something, but when he had arrived in Augusta that afternoon, she had been guarded and distant. When she welcomed him into the house, he thought he had glimpsed affection in her eyes, perhaps more, but he hadn't been certain.

The woman was a puzzle. Kirkcaldie had believed that at some point she had vowed never to be hurt again; although she was willing to share her son with him, he had been sure that she would not share her heart. As he considered what had brought about the change, she rolled towards him and pressed her face against his chest, kissing it softly so that goosebumps rose along the length of his body like quills. With eyes still closed, she stroked his back, her fingers halting occasionally to probe a scar or puckering of skin as though reading his past. They were both defined by their scars, he realised. Leah and Palgrave, too.

Kirkcaldie sighed, closed his eyes and enjoyed the lightness of her touch against the rutted and ridged contours of his skin.

'Your body tells me that you have suffered enormously,' she said as she took Kirkcaldie's head in her hands, looked deep into his eyes. 'Your mind has been injured as well, I warrant.'

He raised an eyebrow in question.

'Your thoughts are as turbulent as the ocean. I can feel it.'

What is she seeing? he wondered, amazed. It felt as though she was looking into his soul.

'How?'

She shook her head and released him. Rolling over onto her back she was silent for a moment, attempting to articulate what she had never spoken before. She twisted a strand of her golden hair around her finger before speaking.

'I don't know. I began to sense these things after Silas raped me.'

The candidness of her language stunned him for a moment. But this was her nature, he supposed; Maria did not abide by usual conventions. The very fact that she had fallen in love with him when she was just a girl was proof of that.

'I could not find meaning in anything then, so I looked for it in other ways – in the flow of a fast-running stream, in the boughs of a tree or in the formation of the clouds. We are created from water and air, we are rooted in the ground and gain sustenance from the sun ... I suspect I draw knowledge and energy from the world around me, but I don't know for certain.'

She turned to face him. He brushed his fingers against her cheek.

'You frighten me, Maria. But I am drawn to you in a way I don't understand. I always have been.'

They gazed at each other, acknowledging the closeness they now shared.

'I knew it from that first day on the green,' she said. She lay her hand on his chest once more. 'Do you love me, Samuel Bellamy?'

His reply came without hesitation.

'Yes, Maria. I love you with all that I am, body and soul.'

18

BOSTON, MASSACHUSETTS

Once Kirkcaldie departed Boston, John gave in to his nocturnal cravings, unable to heed his father's advice. Not since before the wreck of the *Whydah* had he slept soundly, but recently his night-time restlessness had grown much more persistent. He was plagued with recollections of his crime as well as the unceasing urge to do it again. What was he searching for? A victim, a man to beat and maim? He wasn't certain.

Each evening, he would walk to Summer Street first and stand in the shadows at a safe distance of Bowman's house and watch. Eliza cared for her father for ten days. John could see her form in the window as she moved about the house. His eyes tracked her up and down stairs and from room to room. Her movements seemed light and effortless. Watching over her calmed the turmoil that raged inside him. John had been burdened with guilt since his attack on her father; contemplating her feelings as he watched her, it occurred to him she must be equally burdened, caring for a man she despises.

Distracted and finding it difficult to put his mind to the

law, he had spent his days discovering more about her. She was six and twenty, unmarried and taught for a living at the South Writing School on the corner of West and Common Streets. He had watched her there as well, again from a distance. She was well-proportioned and extremely attractive – in John's opinion – with an olive complexion, serious brown eyes and a back that was ramrod straight.

Eliza was not, however, a school dame – she instructed both girls and boys in writing, English grammar, geography and double-entry bookkeeping. From a neighbour at the boarding house, he discovered she even had a strong grasp of Latin, although she was not currently teaching the subject. According to the neighbour, the Latin master refused to allow a woman to instruct the students in classical languages, an immense source of distress for Eliza which she complained about frequently.

John sought out other people in Eliza's life, too, explaining he was a lawyer representing her grandfather's estate. The old man, who had never met his granddaughter due to an estrangement between certain members of the family, 'wished to discover whether Eliza was of honourable character before leaving her an inheritance'.

'However, it would not be wise to discuss my visit with Mistress Bowman. We don't want her to get her hopes up, do we?' John would explain, smiling, handing over a calling card that seemed to legitimise the inquiry.

Kirkcaldie had been a model tutor in the art of deception. 'You have to believe the falsehoods, John,' he had advised on many occasions. 'If you don't, others won't either.'

According to Eliza's landlady, a polite, sensible widow, Eliza Bowman was a model boarder. She kept her room tidy and always paid her rent on time. Most importantly, she never invited friends into her room or had attempted to smuggle male acquaintances into the boarding house as had been a habit of a number of previous tenants. Eliza Bowman, it seemed, was the perfect Bostonian citizen, too good to be true. Like Kirkcaldie, John did not trust willingly. But he wanted to trust Eliza.

His meandering thoughts returned to her relationship with her father. Was it Bowman's extreme opinions that had forced her estrangement from him or something else? Despite his searching, John could not find answers to these questions. Most of those he spoke with were unaware she had any family at all.

Each evening, he would follow her from the writing school to Summer Street, and later, when she left her father, to the boarding house. Then one night she stopped abruptly on the road, before John was able to duck into the shadows. She turned quickly. Her frosty stare pinned him to the spot. Raising an eyebrow, she strode in his direction, halting only inches from him.

'Why are you following me, Mister Kirkcaldie? Has it something to do with my father or do you have a more sinister motive?'

She had a flair for the dramatic which he liked. He opened his mouth to speak but she interrupted.

'And do not attempt to tell me this is a coincidence. I have noticed you before – at the school and outside my boarding house. You are too striking a man to hide in a crowd.'

She paused, her eyes glinting steel. John was unsure whether her statement was a compliment or an insult.

'Furthermore, Mistress Forsythe, my landlady, informed me a lawyer had stopped by, asking questions. She said you were exceedingly interested in my comings and goings. She's a suspicious woman, Mister Kirkcaldie, and I would not be surprised if your prying will become the root of my future homelessness.'

John stood astounded. Never having been confronted by an educated and well-bred woman in such a brazen fashion before, he found that he enjoyed being challenged in this way.

She reached into her drawstring bag and produced a pair of spectacles. John's heart stopped. They were his. He stood staring at the object like a fool, speechless.

'I assume these are yours. The first time we met, I noticed you had a line on the bridge of your nose – the tell-tale mark of a man who wears such an item.'

She placed them in his hand. His composure returned.

'I found them in a crack between the cobblestones and the front door. You must have dropped them when you came to visit after my father was beaten. Or perhaps one evening when you were spying.'

Curious, logical, direct. *She would make an excellent lawyer, if women were permitted into Harvard,* John thought.

'Have you been walking the streets blind for over a week?' she finished.

'Not quite ...' replied John with an involuntary laugh. Embarrassed, he soon recovered himself then altered his tone, growing serious.

'I have been concerned for your welfare.' John said, attempting to distract her from his real purpose, although his statement was partly true. 'Your father's attacker might return, and I fear you will be hurt.'

It had struck John in the days he had been watching her that Eliza Bowman was most often alone. What's more, she took no care to limit the likelihood of an attack from another quarter. It was not safe for a woman to walk the streets of Boston alone at night. Even though she was forthright, independent and exceedingly intelligent, there was a vulnerability about Eliza Bowman that made John want to protect her.

'I see,' she responded doubtfully.

'Please, forgive me. May I walk you home?'

He placed the spectacles on his face.

'Ah, that's better.' He smiled at her. 'Now I have my eyeglasses, I might have a better chance of finding my way.'

Eliza stood in the street for some minutes considering John's request. Finally, she nodded, softened, returned his smile. She turned and continued on her journey home, John by her side.

'How is your father's health?' he inquired.

'He has much improved.'

'Is he able to identify his attacker?

'No. The assailant wore a mask, or something like one, to conceal his identity. Nothing has been stolen. Even the poisonous pamphlets my father pens were left untouched.'

'Pamphlets?'

A shadow fell across her lovely face. 'Messages of hate.'

That was all she said on the matter, but John could piece together the rest of the story. The pamphlets were a vehicle for Henry Bowman's extremist views on immigration and foreign workers. He had glimpsed one briefly himself before Bowman had scrunched it into a ball and thrust it in his pocket. John wondered how large a following Bowman and the Colonial Vanguard had managed to gather.

'Then you suspect your father's attacker may have been a person who did not share his views?'

'I am 100 per cent certain of that, Mister Kirkcaldie. If I were a man, if I were capable of such an act, there have been many times when he and I would have come to blows.'

Although they should not have, Eliza's words comforted John. They were no excuse for his behaviour in attacking Bowman, but it was obvious the man provoked extreme reactions in others as well.

'I suppose you find me shocking?' she went on, her temper rising. She had mistaken John's reticence for horror. 'How could a daughter speak about her father in those terms? You must think me monstrous.'

John stopped. 'Not at all.'

Eliza turned. John noted tears in her dark eyes. They were full of mystery, inscrutable. It reminded him of looking into the sea on a moonless night. How many hours had he spent doing just that on the deck of the *Whydah*, willing his mother to return? He could still feel the smooth oak of the ship's railing gripped tight in his small hands.

'It is he who is the monster!' she declared.

John looked into her pooling eyes, searching for words to console her.

'We do not choose our fathers or our mothers,' John responded.

He was reluctant to share his story with her but seeing her distress, he wanted nothing more than to be able to comfort her. He knew her rage and her frustration at a situation which she had no power to alter.

'I do not know who my birth father is, but I was raised by a man who became a father to me. I could not have wished for a finer example. Neither could I have wished for more love or care than I received from him.' He shrugged. 'At the same time, without knowing why, I have missed my actual father. I have longed for him, feeling that our blood connection might be the source of the true contentment that eludes me. It's what we are encouraged to believe, after all, but perhaps it is a lie.'

'"The blood of the covenant is thicker than the water of the womb",' she quoted.

He paused. He was impressed and flattered that she had understood his perspective so clearly. They walked on in silence as John considered his relationship with Kirkcaldie. Their bond was unbreakable due to the blood they had shed together in battle – the trials and challenges they had faced together.

'Familial ties mean nought. Blood can be shared in other ways,' he murmured.

Eliza nodded. 'You must be a very fine lawyer, Mister Kirkcaldie.'

'I don't think my partner would agree.'

When they reached her boarding house, the pair stopped for a moment on the street outside.

'I promise not to follow you anymore. However, if there's anything I can help you with – legal or otherwise – please do not hesitate to contact me.'

John reached into his cloak pocket and produced a card. Eliza read it thoroughly, before placing it into her bag.

'I will,' she said, taking his hand and squeezing it gently in thanks.

ON HIS JOURNEY back to King Street, John contemplated all that had passed between himself and Eliza Bowman. He had probably said too much, inviting questions in the future, but he had wanted to confide in her, hoping his words would provide solace for them both. John had never confided in anyone, not even Joshua.

John had been just a child of nine when Sam Bellamy had entered his life. Had he made connections to anyone else he had met since then? Yes, but Kirkcaldie had sworn Palgrave, Leah, Maria and the older children to secrecy.

Yet John needed to tell her something of himself. He wanted to offer a glimpse of the truth. Although he understood the reasons for the deceptions, he was Kirkcaldie's creation and, he believed, he was beginning to lose sight of himself, his mother's son. He had been told by Joshua on numerous occasions that it was his earnestness that scared women away ... but perhaps they fled because he had never wanted to let them in, tell them his story.

Having stared into the liquid depths of Eliza's eyes, he was certain she would understand his past. Thoughts of his new acquaintance warmed him as a gentle flight of snow began to fall. Eliza's flawless olive complexion, her raven hair and the unreachable depths of her eyes were at the forefront of his mind as he walked.

Passing an alleyway, he was distracted by a noise, the sound of a fracas – the muffled cries of a woman and the low, husky voice of a man. Goosebumps prickled the back of his neck. He stopped. Living in close proximity to Long Wharf, John was no stranger to the sounds of violence but where they had once repelled him, they now enticed him. He peered into the darkness of the narrow laneway. An anguished whimper emanated from the black and he hastened towards it.

'Take your hands off her,' John called as he took in the scene awaiting him.

A young woman was being held against a wall. She struggled under the weight of her assailant's arm which was pressed against her neck. Her attacker was slight but even in the shadows John could tell by his stance and wiry physique that he was strong. John guessed he was a seaman, judging from the Monmouth cap he wore.

'Keep your shirt on,' the man said. 'She's a punk. All I want is the flourish that I am owed. Leave us be!'

The area was ripe with the stench of refuse and piss. John pulled his scarf up over his nose, sensing the creature within him wakening. He did not try to soothe it back to sleep. He removed his eyeglasses and placed them in his pocket.

'He says he paid me, Sir. He says he paid me a shilling, but he has not,' the girl screeched.

John could not see clearly in the dim laneway but she sounded no older than a child.

'Move away from her,' John directed in a low voice. Muffled by the scarf, it took on a menacing tone. 'Whether you have paid her or not, the young lady clearly is having second thoughts.'

'A punk is not entitled to "second thoughts",' the seaman muttered sarcastically.

As John took a step forward, he felt the now familiar surge of rage and blood grow warmer, ever warmer. He drew in his breath, releasing it slowly, attempting to control himself. Giving the man a chance to walk away.

'Fortunately, I do not mind an audience,' the attacker quipped then proceeded to lift his victim's skirts, his body pinning her to the wall.

His heat flaring anew, John approached, gripped the man's shoulder and wrenched him off his feet. To the girl he said but one word: 'Run.'

She fled in an instant.

Surprised to have been halted in his assault, the seaman regained his wits, rose and came at John, ramming him against the wall, winding him. *This man is a fighter*, thought John. Knotted and muscled, he was a tightly packed round – a savage, a baiting dog.

Henry Bowman he was not.

Although John's breath had been knocked from his lungs, he managed to push his opponent away. John readied for the fight ahead, breathing in huge swathes of air, exhilarated.

Then he smiled. *A challenge.*

He balled his hands into tight fists. They were still tender but he didn't care. The seaman ran at him, red and furious. John swung back his arm and caught the man on the chin. Pain shot through his hand like a quarrel. Dazed, the seaman came at him again, fists swinging wildly. As he had seen Kirkcaldie do hundreds of times, John focused on his opponent's body. Although the effort was greater, it would preserve his knuckles.

John landed two or three solid punches to his opponent's belly before the man fell to the ground. John kicked him hard in the ribs. The man coughed. Then he was still.

Watching, waiting, nearly sated, John kicked him once more for good measure.

19

AUGUSTA, MAINE

Leah enjoyed her walk into town each week. It gave her the opportunity to purchase any provisions the household required, send Palgrave's correspondence and collect the mail that was waiting for him and, occasionally, for herself. Even in the chill of a winter's morning in Augusta, she valued this rare time alone, time to meditate on the events of the week.

Palgrave found the crunch of snow beneath his feet displeasing, but Leah relished the noise. It was a satisfying sound as though each step was being recorded for eternity. Now a light fall of snow dusted her dark cloak and, as she approached the Kennebec, she spied through the snow-laden spruce trees the ice harvesters at work, sawing through large blocks of ice while their horses waited patiently, if not a little bored, as if to say, 'When might we leave?' This morning, she was carrying a number of woollen blankets she, Sarah and Maria had knitted. They were for the hospital, always overrun during the winter months. She would call by after she had collected the mail.

Usually, during the hour-long trip Leah would be able to

reach an accord in her mind about any event that might be troubling her. But this morning was different. Her thoughts still eddied and swayed by the time she placed her foot on the frozen surface of the river. She suspected her husband was lying to her and she hated herself for it. *Am I naturally distrustful?* she wondered. *Do I read more into his moods than other wives might?*

She recalled the events of that morning. From the vantage point of their bed, she had watched her husband dress. He was always careful in every aspect of his attire, fond of quoting to his children 'the apparel oft proclaims the man'. Even when they had lived in Eastham, penniless and exhausted each morning from the previous day's work and worry, Palgrave had dressed with the dignity and care of a gentry man.

Turning, noticing her eyes on him, Palgrave walked to the bed and kissed her softly on the mouth.

'Good morning, my love.'

She smiled and stretched her legs catlike in the bed.

'I'm heading to Portland on the third with Kirkcaldie.'

She looked at him expectant of further information.

'It's a fishing expedition, I suppose, to see if there's not a way around this damn Molasses Act.'

'I see.'

Leah pushed back the blanket and swung her feet to the ground.

'And why is Kirkcaldie accompanying you?'

'Oh, he has some acquaintances there among the governor's men to whom he is willing to introduce me.'

Palgrave concentrated on his reflection in the looking glass as he tied a cravat around his neck, ensuring the knot was symmetrical at his throat. His gaze flicked for an instant in Leah's direction.

Leah walked to the ewer and poured water into the basin.

'How long will you be gone?'

'A few weeks.'

'A few weeks,' she repeated. 'That seems a long time considering the nature of your endeavour. Portland is not but two hours away.'

Palgrave cleared his throat.

'If I can find no contentment in Portland, we were considering travelling on to Boston, to visit the governor himself.'

'Even still ... a few weeks ...' she protested as she leant over the basin.

'I simply want to ensure all contingencies are catered for ... time spent visiting with Joshua, heavy snowfall, et cetera,' he said, feigning indifference. 'In any case, it has been decided.'

That had been his final words on the matter. He had exited their chamber with the strong tread of purpose. What remained in his wake was a heavy feeling of dread in the pit of Leah's belly.

When Leah arrived at the Green Dragon, she pushed open the oak door. The place was empty and dark. Morning board was long over. Leah looked around; it was not yet ten in the morning and only a few candles burned in the sconces. A large fire in the hearth had been lit and the space was resonant of sandalwood.

Leah recalled her trepidation the first time she had stepped foot in a tavern – the Garvey's ordinary in Eastham. Distrustful but determined, she had sought out Mary Garvey in order to secure her family's escape from the town. Now Leah was filled with a similar anxiety – she was concerned the heavy snow may have impeded the passage of the postal riders.

Riyogi curled his neck around the curtain that led to the kitchen, catching sight of her.

'Mistress Williams,' he called happily. 'I wasn't expecting to see you this morning. The snow fell in sheets last night. I will make you tea.'

Her friend disappeared once more. Leah could hear the low scrape of his moccasins against the wooden floors as he moved about the kitchen.

'It takes more than a little snow to stop me collecting the mail,' she called as she removed her muff and cloak. 'You must know by now, Riyogi, that this is my favourite part of the week.'

Besides Ben Shute, Riyogi was another person benefiting from Tabby Post's legacy and riches. After Tabby vanished, Riyogi transformed the Green Dragon into a refuge of sorts for those who were in danger and in need of shelter. The idea had germinated when Tabby had placed Polly Cool and her children, along with Jeremy Cool's 'disciples', in his care after she had shot an arrow through Cool's neck and led them to freedom. Those families, refugees from the depraved man's settlement at Harper's Creek, had since moved on; Palgrave and Kirkcaldie had helped them secure land and loans that ensured each a new life. Later, months after Tabby had disappeared, Leah convinced her husband to invest part of Tabby's wealth in Riyogi's charitable venture, despite the unlikelihood of a financial return for his client.

Now Riyogi's boarders were mostly women with children fleeing husbands who were either drunkards or violent or both. He had even housed a number of runaway slaves – both Negro and Indian – for a time. For these fugitives, he had established special lodgings in the basement. Then there were those like Charlie Purse. A gypsy of sorts, he had been in Riyogi's employ since his recovery from the dreadful beating he sustained when he was first passing through the town. Riyogi did not discriminate. Any lost or desperate soul – no matter their gender, colour or circumstance – was welcome at the Green Dragon.

Riyogi returned with a pot of the green-as-grass tea he liked so much. Leah did not care for the taste but it was warming and it seemed that Riyogi took great pleasure in making it for her, utilising his cups, whisk and ladle. They sat together at the table and Riyogi poured for them before producing a number of letters from the pocket of his loose-fitting jacket. Leah flicked through the pile, her eyes stopping on one envelope longer than the others. She gazed at the well-formed letters of the address and smiled.

It has been months, she thought, drawing in her breath. She slotted the correspondence back into the middle of the pile then placed the letters to one side. Opening it was a pleasure she reserved for later in the day, when the house was quiet – the children resting and Palgrave occupied in his study. She could then pore over each word at her leisure.

Riyogi brought a cup to his lips, drawing in the hot liquid through his teeth.

'Tell me Riyogi, what news do you have?'

'I visited my friend Charlie at the hospital,' he began.

Leah nodded.

'He is still quite ill.'

'Strange. The day before last he was on the mend. Have the fever and cough returned?'

Riyogi smiled. 'No, they have abated. I am afraid he is heart sick.'

Leah placed her cup on the table and gave her friend a questioning look.

'It seems your daughter is the source of this malady.'

'Elizabeth?' Leah asked surprised. Her eldest daughter was recently married to an accountant from Albany. Leah supposed it was possible that Elizabeth could have turned the unfortunate young man's head, leading to him being heartbroken at the loss ... However, she could not imagine Elizabeth taking an interest in a roamer like Charlie.

Riyogi shook his head. 'Sarah.'

Leah raised her eyebrows in surprise.

CHARLIE HAD FOUND sleep difficult to come by. His cough kept him awake during the night. When he finally dozed off in the morning from sheer exhaustion, he was always disturbed by the hustle and bustle of the ward – the patients receiving their breakfast, Doctor Shute attending to his morning rounds. He sensed the doctor at his bedside now, but Charlie refused, out of natural-born stubbornness (a trait inherited from his father) to open his eyes.

Shute slid his cool fingers around Charlie's wrist, checking his pulse. Charlie could hear him breathing, waiting. Satisfied, the doctor removed his hand then slid the bed clothes quietly from his patient's chest. They barely rustled. Even when the ice-cold ear trumpet was placed against his bare skin, Charlie refused to stir.

Then a woman's footsteps.

Sarah? he wondered, hopeful.

The ear trumpet lifted from his chest, the bed clothes drawn up to his neck, the creak of a chair, the scratch of a pencil on paper. Charlie was still aware of another person's presence by his bedside.

'Good morning,' Shute whispered.

A woman's voice in greeting. Leah Williams.

Sarah's mother came into the hospital frequently to lend her time to the overworked Doctor Shute. Charlie had seen her many times at the tavern too. She was a good friend of Riyogi's. They both seemed to enjoy her visits, their private banter and easy laughter told him this. Charlie wondered what connected the unlikely pair – an Oriental and a wealthy Puritan goodwife – and how their bond had formed.

Charlie could only guess at the age of Leah Williams but, with her buttery complexion and thick honey-coloured hair, she was extremely fetching. Yet in Charlie's eyes, although she shared none of her mother's fine looks, Sarah was the prettier. The daughter's delicate features seemed chiselled by a master sculptor and her bearing was proud, regal even. Fortunately, Charlie was a long-legged individual himself, so a tall woman did not scare him as it would a man of lesser stature.

Any fool could see (apart from the fool who Sarah most often directed her thoughtful and kindly gaze to) that she was in love with Benjamin Shute.

'Poor man is dead to the world,' Leah remarked.

Fortunately, not, Mistress Williams, Charlie thought. *Or perhaps I'm not so lucky ...* It had been Charlie's plan to slip in and out of the area unnoticed. Then he had been done over and left for dead. While grateful for Riyogi's help, now, without him even wanting it, he was part of the community, never to go unnoticed again. At first, his loss of anonymity had complicated things. However, the more he became acquainted with Sarah Williams, the more his original scheme lost its shine.

Still, he was stubborn and he refused to renege on a promise, even if it was one made only to himself and the dead.

'He hasn't been sleeping. The cough, you understand.'

He heard Leah come to his bedside. She paused for a moment. He could hear the measure of her breathing and smell the scent of her hair. He felt as though she was inspecting him. Then she drew away.

'Where would you like me today?' he heard her ask the doctor.

The doctor didn't answer. Distracted.

She came closer and said in a low voice.

'Ben, you are exhausted. Go and rest.'

The doctor sighed. Still the scratch of the pencil.

'There are the accounts I need to see to. Perhaps after that ...'

'Sarah can manage the accounts. She is extremely competent with figures.'

'Do you think she ...?'

The pencil ceased. Charlie imagined the doctor looking up at Leah Williams from his seat, the woman poised like a guardian angel.

'Sarah could help with a great deal around here, much more than she does already.'

Charlie feigned stillness, although the urge to leap from his bed and clasp his hand over Leah Williams's mouth was desperate. He knew what she was playing at, but her daughter deserved a better man than Ben Shute. There was no denying he was hardworking and compassionate – a fine doctor in all respects. Furthermore, he was handsome and his family well-connected, Charlie had heard. There were any number of Augusta's women who'd take him, readily, eagerly. However, he was the type of man who could never be attentive in the way a husband needed to be.

Not many memories remained of his father, but Charlie could recall his consideration of his wife, the gentle caresses, soft kisses and loving words in her ear when he thought Charlie wasn't watching.

For the life of him, Charlie could not fathom how the doctor had overlooked Sarah Williams, especially when it was obvious how much of herself she was willing to give to him. If Ben Shute did not spend every waking moment at the hospital and with his patients, Charlie would have said that he was already in possession of a sweetheart. The man was completely immune.

Charlie wasn't certain why he was angry with the doctor. After all, the less attention he paid to Sarah the better, as far as Charlie was concerned. But it rankled him no end that the man Sarah loved was ignoring her affections. *But who can explain the workings of the human heart?* he concluded. He gave an involuntary sniff of disgust.

Suddenly the space around him closed and he felt the gentle press of a damp clout to his forehead.

'He's perspiring, Ben,' he heard Leah say. 'The fever again?'

'Most likely too many bedclothes,' the doctor replied.

An instant later, Charlie felt an unwelcome rush of cool air as the quilt was whisked from his bed.

20

BOSTON, MASSACHUSETTS

John stood over the body of the seaman. The alleyway and the street beyond were deserted, so he was able to listen hard for the sound of breathing. He moved closer, got lower, then held his hand very near the unconscious man's mouth. John felt warm breath against the back of his palm.

Rising, he moved calmly towards the entrance of the alley. When he looked back into the dark, the man could not be seen, hidden as he was in the shadows.

John located his spectacles, put them on then plunged his injured, shaking hands into the pockets of his cloak. Then he walked with as much self-possession as he could muster towards King Street.

As he walked, he ruminated on events, attempting to calm himself. His body still surged and his legs felt weak, as though he had run for miles. He did not experience the same sense of guilt and fear that he had after his attack on Henry Bowman. In fact, he was possessed with a powerful sense of purpose. He had saved a girl from harm. Although that had not been the sole reason for his actions, it offered him a means to justify the violence.

John had seen wrongs committed throughout his boyhood in Nassau and during his years with Kirkcaldie. Benjamin Hornigold, the Flying Gang and the atrocities they had committed in Nassau; the hanging of Kirkcaldie's shipmates. Those men he knew only from the few days he had sailed on the *Whydah* but they had accepted him as crew and cared for him like a younger brother. They had been good men who were executed unjustly.

Then there was the man from Kirkcaldie's story. With some emotion, Kirkcaldie had once told him of a midwife he had known whose father was wrongly accused of the murder of his own brother. The weight of the burden had driven the poor soul insane.

It was for these innocents, and those like them, that John had chosen law and not the Church when he was accepted into Harvard University. However, it had become glaringly evident to him in recent months that in a colony where the only authority was a monarch who cared not for the people but for his coffers, justice was a hard commodity to access. *Especially*, thought John, *for the poor and powerless – prostitutes, immigrants, Negroes, women ...*

The injustice he witnessed daily was responsible for his feelings of fury and helplessness. But he had come to understand that there was more to what stoked his rage. Since his chance meeting with a nameless man a few weeks ago, his long-buried anger over Tamesine's murder and Hornigold's lack of punishment had awakened something in him – something fierce and angry – a wild animal that needed nourishment or it would surely consume him. John sensed its presence as keenly as the bitter wind that blew off the ice-coated harbour.

OVER THE NEXT FEW DAYS, John attempted to shift back into the steady rhythms of his life, rhythms that had been disrupted since Joshua had led the ill-fated Felix Schleck to his room more than a fortnight ago. He and Joshua visited taverns and the courthouse, hoping to procure clients. It was on the fourth day, when they had only managed to engage three clients – all involving the non-payment of bills – that John realised he had become nothing more than a debt collector.

So when Joshua returned one day with the *Boston Gazette* suggesting they scour the obituaries in search of a possible wrongful inheritance or deathbed confession, John groaned in frustration and discontent. Dutifully, reluctantly, he flicked through the newspaper. An article caught his eye.

'Masked Angel Saves Woman'. John skimmed the news report quickly. It seemed that the young woman whom the 'masked angel' had saved was Sara MacArthur. From the gist of the article, it appeared that she had approached the publication with her story. *To what end?* John wondered.

Money, most likely.

He had heard of the *Gazette* paying for news. The article was not incendiary, merely reporting the facts of the event. The story did not mention Sara's employment only that she was 'dragged into the alleyway against her will by a ruffian who threatened to rob her'. The seaman with the Monmouth cap would disagree, John was certain.

The article described Sara's attacker in great detail – short of stature, pale complexion, whiskered. He had not been found by the authorities. *Probably on a ship bound for the Indies by now*, John thought. Even in her 'distress', Sara had managed to recall her attacker's eye colour – brown.

However, the description of her saviour was scant – only that he was tall, dark-haired and wore a mask. John supposed that in the dark alleyway his scarf might be mistaken for a mask ... Nevertheless, he was thankful for the lack of detail. John briefly speculated on the welfare of the seaman but the thought was soon lost when a knock happened upon the door.

The lawyers looked at each other in confusion. It was a gentle knock, not that of a Red Coat or John's landlord. As far as they could recall in their time as partners, a client had never come to the door of their own volition, despite the address on the calling card.

John rose, donning his coat and checking his cravat was straight. He waited a moment for Joshua to do the same before opening the door.

It was Eliza. John's heart lifted at the sight of her. It had been almost a week since he had last seen her but he had not forgotten her eyes. In the gloomy light of the hallway, they were the colour of cinnamon. They enlivened John's downcast mood.

John invited her into the room and a series of awkward introductions ensued. He could see by Joshua's expression that he recognised her surname, so John quickly hastened to discover the reason for her visit, offering Eliza a seat. He sat beside her with Joshua behind the desk. Theirs was not the picture of a successful law practice, but John did not offer excuses for the shabby environment. He judged Eliza Bowman the rare type of woman who would neither be distressed nor impressed by the surroundings in which she found herself.

'There are siblings in my class – sisters – Joanna and Jessie Brown,' she commenced without invitation. 'They are both very clever and delight in all the joys of learning. Their father, William Brown, is a wheelwright. He's an extremely forward-thinking man who sees value in educating his daughters, but it is their mother who steers the focus of the household. She is an educated woman herself and is able to read and write. She keeps the account books for her husband's business. Joanna and Jessie have inherited their mother's understanding of numbers and Mistress Brown hopes to see them well-prepared for whatever lies in their future.

'However, the family have recently been the victim of a reprobate landlord by the name of Penn. He has raised the rent twice in the last six months. While Mister Brown's services as a wheelwright are much sought after, as you can surely understand, a raise of sixteen per cent in six months is quite scandalous. If he does not pay, the landlord has threatened the family with eviction.

'While this is not so bad in itself – the Browns could perhaps find more suitable lodgings owned by a more scrupulous landlord – the yard where Mister Brown operates his business is also owned by Penn. The family live adjacent to their business, which itself lies next to the blacksmith Brown works closely with.'

Eliza looked at the two men.

'Do you see the nature of Mister Brown's dilemma?'

'Of course,' the lawyers remarked in unison.

'Mister Brown,' continued John, 'cannot afford the rent and the upheaval and cost involved in relocating his family and business elsewhere in the city would be too great.'

Eliza nodded. Joshua glanced at John before speaking.

'But unfortunately, Mistress Bowman, as unscrupulous as the situation surely is, Penn is within his rights to raise the rent. Likewise, he is also within his rights to have Brown evicted if he does not agree to payment. Furthermore,

Mister Brown could well end up in debtor's prison if he does not produce the arrears.'

'The most distressing news about this entire affair,' Eliza went on, ignoring Joshua's summation, her colour rising, 'is that Mister Brown will be forced to move from Boston to the countryside where land is affordable. He has even grown fond of the idea of owning his own premises. Sadly for his wife and his daughters, the only schools to exist that allow female enrolments lie in Boston. Mistress Brown, in particular, is immensely disheartened.'

Eliza cleared her throat. John observed her, noticing her face tense slightly.

'She would go to *any lengths* to remain in her own premises.'

Eliza's eyes were locked on his. It was if she were trying to convey something more to him, but he could not glean the meaning. He raised an eyebrow in question but she said nothing more.

When the partners in law glanced at each other again, they each understood the outcome of Eliza Bowman's visit. John rose. Eliza was his acquaintance. He would have to be the one to disappoint her.

'Mistress Bowman, there is no way we are able to proceed. As Mister Williams pointed out, the law is on Penn's side. If the only injury that results from his decision to evict the family is that two girls cannot continue with their education, then I fear that a judge would not even entertain such a petition.'

Her face hardened. John could see how unhappy this news made her and he wanted nothing more than to be able to help. His heart moved into his throat and he swallowed hard.

'This is the law and, no matter what the opinion of

Mister Williams and myself, it would be a futile effort,' John said. 'I wish it were not so.'

'I see,' she said, looking down at her fingers fiddling with the cord of her drawstring bag. 'Instead of bookkeepers and clerks or teachers, young women capable of earning a living independent of men, the Brown girls will become the wives of farmers, their sharp minds blunted by the drudgery of their lives.'

She took a deep breath, as if to fortify herself.

'Please trust me when I tell you that Penn is the most despicable of men.'

Eliza's final statement was tinged with earnest sincerity.

'Perhaps these girls would *like* to be married, work side by side with their husbands,' Joshua considered. 'My own mother has done so for her entire married life. Her mind has not dulled in the slightest.'

John nodded, thinking of Leah Williams and her outspoken, confident ways. Joshua was correct, but his experience of women was skewed. His mother and his aunt were not typical of most females.

'Well, your mother is extremely fortunate,' Eliza uttered, chin raised. Her tone hinted that Joshua knew very little about the lives of women in a city such as Boston.

She rose and moved to the door.

'I will show you out,' John said.

As he followed her down the stairs, he rapidly inventoried various options in his mind, quickly dismissing each. There was no room within the law to manoeuvre. Unfortunately, the rights of tenants in the Massachusetts Bay Colony were limited at best.

They stood on the frosted cobblestones as Eliza slipped her slender fingers into her bright red woollen gloves. She caught him gazing at them.

'I am not a very accomplished knitter,' she said, holding her hands aloft. John noted the holes and irregularities in the stitches. 'My mother died when I was quite young. I was raised by a man with little sympathy for the feminine arts.'

John pressed his hands into his pockets.

'I am sorry I could not be of more help. The law ...'

But before he could finish, she turned and walked away.

∾

THAT EVENING, after the odious chore of tending to her father, Eliza retreated to her room at the boarding house. Seeking solace, she pulled a large box out from under her bed and placed it on the dresser, opening it with reverential care. She picked up the pair of calfskin gloves that lay within. After stroking the fine leather, she slid the gloves onto her slim fingers. They were a perfect fit. Then she removed the garment the box contained.

Eliza donned the heavy red cloak and fastened the ribbon in a neat, even bow beneath her chin. Breathing in deeply, comforted by the weight of it on her shoulders, she stared at her image in the looking glass and contemplated her visit with John Kirkcaldie and Joshua Williams. She had been disappointed, especially by John. Eliza was profoundly aware of what a mother would do for her children.

Since caring for her father, fleeting visions of the past had surfaced in her mind then just as quickly disappeared. A woman being taken away. No, dragged away, screaming. The cries that had echoed like a tragic melody in her mind in recent weeks had been her mother's, Eliza was certain. It was the one memory around that loss which had stuck, along with a feeling of being protected in some way. She could sense others, but they hid in the shadows, beyond her reach.

The visit she made to the young lawyers had brought her mother to mind unbidden, triggering tiny sparks of recollection with only a few catching. There were no portraits of her, no likenesses, so Eliza didn't know whether she resembled her or not. There had been times when her father, after a drink or two, had chided Eliza's appearance, calling her a 'dark-skinned gypsy'.

'Just like your mad slattern of a mother,' he'd spit.

Now, as she stood in her mother's red cloak and tan calf-skin gloves, she struggled to recall her at all.

Stella Dufort had arrived in the Massachusetts Bay Colony when she was twenty-one years old. The opéra-ballet company of which she was a member had caught the eye of Governor Joseph Dudley when he visited Paris on a diplomatic mission in an effort to stop the raids the French had begun on the New England frontier. The governor's mission was unsuccessful, but the ballet did appeal to his cultural sensibilities and, at his invitation, the company toured Massachusetts. During a performance of *The Merry Sisters of the Indies* in Boston, Stella landed badly while executing a cabriole, breaking her ankle. A bonesetter was summoned.

Henry Bowman was attentive during her recovery and seemed to do everything in his power to affect a positive outcome. *And why would he not?* thought Eliza, bitterly. Gleaned from her memories, from the brief flashes of images Eliza possessed of her mother's appearance, Stella was a striking woman – slender with chestnut hair and eyes the colour of chocolate, straight-backed, her neck as lithe and graceful as a swan's. A woman like that would surely gain the attention of any man.

Henry would visit Stella in the boarding house where she was residing, demonstrating exercises in order to aid her recuperation. She was to twist her ankle this way and that, three times a day. Once the splint was removed, he would massage her ankle and long slender foot with lavender oil, pressing his thumbs into the soft pockets on either side, making Stella wince and giggle. Henry's gentle care impressed her greatly and she began to look forward to his visits. As they got to know one another, she encouraged her admirer to advance his studies. Bowman soon became apprenticed to a physician, intending to balance his paid work as a bonesetter with his new endeavour.

Yet despite Henry's attentive ministrations, Stella was never to stand on point again. Her company returned to Paris without her. Encouraged by the governor, who felt a sense of responsibility at having had a hand in ruining the promising career of this native French woman, Stella worked as a ballet teacher to the daughters of the colony's most wealthy. During this time, Henry Bowman, quiet and respectable, became as attentive a suitor as he had been a bonesetter. He showed interest in Stella's teaching and discussed his studies with her regularly. She enjoyed hearing of his progress. He showed her consideration and tenderness and talked of the future, perhaps one they might share together.

Henry's focus on her did not wane in the three years it took her to accept his marriage proposal.

Still, Eliza could not help but be bewildered by her mother's choice. Although lovely and not yet twenty-five, perhaps Stella – her career over, an immigrant alone in the colony – felt that the familiarity of the bonesetter's face, along with his patient attentiveness and her memory of his earnest care, would make Henry the safest port in the storm of her young life.

And following their marriage, they did seem happy. Eliza liked to imagine that Henry had been a source of happiness for her mother at some time in their past together, even for a brief period. If so, it would mean that Stella had not been entirely foolish in agreeing to marry him. But things soon changed. Soon after Eliza was born, Henry began to imagine that other men were appraising Stella, and that she returned their interest. So he took to watching her. Then the drinking and abuse began. He gave away his studies, deciding he could not spare the time away from her. Stella's hope that her husband might become a physician was crushed.

While Bowman was never violent to Stella, if he noticed a man cast his eye her way, he became vengeful and threatening, accusing her of inviting attention. Then one day he informed her that if she was ever to leave him, he would keep their daughter.

Eliza had learnt all this only recently, from a letter she found hidden in the folds of the red cloak she now wore. *When had it been written and concealed?* she wondered as she gazed in the mirror. *What was its original purpose?* Although the letter was lengthy, for Eliza there were still countless gaps in the story of her mother's life. Stella Bowman was a portrait only half executed.

Since Eliza had discovered the cloak and the letter, she frequently tried to imagine herself in Stella's predicament. Taking in her mother's familiar jasmine scent, still imbued in the garment, Eliza believed she understood Stella's loneliness and pain.

The cloak was all she had of her. There were no costumes or programmes from her mother's performances.

No mementoes. Eliza was certain there had been once. She remembered a miniature of her mother in a costume of gold, and a pair of pearl earrings ...

Whether Stella had hurled all of her past into the fire one day, cursing her wretched existence as the wife of Henry Bowman, or whether Bowman had done so after Stella was taken away, Eliza did not know. But she had been gladdened, more so than she could have imagined, when she discovered the cloak, gloves and letter in the attic of her father's house. It was the only good thing that came of her enforced stay with the man she hated.

21

THE CARIBBEAN

Palgrave and Kirkcaldie stood at the stern and watched Santo Domingo disappear in the distance. Dawn had only just happened upon them and the sunlight lightly caressed the ocean, turning it a brilliant shade of indigo. Palgrave had successfully procured twenty-five hogsheads of molasses. The barrels were stacked and secured neatly in the hold, behind a lesser number of hogsheads that housed tobacco leaf and coffee. Although Palgrave was in no need of either commodity, they were part of their ruse, in case the ship was boarded by the custom official in Casco Bay, Portland. However, American smugglers in the Caribbean were many. All agreed that the officials at the ports along the eastern coast were shiftless types, happy for the captain of a vessel to merely swear an oath on the Bible that they carried no contraband.

Now, as the Spanish island diminished to a pinprick on the horizon, Palgrave willed their words to be true. To their advantage, Kirkcaldie was the captain. It was he who would do the talking when they reached Portland's busy harbour. Palgrave had witnessed Kirkcaldie's charm a hundred times before. He was expert at fabrication and never displayed even the trace of a tell.

It would take four days to reach Portland. They had encountered a storm one evening, only a day after their departure. It was not a vicious storm, nothing like the tempest that had claimed the *Whydah*, but for most of the night it was squally and rough. The ketch they sailed in was small and bobbed like a cork in the heavy swell. Kirkcaldie had remained composed, although Palgrave noted that his friend's jaw was clenched tight and his movements on deck clumsy.

Distracted by an untethered barrel, Palgrave had not noticed his friend disappear. He had discovered Kirkcaldie below deck, sitting on his bunk with his eyes closed, breathing deeply, as though mustering his courage. Palgrave remained silent in his concern, watching. As the vessel pitched and rocked, Kirkcaldie's expression did not alter but he seemed to grow larger, broader, stronger. Together, they returned moments later to the quarter deck, Kirkcaldie calm and in control, issuing orders as though they were sugar plums. A changed man.

Recalling the event, he turned and looked on Kirkcaldie's serious profile for a moment, wondering what thoughts occupied his mind. During their recent time in the Caribbean, Kirkcaldie had been more like the man he remembered than ever before. He had laughed more freely, jested with the crew. Palgrave had offered Kirkcaldie payment for his services. He had refused with a smile. 'Your continued production of Eight Bells rum is payment enough,' he had said.

On the travellers' return to Augusta, Kirkcaldie and Maria intended to wed. Adhering to tradition, Kirkcaldie had formally asked Palgrave for permission to marry Maria as Joseph Hallett had died some years before. Palgrave was delighted by the news, heartened that both parties had finally taken his advice. He had happily and readily agreed, offering the groom-to-be a handsome dowry. Kirkcaldie had brushed the suggestion aside, again with a smile.

Palgrave had never discussed finances with his friend. Kirkcaldie's refusal led Palgrave to puzzle over the source of his income. What had Kirkcaldie accrued as Captain Grand? What did the governor's surveyor earn? Palgrave could not guess. He had made no investments on Kirkcaldie's behalf and, while living an extremely quiet life, for as long as Palgrave could remember, Kirkcaldie's was the life of a wealthy man. He had, after all, enrolled his son at Harvard University and kept a large home outside Hallowell for many years.

Kirkcaldie had confided that the enormity of the *Whydah*'s riches rested at the bottom of the Atlantic Ocean – he and John had leapt from the ship holding nothing but each other. The beach near the wreckage, under the cliffs of Wellfleet, was searched the day after the wreck by the authorities. The only flotsam to wash ashore were the drowned, blue bodies of his crew mates.

Yet to Palgrave's knowledge, Kirkcaldie had never been in want of funds. It seemed to him that the longer he knew Kirkcaldie, the more of a mystery the man became.

On their departure from Augusta, they'd left Maria and Leah to make the wedding preparations. At sea, Palgrave learnt that Kirkcaldie and Maria had chosen not to tell Bell of their plan to marry until his father had returned safely. While Palgrave could not bring himself to tell all of their venture to Leah, Kirkcaldie had confided in Maria about the true nature of the trip. He told his friend that he'd been unsurprised to find she already knew, having sensed it some weeks ago. Kirkcaldie and Maria therefore agreed that, given the danger involved, they did not want Bell to be saddened should something happen to prevent the wedding.

Knowing that the betrothed couple had confided in each other, Palgrave wondered again why he had been unable to tell Leah of his plans. He looked out at the blue waters, deep in thought for a moment, then turned to Kirkcaldie.

'Are you sorry our adventure is nearing its end?' Palgrave asked. 'We may not return to these islands for some time.'

'Not at all. I have a great deal to look forward to in Augusta – a new life with Maria and Bell. And you?' he returned.

'To be truthful, my feelings are an odd combination. On the one hand, I'm sorry to be leaving the sea. I have missed this life – its vagaries and freedoms. But on the other hand, I am also happy to be returning home. There is a certain comfort that comes from the routines of family life and those of business. Columns of figures in a ledger can be extremely soothing for a restless mind.'

Kirkcaldie laughed quietly.

'However, I still yearn for the thrill of adventure ...' admitted Palgrave, lowering his eyes. 'Childish, I know.'

Kirkcaldie studied his friend's face for a moment.

'Not at all. Other men play at cards and gamble away their livelihoods to gain the sensation you describe. Or they play false with their wives.'

Palgrave nodded. 'That I will never do.'

'What will you tell Leah of your bronzed complexion?' asked Kirkcaldie.

Palgrave looked at his friend, a smile growing on his lips.

'I will inform her that the weather in Boston was unseasonably fair.'

Together they laughed at the ludicrousness of the comment.

'WHERE ARE THEY, do you suppose, sister?' Leah asked as she embroidered a fine linen tablecloth she had made for Maria's dowry. Even though Kirkcaldie wanted nothing, had declined Palgrave's offer of a dowry, Leah refused to send her sister into his home empty handed. 'Did he tell you anything?'

Maria placed her sketchbook on the ground and moved to the hearth. Leah glanced at the sketch. It was a drawing of the scene outside the window – the summer kitchen with Leah's vegetable garden in the foreground, all of it washed by snow. Art was to Maria as air was to others. Apart from the terrible period in Eastham when Maria was imprisoned, Leah could not recall a moment when her sister did not have a pencil, pastel or paint brush in her hand. It was how she always pictured her sister.

'Trust your husband, Leah. It should not matter to you where they are. He will return to you,' she said firmly, poking at the fire to rouse the flames.

'Do you trust Kirkcaldie?' Leah returned.

Maria nodded.

'Wholly?' she added, raising an insinuating eyebrow. Leah would not go so far as to mention John's mother by name. Tabby was different – she belonged to Kirkcaldie. Maria belonged to Bellamy.

'Wholly,' Maria said firmly.

Leah found it difficult to believe. She found her sister's faith disconcerting. After the crucible they had endured due to the rash actions of both Palgrave Williams and Samuel

Bellamy, Leah was sceptical of her sister's sincerity. But this was her sister – Maria trusted Kirkcaldie, even when he had given her every reason not to.

'It's your greatest fear, is it not?' Maria said, rising and moving back to her seat by the window. She picked up her sketch book and began to draw.

Leah lifted her eyes from her stitches and looked at her sister.

'That Palgrave will leave you, abandon you as he did before.'

Maria had a way of slicing through to the core of an issue, refusing to temper her words in order to lessen their impact. It was brutal and painful and bloody. Maria never insinuated or implied. *This was the nature of truth*, Leah reasoned.

Leah did not answer the question but focused on her work, thinking. She could feel Maria's eyes on her, waiting for a response. When none was forthcoming, she heard the sweep of her sister's pencil against the paper.

On the rare occasion Palgrave had travelled to Boston for business, he had always done so reluctantly. This trip, he had been different. She had sensed him attempting to contain his eagerness to leave. The awareness of it had filled her with terror. Typically a still man (Palgrave could sit for hours without a movement), in the days before he departed he appeared increasingly distracted. She had watched his foot beat a constant rhythm on the floor and his fingers tap staccato on the table during supper.

She had long wondered what it was in his nature that drew him away from her. After many years of reflection, Leah eventually realised she was partly responsible for him leaving her all those years ago. She had saved him when she had forced her way into his life after the death of his first wife Anne and his children, but she had never allowed Palgrave to save her and their family. In a sense, she had gelded him. At that time, the only way he could become the man he needed to be was to leave her.

When he had walked away from her in Eastham – when she had seen him walk into the woods, the trees closing behind him – she had been pushed from a cliff and had broken into a thousand pieces. But Palgrave had returned. Slowly, cautiously, she had recovered. As one, she and Palgrave had eventually put the pieces of her soul back together, although it had taken another crisis to act as the catalyst.

Now neither of them needed saving. They were comfortable financially and as husband and wife, or so she believed. This latest trip had left her in turmoil once more. *Is it a flaw in my own nature that repels him or merely a lust for adventure?* she wondered.

Diverted by her thoughts, she pricked her finger on the needle. Annoyed, she hastily buried the wounded digit in her apron so as not to sully the tablecloth. If Palgrave were to leave her again, she was not certain she would be capable of a second resurrection.

When Leah finally placed the cloth aside and her thread in the basket by her feet, she sighed.

Maria lifted her eyes to her sister.

Unable to withstand Maria's gaze, Leah looked away.

22

BOSTON, MASSACHUSETTS

Joshua arrived at midday, bringing with him cheering news – damages had been awarded to Felix Schleck to the amount of 370 pounds.

'And Bowman?' John had asked.

Joshua shrugged.

'You know he cannot be prosecuted. However, the Dutch East India Company were hasty with the agreement which suggests –'

'That they want Felix Schleck to disappear and, hopefully, Henry Bowman along with him.'

'I am confident Bowman's employment will be terminated,' agreed Joshua, nodding.

The younger partner released a rueful sigh. The action expressed John's feeling that while Felix Schleck had received a type of justice, it was unsatisfactory. Still, it was the best that they could hope for under the circumstances. Although the result of their case was a win, both lawyers knew it was not true justice. John immediately began to ponder how this might affect Eliza.

A few moments later, Joshua departed in haste,

informing John he was meeting Schleck so they could head to the company offices together and collect the funds. Joshua's urgency to have the money in his pocketbook was as desperate as Schleck's.

'Would you care to join us?'

The handling of paperwork, the signing of documents and writing of petitions – the minutiae of the law – had become Joshua's domain in the years they had worked together. He possessed a sharper eye for detail than John. As a result, his partner was not disappointed when John responded in the negative.

With his thoughts still circling Eliza and the taste of discontent bitter on his tongue, John donned his cloak and scarf and walked to Prince George Street, the location of William Brown's wheelwright shop. Once he reached the street, the place was easy to find – John simply followed the sound of hammer against metal.

Standing at a distance, he watched Brown perform his task. The wheelwright stood with a younger man of about fifteen years in a courtyard surrounded by a mix of low stone cottages. John judged the fellow to be Brown's son; they shared the same stocky build and jutting jawline. Despite the cool weather, both men had their sleeves rolled to above the elbows of their muscled arms. Wood was piled in a heap on the ground and a healthy fire burned.

The younger man waited, tongs in hand, for a number of heavy strips of iron to be ready while Brown waited nearby, holding a large wooden wheel that partially sat in a shallow ditch in the ground. When the iron was ready, hot and red, it was brought to the wheel and the two men proceeded to hammer it fiercely onto the wheel with fast, frantic, heavy strokes before the iron cooled. The sound pealed out in the courtyard; John could feel it in his teeth.

Just as quickly as the hammering began, it ceased. The iron was secure. Water was poured into the small trench where the wheel sat. Brown turned the wheel so the hot metal was instantly cooled; stream rose like a phoenix, enveloping both figures. When it cleared, Brown inspected the work, nodded. His son returned to the fire and retrieved another strip of the curved iron.

Two young girls swept past John and entered the court-yard. These were Eliza's students, John guessed. It appeared that they had finished school for the day and came to bid their father and brother a good evening. They were dressed in dark woollen cloaks and heavy stockings. Hooded, capped and scarved, their faces could barely be seen. The men were still occupied with their task so after a brief greet-ing, the girls retreated quickly into one of the cottages.

From what John could observe, they were a hardworking family who were being taken advantage of by their landlord, Penn. But taking advantage was not a crime. He watched the scene for several minutes then left the father and son to their business, continuing along Prince George Street, stop-ping at a tavern. He bought a pot of ale.

As the innkeeper cleared a table, he called to a customer.

'Penn, how is the pheasant pie this evening?'

Startled by the fortuitous encounter, John swivelled on the stool, taking in the man seated at a table in the corner.

Penn sat hunched over a meal and a cup of cider, his forehead resting against his hand. He was a measly sort of man; he appeared thin and wretched-looking to the observer, but John could not determine if it was bias that was tainting his opinion or fact. If he had no knowledge of Penn, would he simply view the man as another Bostonian taking a meal before returning home for the evening?

John frowned. Before he'd acted in the Bowman case, he'd had evidence that Bowman was corrupt. Similarly, John had witnessed, with his very eyes, the seaman attempting to molest Sara MacArthur. The situation with Penn was different. He trusted Eliza when she described Penn as 'despicable' but how objective could she be? John drank his ale and departed, stopping a little further up the road.

It was nearly an hour before Penn emerged from the tavern. John checked his pocket watch – eight o'clock. Penn walked briskly in the opposite direction, back towards the wheelwright's shop. John saw him stride into the courtyard and enter a door opposite the one he had seen the Brown sisters enter earlier.

John stood watching, waiting. He speculated on how he should proceed.

Penn had not broken the law. He had not committed a heinous crime, any crime in fact. As distressing as his actions were, Penn was not a criminal – legally – as far as John could discern. As difficult as it was for Eliza to bear, John felt there was nothing he could do.

Staring at Brown's house, as though he might gain comfort from merely watching over the family, he saw the windows grow dark, the final candle snuffed. He turned to leave. He was almost to the street when he heard the sound of a door open then close. John halted. He heard footsteps on cobblestones.

Turning, he hurried back to the courtyard's opening. A woman crossed the yard at a frantic pace, lifting her skirts to avoid the puddles left from the melted snow around the wheelwright's fire. John could see the embers still glowing.

The woman moved swiftly from Brown's house to Penn's. *Mistress Brown*, John thought. A handsome woman, no older than Maria Hallett and just as attractive. She rapped softly at Penn's door. Within a moment, it was opened. Mistress Brown entered.

His interest piqued, John emerged from the shadows, moving further into the courtyard. From a distance, he stared at Penn's windows but could see nothing. Glancing around, certain he could not be seen in the dim light of the evening, he walked closer to the house and held his ear against the door. He could hear voices but to distinguish them was impossible. Lifting his scarf over his mouth and nose, he edged around the side of the house to a window. The curtain was open just a crack. Moving slowly, silently, he peered through the opening.

John drew in his breath at the scene before him, turning away in an instant. Sickened, he could stomach the sight no longer than a few seconds.

Mistress Brown was bent over the table, her skirts lifted. Penn stood behind her, rutting like a ram. With his spindly hand, he pressed her pretty face against the table, a pitiful expression of blank resignation resting upon her countenance.

Standing in the blackened courtyard, pressed hard against the wall, John waited for his breathing to steady. This was Penn's crime. Eliza had known; it was her female sensibilities which forbade her from giving voice to the knowledge before Joshua and himself. Recalling her visit and their conversation, John now realised that Eliza had hinted towards the reality of the situation; she had plainly told them Mistress Brown would do anything for the sake of her daughters. However, John and Joshua had been so preoccupied by the legal aspects of the circumstances that they had not considered the moral.

A few minutes later, the door opened. John pressed his back further against the wall. Mistress Brown scurried back across the cobblestones to her own door and let herself in.

How long have these nightly visits been occurring? John wondered. Mister Brown would be so intensely exhausted from his work each day that he would not miss his wife when she slipped out at night. Eliza was correct. Penn *was* despicable.

John took a deep breath, feeling the beast in him stir. He closed his eyes, breathing fast. Tamesine's face drifted into his mind, free and proud. How hard she had worked, the indecencies she had endured for her son ... He stood for some moments, breathing deeply, knowing he should attempt to temper whatever was waking within him.

But he did not want to.

John glanced around, seeing if he could spot anyone near, but Prince George Street was deserted and the windows of the surrounding cottages were dark. He removed his spectacles and secured his scarf over the lower part of his face then moved to the front of the house. He didn't knock at the door. Instead, he turned the door handle. The shameless nature of breaking in and trespassing into another man's home did not even occur to him. For years he had studied the law. Now each appeal, writ and rule were lost to him like stars in the daylight.

The door opened smoothly without a creak and John stepped inside, closing it softly behind him. No lights burned in the house. The crackle of the dying fire was all John heard as he stepped lightly down a hall, past the parlour that housed the table where Penn had had his way with poor Mistress Brown. John wanted to take to it with an axe in the hope of somehow erasing the gross violation.

He took a deep breath then kept moving through the darkened rooms. John found Penn's chamber at the back of the cottage. He could hear his throaty snore as he approached the open doorway. John moved to the bed and stood over it, staring down at the slumbering Penn who was lost to the world in the sleep of a satisfied man.

Reaching towards the body, his hand towards Penn's throat, John stopped. Thought. He moved his hand lower and snatched the landlord's balls, twisting them hard. The landlord's eyes shot open. He screamed in pain, squirmed in agony like a caught fish on a jetty. With his left hand, John grabbed Penn's pillow and pressed it against his face.

'Quiet!' John commanded. 'Cease floundering and it won't pain you as much.'

Penn did as he was told. John removed the pillow but tightened his grip on the man's bollocks. Penn grimaced, seethed, but remained still. In John's large hand, the man's balls felt like chicken gizzards. John could rip them off if he chose; a part of him wanted just that.

Mistress Brown had no choice but to do as Penn demanded if she wanted her daughters to remain at school. If she told her husband, he would likely murder Penn and be promptly sent to the gallows. If she turned to the law herself, Penn would paint her as a harlot and she would be cast out by her husband with nothing, with no means of survival. Penn had placed her in an impossible situation.

John squeezed harder. Penn struggled to draw breath.

'Stay away from Mistress Brown,' John said in a low voice. 'Do not raise the Browns' rent. Ever.'

The terror that enveloped the landlord's eyes cleared to understanding.

'Do not go near the family again.'

The man nodded.

John released him but balled his hand and thrust his

knuckles into Penn's face. The landlord was unconscious in an instant.

John departed the house and then the courtyard, surging and intoxicated once more.

THE NEXT MORNING, John rose early, more out of habit than desire. Kirkcaldie had always risen at dawn, citing a particular liking for that time of day. John dressed then made his way to Eliza's rooms through the silver-grey of a February morn. In truth, he too had a particular liking for this time of day, especially in winter. With the streets barren of people and sunlight, to John it was like walking through a dream, as though the setting and everything around him, weren't quite real. He looked down at his cloak. A light dew rested on its fabric, giving the appearance of a fine glistening spider's web.

Despite the early hour of the day, he was concerned he would miss Eliza's departure from the boarding house. She seemed likely to be an early riser, a perpetually organised person who refuses to waste even a minute of the day. John admired people like that for he was the very opposite. He was able to while away many hours lost in his own thoughts.

Correct in his assumption, John caught Eliza's attention as she walked out through the boarding house door. He jogged across the street to join her. She wore a red cloak with a scalloped collar that fastened under her chin with an equally red ribbon. He had not seen her in this cloak before; it was quite beautiful and unique. The hood framed her face perfectly and the colour of the garment brought out the minute flecks of dark claret in her eyes.

He offered her a bow and she responded with a quick curtsey.

'May I walk with you?' he asked.

Eliza nodded and continued on her way. While she did not seem pleased to see him, John could detect no displeasure in her manner. They walked in silence, John enjoying the purposeful *click* of her shoes on the cobblestones and the soft *swish* of her cloak. Occasionally, he glanced her way and caught the merest glimpse of her profile as her head was mostly shrouded by the hood. She reminded him of Little Red. *Although Eliza would never be so naive as to be deceived by a wolf*, he thought.

He wanted to speak. He wanted to tell her how he had stolen into Penn's home. John wanted to explain what he had done but he could not. It wasn't until they reached the school that he finally spoke.

'Yesterday, after we parted, I spent some time investigating the circumstances of the Brown family and the landlord Penn.'

Eliza looked at him squarely, desiring more.

'You were absolutely correct when you described Penn as "despicable".'

Her eyes widened.

'I witnessed his contemptible nature. I also witnessed the hardworking family who he has so cruelly treated, and your students, who appear most well-mannered and scholarly.'

He paused, wondering if he needed to say more. He wanted her to realise that he understood.

'What is to be done, then?' she asked, eagerly.

John pondered her question for a moment.

'The situation has been dealt with.' He offered her a slight smile.

She tilted her head. 'How?'

He kept his eyes on her, willing her to understand.

'Please ... Put your trust in me that it has. Penn will neither raise the Browns' rent nor evict them. But I encourage you to counsel the family to find more suitable lodgings. For the sake of Mistress Brown and her daughters.'

Eliza's eyes suddenly shone in comprehension. She took his hands in hers.

She wore soft calfskin gloves – not the woollen gloves she'd knitted herself – but John could feel the press of her fingers against his own. He watched as relief and gratitude filled her eyes.

She swallowed hard in an effort to stem her tears before raising his hands to her mouth and kissing them quickly. Then she turned and hurried through the gates of the school like a flurry of crimson linnets.

AS HER CLASS copied neat columns of numbers in their workbooks, Eliza walked between the rows of desks, checking the neatness and accuracy of her students' work. However, she found it difficult to concentrate on the figures on the pages. While Mister Kirkcaldie's news about Penn was most heartening, the situation had given rise to thoughts of her own mother and her inability to gain justice after a life lived with a violent man.

When she had discovered her mother's cloak and gloves in a box in her father's attic, they were pristine, uneaten by moths and flies. Donning them in the dusty, dark confines of the small space, she had felt free, as though released from the burdens of her past – and as though she were releasing her mother in some way.

Looking towards the window now, Eliza became mesmerised by the snowflakes grasping at the windowpane, forming ice-laced patterns.

They'd dissolve quickly if the sun were to ever come out, she thought.

23

AUGUSTA, MAINE

Maria climbed the stairs, her arms laden with washing freshly laundered. Hearing the voices of the children, she stopped on the landing. The door to their chamber was open. Listening to the pair converse was one of her great pleasures. Their firm opinions and untainted thoughts were so refreshing, they filled her with hope that despite all the evils in the world, goodness would prevail.

While Patience was less than a year older than Bell, she took all the liberties of the eldest sibling, although they were not brother and sister – they were cousins, born within the same year. Patience arrived first, at the end of one summer, and then Bell at the beginning of the following. They had grown together in the same house, with the same family, side by side as siblings would. They even shared the adults in the house – Leah was as much Bell's mother as Patience's and Palgrave had played father to them both. In Maria's mind, although Patience was frequently bossy and often quarrelsome, Bell viewed her as his beloved older sister. As a result, the children were marvellous friends.

Maria felt it was a credit to Bell that he managed their relationship in such a mature manner. She realised that it couldn't be easy for a child so young to do so.

Maria stepped out of her slippers and crept up the remaining stairs. She stood to the side of the door, able to see the children reflected in a large cheval mirror. They sat together in their chamber – for they shared a chamber still – the one that had belonged to Leah's oldest son Joseph before he wed and moved into the township with his wife.

When they weren't being schooled or assisting with the household's numerous chores (Leah resisted the hiring of a maid or groundsman still) the pair delighted in each other's company. In the springtide and summer, they enjoyed fishing and playing tennis, but hide and seek in the woods behind the house remained the cousins' favourite game.

When the weather was not as clement, the pair would often write stories together. These were usually adaptations of tales told to them by Kirkcaldie. Bell, who had inherited his mother's artistic talents, would illustrate these novellas.

This was the task they worked at now. Bell was sketching a small portrait of Captain Grand for a page previously written while Patience wrote on. Maria had aided Bell in the rendering the day before, sketching an outline of the character's figure for her son. Maria had no difficulty calling to mind the shape of Kirkcaldie's face and body.

The story the cousins were writing was titled *Captain Grand and the Mystery of Mister Dalrymple*. Maria had helped them with the title too. The children had been unable to agree on a suitable mystery, or to establish who Mister Dalrymple was, but they were confident Captain Grand was capable of solving whatever they came up with.

Bell planned to have the novella finished by the time of Kirkcaldie's return. The boy hoped his friend might read it aloud to the household. Maria hoped so, too – Kirkcaldie had such a wonderful voice, one that resonated long after he grew silent. She recalled the first time she heard it, outside the ordinary in Eastham. Her heart had instantly melted. Although she did not need comforting very often these days, Maria found drifting into sleep with Kirkcaldie's mellow tones echoing in her mind as soothing as a warm bath laced with peppermint.

Bell shared his entire life with Patience – mother, father, siblings and cousins, lessons and spare time. Maria often imagined her son's world as a prism of sorts, in which his life and that of his cousin's were continually reflected, one another's joys and hardships sometimes distorted. Their lives shared a sameness. For the most part, Maria was certain that Bell found a comfort in that familiarity.

Bell was not as questioning as his cousin but, Maria warranted, just as curious. He had wondered about his own father at times, but not frequently. Until he was three, he believed Palgrave was his father. When eventually corrected, Bell asked, 'Well, who is my papa?'

'He is an angel, Bell,' Maria had replied. 'That is why he cannot visit you.'

While it was a satisfactory response for a three-year-old, Maria was aware that the reason that comes with age would soon prompt her son to query her response. As yet, he had not sought out the truth from her of how he came to be born, or seem to feel the lack of a father to call his own. However, she had occasionally observed that her son was sensitive to the absence of a sense of specialness a father might give him. While Palgrave did a remarkable job of caring for both Bell and Patience, on occasions such his birthday and Christmas, Bell seemed to want something more than what lay beneath the wrapping of his gifts.

Of course, she, as his mother, loved him dearly, but she was as much focused on Patience as she was on her own son. It was simply the way the household operated. It simply *was* ... whether he and Maria liked it or not.

Bell had simply learnt to delight in the immense benefits of his upbringing in his strange and wonderful prism – he had a constant companion and numerous adults to run to when he fell from a tree or cut his knee. To Maria's mind, this sense of security appeared to make what annoyances Bell experienced easier for him to bear.

It was when Kirkcaldie came to visit that Bell experienced being loved singularly, Maria believed. Kirkcaldie always spent hours with Bell and Bell alone. Although he had never ignored Patience, never been rude to her or ill-tempered, it was obvious that he favoured Bell. Patience was forced to amuse herself.

Kirkcaldie not only instructed Bell in knot tying, but also fishing and hunting. It was Kirkcaldie who taught Bell to load and fire a rifle. One fall, they had shot rabbits and foxes together then made Maria a dark amber fur muff. Thereafter, she regularly boasted to Bell and the family that it kept her hands 'as warm as sunbeams'.

Maria watched her son now as his hand moved about the page. His style was so similar to her own that she often felt as though she were watching herself. Maria mused on her son's peaceful countenance as he stared at Captain Grand's rugged profile on the page. He had drawn a tall man with wild dark hair, broad of shoulders and fierce. Bell turned briefly to the looking glass before continuing his drawing. Maria took a step back so as to go unnoticed.

Recently, Bell had informed Maria that he had begun to notice the silences and pauses that often halted the flow of adult conversation and also the looks, the fleeting, gossamer-fine glances that filled those spaces. He had not known what to make of them so had spoken to his mother about it. She explained that he was maturing and becoming mindful of the thoughts and feelings of company.

'All children are extremely unaware of what is happening around them,' she stated plainly. 'It's a sign you are growing older and developing more adult sensibilities.'

Maria peeked around the doorway. Bell lifted his pencil from the paper then turned to his cousin. She wrote feverishly, an expression of panic on her face, as though if she did not commit the words in her head to paper immediately something immensely significant would be lost to the world forever.

'Patience,' he said.

She ignored him, lost in a world of duels, fisticuffs and the barest survival.

Bell repeated her name twice more, louder each time, before she looked up from the page, lips pursed, irritated at the interruption.

'What is your opinion of Kirkcaldie?' he asked.

Maria's eyebrows rose at Bell's unexpected question.

'Oh, he is extremely *interesting*. Handsome, too.'

Smiling at her niece's answer, Maria could not but agree.

'Do you think Kirkcaldie might be my father?' Bell went on.

Maria's heart seemed to stop. Clutching the washing to her chest, she stifled a gasp.

Patience lay down her quill immediately.

'What an *interesting* question.'

Maria noticed the subtle roll of her son's eyes. 'Interesting' was a word Patience had taken to using recently, in lieu of 'strange' or 'foolish' or 'magnificent'. Bell believed, he had informed Maria, that Patience thought the use of the word made her more 'interesting'.

Maria could see by Patience's gleaming blue eyes, bulging with excitement, that Bell's unusual question had been a topic to which she had given much thought.

'If resemblance counts for anything, I would say unequivocally yes,' she said. 'Apart from your fair hair, which clearly belongs to your mother, you have his brown eyes and generous smile. I have noticed Kirkcaldie does not smile very often ... but I have seen the similarities when this rarity occurs.'

Patience seemed very pleased with this observation and the words she used to describe it. Maria watched as Bell viewed himself once more in the looking glass. He smiled broadly at his own reflection. Then his features softened, and he stared at himself more seriously. Maria knew that it was his blond hair that was deceptive; it was so easy to see only her in his appearance. One had to have a keener eye to spot Kirkcaldie, but the similarities – eyes and smile – were present, just as Patience said.

'I have noted the looks that pass between Kirkcaldie and my mother,' said Bell.

Patience's face seemed to beam more with this news. Maria felt the heat rise in her cheeks at Bell's words.

'I believe they ... perhaps they love each other, or have loved ...' said Bell, sighing, unable to verbalise his thought completely.

Maria's heart tightened once more. *He has sensed something between myself and Kirkcaldie.* She remembered now that Leah had said as much weeks ago.

'But I do not want to broach the subject with my mother in case I am wrong and the memory of my father – were it not Kirkcaldie – fills her with pain. Perhaps he was killed –'

'It is quite likely,' Patience cut in soberly. 'If your father died tragically it might explain why Aunty Maria told you he was an angel.'

A pang of sorrow passed over Maria. She had not thought Bell could believe his father dead. Now she understood his lack of questions on the subject.

Bell sighed again and returned his gaze to his drawing. Captain Grand – Kirkcaldie – gazed back at him.

'Perhaps I am looking for similarities where there are none,' he said. 'It's just that I admire Kirkcaldie ... I love him *so* much.'

Maria's heart swelled. She wanted to run to her son, hold him in her arms and tell him everything. But this wasn't the time. She must wait for Kirkcaldie's return.

'You should ask your mama,' Patience advised. 'Or, even better, you could ask him. Then you will know for certain.'

Bell cast a doubtful look at his cousin. Suddenly, Patience's eyes brightened further, full of excitement and possibility.

'Would it not be wonderful if Kirkcaldie *was* your father? He is much more *interesting* than mine.'

24

AUGUSTA, MAINE

Sarah held her palm to Charlie Purse's forehead a final time. His fever had broken a week ago, but Ben had asked him to remain in the hospital until his incessant cough began to improve. Now it had and, although he was reluctant to do so, Charlie knew it was time to move on and take up residence once more with Riyogi at the Green Dragon. But while Sarah Williams held her hand against his brow, he relished the sensation and willed her never to remove it.

'You're as fever-free as any healthy man, Mister Purse,' she said, rising from his bedside. The pair locked eyes for an instant and he noted a blush in her cheeks. Her eyes had the colour of irises.

She is such a lovely young woman, thought Charlie, *though not oft complimented.*

Charlie had first noticed Sarah when he was sent by Riyogi on an errand to the Williams house, high on the hill on the other side of the river. She had tended him in hospital before that, after he had been beaten, robbed and left to drown in the incoming tide, but he had not noticed her fully then. At that time, his body had been broken and his mind in turmoil at having his mission scuttled. It had taken him a number of weeks to reconcile his plans for the future with the reality of the present and, while he could not believe it now, he had ignored Sarah Williams.

The day of his errand had been an unseasonably warm April day. After rowing across the river, he had tramped the few hot miles to the house on foot. It was Sarah who opened the door when he knocked, which he thought odd – such a man as Palgrave Williams, with all his riches, not having a maid or footman in his employ was unusual to say the least. In Charlie's experience the moneyed enjoyed flaunting their possessions, fine clothing and servants.

Sarah had stood silent, waiting for him to speak. She'd been cooking, he assumed, for she wore an apron and her sleeves were turned up to her elbows. Her top lip glistened with moisture and Charlie, taken by her beauty, stared at those lips for a longer time than was seemly. He noticed a flicker of recognition in her eyes and this had heartened him. Eventually, she cleared her throat, signalling him to speak. Removing his hat, Charlie introduced himself.

'My name is Charlie Purse, Mistress. You might remember me from the hospital.'

Sarah nodded.

'Riyogi has sent me to collect a document from your father.'

She narrowed her eyes and raised her chin.

'Your injuries have healed handsomely, Mister Purse. Barely a scar.'

Her gentle gaze gliding over his face was as soft and cool as feathers.

Sarah permitted him entry into the house, unsmiling. Oh, how he would have welcomed her smile at that moment. She lifted the corner of her apron and wiped her brow.

'My father keeps no servants. A blessing on the one hand but also a curse, especially on sultry days such as this. Usually, we have no need to occupy the summer kitchen 'til May.'

The way she said ''til' comforted him. Although to his eyes her mannerisms and gestures appeared queenly, Charlie discerned she was a compatriot, a country woman at heart. And as he followed her along the corridor to her father's study, he could not help but admire her straight back and the gentle swing of her hips. When she left him at the door, he had felt a faint flush of disappointment.

He did not see her again until some weeks later when she nursed him through his illness. Charlie was sure her tender ministrations had contributed to his recovery. Now, she led him through the hospital and out through the entrance.

'What are your plans, Mister Purse?' Sarah asked as they stood for a moment, taking in the snowfall.

Charlie shrugged. 'The Green Dragon for the time being.'

'For the time being?'

Instantly bolstered by her query, he went on.

'It suits me for now and I'm hoping some prospects for the future might arise that would see me prolong my visit. I have in mind a venture.'

'A venture?' she echoed, thoughtfully. Then she took his hand and squeezed it gently.

His heart leapt.

'Take care, Mister Purse. And you mustn't forget this ...' Sarah handed him a package wrapped in paper. 'It is the tonic Doctor Shute prescribed.'

He took the parcel and measured its weight in his hand. About the size of a rum bottle. He smiled. *Well, a man could hope ...*

'Something amuses you?'

Charlie shook his head and tucked the package under one arm. He did not think it would be wise to mention his preference for rum to Sarah Williams.

His eyes followed her (and the gentle sway of her hips) as she pushed open the door and disappeared into the hospital.

Benjamin Shute leant over a patient, holding an ear trumpet to the woman's chest. His brow was furrowed in concentration as he stared at a spot on the wall, listening to her breathing. Sarah loved to watch him at work. His concentration and focus were palpable, they pulsed from him in silent, rolling waves (which she imagined to be bronze in colour and sounding like the lowest note on a cello). She was moved each time she witnessed such a scene. Shute straightened and looked towards her.

'Charlie Purse has just departed,' she informed him.

He nodded. 'Good. He will be fine. It was a nasty bout of influenza but he is young and fit. He will continue to improve. Did you remember to make up the tonic?'

'Of course.'

She waited for him to continue. When he did not, she searched her mind for topics with which to engage his attention.

'Is there anything else I'm needed for? My father is in Boston and I ...'

'Yes. Leave before dusk. Return home. Your mother ...'

Ben turned back to the patient. Sarah sighed. He often spoke in truncated sentences, snippets of phrases when his mind was occupied. *Was it this patient or someone else who has stolen away with your thoughts?* she wondered.

'I will see you tomorrow,' she said.

'Of course,' he replied without glancing her way.

She hovered in the doorway for a moment like a moth around a flame then turned to leave.

'Sarah,' Ben called.

She turned back immediately. He was looking her way.

'Your mother informed me you had a head for figures. I myself do not. I was wondering if you might ...?'

Encouraged. Instantly buoyed. Afloat. She had felt a similar sensation when she had once snuck a glass of her father's rum.

'It would mean spending a greater amount of time here at the ...' His words trailed off.

'Hospital,' Sarah finished. 'I understand.'

Ben smiled and nodded then returned his attention to his patient.

As SOON AS Sarah was outside, beginning the journey home, her intoxication at the doctor's proposal began to fade away. Was it the cold? Had it somehow numbed her affection? Sarah had hoped the wonderful sense of anticipation and possibility might have stayed with her longer. Why hadn't it?

In love with Ben Shute since she was thirteen, Sarah was cross with herself for allowing the feeling to vanish. Of course, Ben's wasn't a proposal of marriage ... It wasn't even a suggestion for them to stroll together to Fiddler's Reach and back, an activity common between courting couples. Sarah had frequently dreamt about doing so with Ben.

Nevertheless, it was a step in the right direction. More time at the hospital meant more time in his company which could possibly lead to ...

Charlie Purse.

An image of the young man darted into her mind.

His thoughtful manner.

His ready smile.

The way his hazel eyes observed me ...

She shook her head. The greater her attempts to rekindle her excitement for Ben's plan, the stronger Mister Purse's image took hold. Sarah frowned and closed her eyes for a moment, determined to dislodge the uninvited vision.

25

BOSTON, MASSACHUSETTS

It was a Sunday morning when John saw her on the staircase of his lodgings. He peered over the edge of the landing and followed her journey. Eliza was on her way up to his room, he presumed, her head down, the hood of her cloak shielding her face. When she reached him, she gasped, even though his presence there should not have been a surprise to her.

'I was daydreaming,' she said by way of excuse for her reaction.

'About what?'

She smiled, brightening the gloomy stairwell in which they found themselves.

'Not daydreaming. Thinking.'

He nodded. A silence grew around them until they heard a door shut and the sound of footsteps.

'Would you like to speak with me? I have nothing by way of refreshment to offer you but my room is warm.'

'You were just leaving,' she said. 'I don't want to disturb your plans.'

'It was nothing important.'

It was the truth. Now that Eliza was in his presence, John could not even recall the errand on which he had set out.

Eliza allowed him to lead her to his room. Fortunately, they passed no-one on the short journey. John was aware how a woman's reputation could be easily tarnished. The image of the wretched expression on Mistress Brown's face in Penn's parlour darted across his thoughts like a skimming bird.

John removed his hat and cloak in the hope that the exchange would be a lengthy one. Eliza did not. Instead, she strolled around his meagre, shabby room taking it in as though it were a sultan's palace. He had not fixed his pallet to the wall yet. It was Sunday morning, after all.

'We live lonely lives, we two,' she stated, unexpectedly. 'My lodgings are not dissimilar to your own, although slightly cleaner,' she offered with a pleasant smile, running a fingertip along the edge of his bookshelf, leaving a track in the dust. 'I have chosen my life of solitude and wonder if you have done the same ...'

This final statement seemed to be more than she had wanted to say. She turned sharply and looked at him.

'I couldn't express my gratitude when I saw you last, Mister Kirkcaldie. I feared I would be overwhelmed by relief, absolute and total freedom, to be no longer encumbered by such a secret.'

John nodded in understanding. 'How did you know?'

'One day, the girls mentioned seeing their mother hurrying to Penn's at night, after their father and older brother were asleep. The sisters were woken by her leaving the house so, curious, had gone to their window. That's when they had spied her entering his home.'

Eliza still wandered about his room, seemingly captivated by his modest belongings. She lifted the quill from his desk to examine it then removed a legal tome from his bookshelf, scanning her eyes over the cover in a cursory manner before replacing it.

'It was an offhand comment. Today, I cannot even remember the context of it or why it struck me as unusual. But after having considered the matter for a time, I realised what was occurring. You see, I know what a mother will endure for her children.'

John watched her movements. They were elegant and graceful as a dancer. He could not imagine her growing up as Bowman's daughter. She touched the brim of John's hat where it lay on a chair, rubbing the fabric between her fingers.

'So I have come here today to express my inordinate gratitude for what you have done,' she said finally. 'Thank you.'

'You are most welcome.'

The pair stood opposite one another for some time. John hated to see her leave but he could not conjure a single sensible word that might tempt her to stay. All he knew was that he'd never felt this way about a woman before and he wanted – needed – Eliza Bowman in his life. His mind tumbled over her words, hoping to stumble by chance on an opening to conversation. She was acting so strangely, her manner distracted yet attentive all at once. Was it possible she wanted to prolong this meeting, too? Was it conceivable that she, too, was as anxious as a mouse behind a wall?

'You were correct earlier when you characterised me as lonely,' he began, deciding the only way forward was honesty. 'I have led quite an unusual life. My father and I travelled a great deal when I was younger. When we finally settled in a home, it was not long before I came here to Boston – first to the Latin School and then to Harvard University. Although I made one or two close friends at both of these institutions, my upbringing has made me somewhat of an outsider.'

She drew back her hood revealing the soft tresses of her hair piled loosely on her head – not the braided style, John noted, in which she typically fashioned her hair. She frowned slightly in contemplation, settling on the edge of his bed. His words had sparked interest.

'Tell me,' she said.

John sighed, pushing his fingers through his hair. His mouth twitched in concern. He had never told anyone his story – not Joshua nor Ben Franklin, or any of his masters or tutors at the schools he had attended. He and Kirkcaldie were the only people on earth to know his tale – his full and complete history. John had kept so many secrets over the years, told so many lies to protect his protector, that it was difficult for him to summon the truth in an instant. But he wanted to. He wanted to tell all he knew and understood about himself to this woman and damn the consequences.

'Have I said something to amuse you?' she asked.

'I'm afraid I cannot fathom where to start.'

Eliza rose, removed her cloak and laid it neatly across a chair, then she took his hands and led him to the bed. They both sat on the edge.

'Begin at the beginning,' she instructed in a tone befitting the schoolteacher she was.

And so he did. His life in Nassau with his mother, the arrival of Sam Bellamy, Benjamin Hornigold, Tamesine's murder and the wreck of the *Whydah* all surged from his lips in an unruly deluge. Eliza sat transfixed by the tale and the teller without saying a word. He produced the brass button, the only keepsake of a father he had never met. Eliza examined it for some time, tracing the embossed crown on its surface with her fingertip.

For John, the release was transforming; he felt lighter, as though cleansed. *Surely*, he thought, *this is what Catholics must feel following confession.*

Without drawing breath, he moved on to his experience after arriving in the colonies and his life with Captain Grand, then Kirkcaldie's role as the governor's surveyor, his own education and the law practice.

'My father is getting married in fact, very soon, to a woman named Maria. He first fell in love with her almost twenty years ago. I am travelling to Augusta in a day or two when events here ...'

And then he stopped, quite suddenly. Eliza looked at him strangely, waiting for whatever was coming next. *Can I go further?* John wondered. *Can I tell her how I persuaded Penn to relent, how I beat her own father into near oblivion?*

'Joshua has a number of cases on the boil ... I don't want to leave him too soon,' he said eventually, smiling. 'There it is. My life on a plate. I am certain it will not be easily digested.'

While he was brave enough to divulge Kirkcaldie's secrets, he was not yet willing to divulge all of his own. He waited anxiously for Eliza to speak. She could run from the room now and straight to an obliging Red Coat who would escort her to the governor's office. 'I have information about the pirate Black Sam Bellamy,' she would say. 'I wish to see the governor immediately.' It had not been two decades since Black Sam had ruled the seas and the Crown's coffers.

His capture would still be highly prized. A governor could make his career on such a score.

John swallowed hard, waiting for her to say something, anything at all. All the while, his belly twisted into tight knots. What had he done? After all these years had he forsaken Kirkcaldie for the possibly fleeting affections of a woman? He waited for her speak.

Eliza smiled at him kindly.

'It is an incredible tale. If I did not know you to be an honourable and circumspect man, I would say you were having fun at my expense. But I know it to be true. I know because of the sincerity in which you expressed yourself and the obvious pain it gave you to share with me your secrets and that of your father. Thank you for telling me.'

She moved closer to him.

'I will never tell a soul.'

With that, Eliza kissed him. It was an unexpected gesture but one he had longed for, even anticipated, since the evening they had met at her father's house.

WHEN SHE WOKE, she was wrapped tight in John's arms. Although he slept, it was a restless slumber. His limbs twitched and his eyelids fluttered like a lark's pinion. *Of what are you dreaming?* Eliza wondered, stroking his chest with her fingertips.

This was the only cure Eliza had for her deep-rooted lone-liness. To lie with a man was an immediate source of comfort, although the peace and solace was never lasting. However, as she lay in John's arms, there was a different feeling about the encounter, something less transient, less fleeting.

Eliza was aware of the risks involved in the life she led. However, she did not consider her liaisons frequent enough to be labelled as habit. Thoughts of disease and violence rarely crossed her mind. What's more, she chose the men very carefully. The first had been the Latin master from school, Reginald Spalding. He was a quiet type, married, with a balding pate of sand-coloured hair and a small paunch sitting in the linen of his shirt, reminding Eliza of a Christmas pudding. Despite his commonplace appearance, throughout her time at the school, he and Eliza had shared wry comments and knowing looks about the headmaster and other matters, such as overbearing fathers and ill-behaved children.

So when she drew Mister Spalding into an embrace in the quiet of her classroom at dusk one day, he had acquiesced quite readily. They had walked to a small hotel in Charlestown where neither of them were known. It was not a passionate encounter by any means. The coupling would be best described as a workmanlike endeavour. Nothing they engaged in that evening in the Charlestown hotel room would be considered ardent. At four and twenty, Eliza had still been chaste. The rendezvous had not been at all what she'd expected. Spalding was oblivious to her situation, ploughing on regardless of the pain he was causing her.

Despite this, when he departed the room an hour later – for his wife expected him home and she was a 'pushful' woman, according to Spalding, that he could not keep waiting – Eliza was left with the bill and a feeling, although somewhat skewed, that there was someone in the world who cared for her. Reginald Spalding had never sought a second tryst. Of this, Eliza was glad. He was clearly afraid of his wife and he was not a man she would be attracted to if she was not so desperately lonely.

Spalding had been two years ago in March. He had since resigned from his position at the Writing School, relocating with his pushful wife and family to Connecticut where he was to oversee a Latin School. Spalding and Eliza had not said goodbye when he departed. A small nod as he walked through the gate carrying a crate of his belongs was all that acknowledged their brief but significant (for her) love affair.

Since the first time with Spalding, there had been a number of men who had attracted Eliza's eye in one way or another. There had been a musician who made a living as an itinerant performer, a young clerk who had come to her assistance one evening when she had tripped and fallen on a loose cobblestone and an older man, a scholar whose thoughtful countenance had garnered Eliza's attentions during a public lecture titled, 'God's Glory in Man's Dependence' conducted by the Reverend Samuel Mather. None of these paramours she had particularly cared for and the only one she had found physically appealing was an acrobat. His body was perfect, as though carved from marble. She could still recall the press of his sinewy arms and legs around her.

These trysts were appealing to Eliza because she was in control. She chose the men, she placed the limits on their time together.

Had she walked to King Street that morning with the idea of seducing John? Eliza did not believe so, but when he confessed his deepest secrets, it spurred along her budding affections into such sudden growth that she was surprised at the power of her feelings. Even so, she *had* sought out his company that morning ...

Eliza could sense her attachment to John developing, spreading like honeysuckle under the sun's sweet strength. Apart from Spalding, she had been strangers to the other men and them to her. In a sense, she supposed, that brought less risk to the encounter. She hadn't even known their names. But John was different from those men.

Eliza sighed in contentment and pressed her body more firmly to John's. He tightened his hold on her.

Yes, he is different, she thought. *And this is different. This is not a tryst.*

26

TAMESINE: THE MUSIC BOX

CORNWALL, 1705

Eseld heard word that afternoon that her sister wished to see her. They were to meet on the path to Boscawen Point. Eseld knew where; Tamesine did not need to state the exact whereabouts. It would be the spot where they often tarried and picked daffodils, by the granite boulders on Carn Barges.

Eseld knew that Tamesine would not be returning to their home in Mousehole. She would be leaving with Lieutenant John King. No-one had informed her of this but she was certain. Although it pained her to admit it, Eseld also knew that leaving Cornwall was her sister's only option for a better life.

She slipped away from her duties at the cove without notice and made her way home. Hurrying up the stairs, she retrieved the music box their grandmother had gifted her only grandchildren before her death. No-one in the family was aware of how their father's mother had come into possession of such an exotic French snuff box, one crafted in what appeared to be gold. Rowena Rosevear had never left

Mousehole. She died a fishwife at the age of seven and sixty. The sisters liked to imagine that a Normandy seaman had fallen in love with Rowena (she was said to have been a great beauty in her day) and given her the box as a symbol of his ardour.

However it happened into the family, the music box was the girls' only belonging of any worth. Eseld wanted Tamesine to have it, both for sentimental and practical reasons; it would fetch a king's ransom if Tamesine ever found herself needing to part with it.

Before placing it in her pocket, Eseld inspected the box one last time. It had once been used for snuff, but in the possession of the Rosevear sisters it was home to the shells, beads and ribbons the sisters had collected. Eseld turned the delicate object over in her hands a number of times, committing each intricate engraving to memory. On the base, the decorations depicted young men building a ship; on the side, the same figures were dragging a ship into the sea. Featured on the glittering lid were couples bidding farewell as the men sailed away. Eseld wound the mechanism which, once released, set two ships in motion on silver waves across a golden horizon. The tune the box played had always been unrecognisable to the girls; fashionable music was not a part of their life.

Now, as Eseld made her way to Carn Barges, she hummed the tune quietly to herself. It was a bittersweet melody and one she refused to forget.

Tamesine stood by the boulders as Eseld approached along the path. She seemed restless, turning this way and that as though watchful. But she was alone, of which Eseld was grateful. Suspecting this might be the final time she saw her beloved sister, she did not want to have to check her words. When her sister spotted her, she ran to meet her. They embraced each other tightly.

'We are handfast,' she began immediately, breathlessly. 'John and I are handfast and I am leaving for Nassau on Thursday.'

'Nassau?' Eseld's breath caught. Despite knowing her sister would leave, hearing her say so was a different matter.

'It is a place in the Caribbean Islands.'

'Is it far from here?'

'Very far. On the eastern side of the American colonies, John told me. It will take at least thirty days to sail there. John said it will be very hot and the seawater will be as warm as bathwater. Eseld, the sun shines there every day!'

To imagine a place thirty days away from their home, where the sun shone every day and the ocean was warm, was impossible for both of them. Even on the hottest day of summer the part of the ocean with which they were acquainted stung like a hornet.

The sisters gripped hands. They only had a short time together for Eseld would soon be missed. Yet with a lifetime of words to impart, both were silent, unable to utter a syllable. Then Eseld remembered the music box.

'I have brought you this,' she said reaching into her pocket. 'You *must* take it,' she added, predicting her sister's response.

Tamesine wanted to protest – it was their most precious possession – but saw the look on her sister's face. She held her tongue and took their grandmother's music box.

Tears pooled in Eseld's eyes as she watched her sister place the treasure in her pocket. She drew in a deep, calming breath in attempt to steady herself.

Her sister watched her, a look of anguish on her face.

'Eseld,' Tamesine said in a tone she rarely used, as though she were talking to a child. 'Do you understand why I am leaving Mousehole?'

Tamesine was attempting to be strong, Eseld knew, to steel her emotions so her sister would not be sad.

'Of course, sister,' said Eseld, smiling. 'This is no place for you. Mousehole is too small to hold you. You will never be happy here. My heart aches at the thought of you leaving but to stay will kill you, that very private part of you that makes you my sister.'

Tamesine's chest heaved with sorrow and tears sprang from her eyes like September rains.

'Will you come with me?'

Eseld embraced her tightly.

'I cannot. Mousehole will be enough for me. I share neither your courage nor your adventurous spirit.'

'I have courage enough for two,' Tamesine whispered through her sobs.

Looking into her sister's eyes, Eseld feared Tamesine would need her full reserves of courage where she was heading.

'I must go now,' Eseld said suddenly, concerned that if she stayed any longer, she would begin to cry as well and beg her sister not to leave.

'Farewell, m'lady,' Eseld said, stooping into an exaggerated, courtly bow. 'Fair weather and still seas. I await your instructions.'

Tamesine choked back her tears and responded in kind with a low curtsey.

'Many thanks, m'lord. Despite my journey, rest assured my heart will remain in Penzance, always.'

The sisters straightened, staring at each other, drinking in their final moments together.

'Dry your eyes and find your husband, sister. Remember me when you play our granny's song,' she said.

They embraced once more. Then Eseld broke away from Tamesine, turned and, at a steady trot, quickly made her way along the path back to Mousehole.

27

AUGUSTA, MAINE

Palgrave watched in awe as Kirkcaldie dealt with the customs official. The man had boarded the ketch when they entered Casco Bay and approached Cape Elizabeth. He was a stern-faced, solemn fellow who appeared to take his role as the governor's representative at the port extremely seriously.

Kirkcaldie had known just by the man's appearance – sombrely dressed, narrow of eye and the grim expression of one who was about to communicate very bad news – that this particular customs official would not be bribed. Earlier, Palgrave had seen Kirkcaldie tuck a purse of coin in the pocket of his jacket for that purpose. In this case, it would not advance their cause to produce it. Kirkcaldie had gauged that in an instant. This would require a different tack, a more subtle approach.

Snow-capped, the rocky coastline stretched before them as the crew went about the business of mooring in the sunlit bay. Palgrave observed Kirkcaldie guiding and directing the official (who Kirkcaldie quickly discovered was named Joseph Baker) to a more pleasing frame of mind. Palgrave listened as his friend described how he had navigated around the rock islands that were a particular feature of the bay. In a concerned manner, as though it were simply luck that had seen him dodge the hazards of the bay on entry, Kirkcaldie sought Baker's advice as to how best manoeuvre the ketch back out to sea. Baker obviously enjoyed displaying his authority and knowledge of the inlet, its secret crannies and unexpected quirks.

Palgrave had watched Kirkcaldie do this many times. He had a gift for reading people, plucking from them the most trivial kernel of information that he could nurture into a more substantial nugget, then into a full-grown partisanship that would work to his advantage. It was these situations when Kirkcaldie reminded him most of Samuel Bellamy. To Palgrave's mind, the man's dual selves were quite at odds. He often wondered about the strength of will Bellamy had required to become Kirkcaldie.

Kirkcaldie managed to provoke the customs official into laughter, always a good sign. They shook hands. Kirkcaldie disappeared below deck for a moment then emerged with a bottle of Eight Bells in his hand, offering it to Baker. The man declined at first, citing the possible perceived unseemliness of such an act. However, Kirkcaldie smiled, joked and pressed a little more – just a smidgeon – until Baker took the bottle with great delight. He descended the rope ladder of the ketch without requesting to see the cargo. Once Baker was rowing towards shore, Palgrave discovered that he hadn't even inquired as to the nature of the freight.

Although Kirkcaldie had many gifts – fighting, strategising, stealth, concealment, rousing men to a common cause – it was this gift that Palgrave admired most as it was his friend's most accomplished. Palgrave had never seen any man coerce and manipulate like Kirkcaldie. The likes of Ben

Hornigold and Jeremy Cool were master manipulators, but their only tool had been fear. Kirkcaldie's most trusted weapon was his innate affability. On a regular basis, he somehow managed to influence another party against their better nature without them ever realising it. At the end of the exchange, they always felt more contented with their lives for having met him.

While amiable and pleasant, Palgrave did not possess this gift. In similar exchanges, the knowledge he was deceiving and manipulating made him conscious of the play acting involved. This awareness turned his amiability to angst and his pleasantness to perturbation. But how he enjoyed watching Kirkcaldie work his magic.

HAVING PAID THE CREW, Palgrave and Kirkcaldie left the ketch in Portland and Smith was instructed to return the vessel to Boston. The pair travelled back to Augusta along the Kennebec by sleigh then took the last three miles by cart. Snow cast their journey in a hazy mantle, neither man certain of what would greet them on their return. When they reached Augusta, they deposited the molasses at the distillery. Desmond, Palgrave's distiller, was pleased, informing his employer he would begin immediately on a new batch.

They arrived home that afternoon, unexpected by the household.

Bell and Patience were in the yard, constructing a lopsided snowman. An entire community of these misshapen forms populated the top of the drive, some of them partially melted. Hearing the wheels of the cart crunch through the snow, Bell looked up from his task and towards the noise. He was the one who saw them first – the boy's face immediately brightened when he realised who was driving.

Both children ran gleefully down the drive, their faces shining, cheeks pink and noses wet from the cold, giving the travellers a boisterous welcome home. Kirkcaldie drew the reins, halting the snow-kissed horses, and Bell and Patience clambered on board. After hugging her father dutifully, Patience rubbed her cold, smooth cheek against his whiskered face and laughed.

'This is interesting,' she commented, pinching his chin between her fingers. It was the gesture of an adult, Leah's gesture in fact. Patience's mannerisms had never been typical of her age.

Bell hugged Kirkcaldie tightly, burying his face into his neck. *Something has changed*, thought Kirkcaldie, surprised. While his welcomes from Bell had always been warm, he would never have characterised them as euphoric. Something was different.

When they reached the house, the children alighted and the men carried on towards the barn to store the tobacco and coffee. Bell and Patience ran inside the house to cry out the news to the rest of the household.

Leah glanced continually at her husband over supper. He was sun-kissed and bearded, his appearance reminding her of another time, although then his hair had been wild as the winds and his skin the colour of a chestnut. She and the children had not even recognised him when he had returned to Cape Cod. At that time, she felt as though she had welcomed a stranger into her home.

They had been *there* again; she was certain of it.

Around the table the men spoke of Portland and Boston. Leah inquired after John and Joshua, demanding to be informed of the minutiae of their lives. Sarah was particularly eager to hear news of her twin, however, she sensed a strange and fraught undercurrent in the conversation so she remained silent. She had been oft disappointed by her brother's lack of communication. He had promised he would write to her each week, but in the ten years he had been away, she could count the number of his correspondences on two hands. Nevertheless, according to the homecomers, John and Joshua were in good health and seemed content living and working in the metropolis.

Patience feigned eagerness when conversation veered in the direction of her brother, but, in truth, she was far more interested in the quality of ladies' fashion in the city.

'We took no note of the ladies' fashion,' Palgrave responded smiling. 'And if I had, I am certain your mother would not appreciate knowing it.'

Leah did not smile in return. Instead, she wondered when her husband had become such a proficient liar.

Each time she passed her gaze around the table, her sister and Kirkcaldie were staring at one another. She looked at their meals. Neither of them had eaten. They had merely pushed their food around their plates with their knives in the pretence of doing so. Despite this, there was a distinct hunger in them, she could tell. She was well-acquainted with that look – loving and lustful all at once – the knowing that their hunger could not be sated unless their bodies were one.

Leah felt no such hunger tonight.

'IT IS ill luck for us to see one another so near our wedding,' Maria whispered when she opened the door to her chamber to see Kirkcaldie standing there. 'To lie with me now would ignite all manner of catastrophe.'

Kirkcaldie leant against the door jamb, smiling, gazing at her with so much longing that she believed she would surely catch alight if she did not close the door immediately. But she wasn't able.

'I thought you had outgrown your Puritan superstitions.'

She shrugged. Despite knowing she should bid her fiancé goodnight, she decided she wanted to hold him there just a little longer. Kirkcaldie was departing the next day for Hallowell. He had not been home in some time, and he wanted to ready the house and the property for his new bride. Maria had never seen Kirkcaldie's house, the home he had built, and she often imagined how it might look – how it might reflect the character of its owner. Although she loathed to see him leave so soon after returning, Maria was touched by his thoughtful gesture.

It would be several days before she would see him again. Despite her misgivings, she was glad he had knocked at her door. Now she could savour him a little more before she bid him a temporary farewell.

From the moment she had first seen Samuel Bellamy on the meeting house green, glistening with pride, she had dreamt of being his. Between then and now there had been so many obstacles to their happiness. Singularly or together, neither of them had ever managed to find real contentment. Surely, she reasoned, that meant they were fated to be married. Looking back at their lives, first her father, who had initially objected to their courtship, then Silas and Reverend Dent, Tamesine and Tabby Post ... they had all played a role in bringing them to this point, a point where they were finally ready to be wed. Everything she saw in his face now verified the truth of it.

As she gazed at his countenance, a shadow passed over his features.

'Maria, in my life I've always needed a purpose,' Kirkcaldie began, changing the mood of their conversation entirely.

He had come to her chamber to confide, she realised. After all these years, he was opening his soul to her.

'I've always needed something to fight for. Without that I am useless. For what seemed like an age, my purpose was freedom. Once that was attained it was John and ensuring Tamesine's dreams for her son were realised. With that done, I was at a loss.'

'Is that why you accompanied Palgrave on his mission? Was it your final fight?'

'I suppose so ... Yet I must confess it was also pride and utter foolishness. My thoughts at the time were filled with you. In truth, they have been for some years. Just the same, I was sure you didn't want me, so I proposed the idea to Palgrave hoping it might rekindle my flagging spirit.'

Kirkcaldie gave a low laugh at his own foolishness.

'But while I was away, all I could think of was you. I could not muster any of the joy I had once felt at defying the Crown. I could not wait to get back to you. Each hour seemed like a thousand. I realise now that my purpose is to love and protect you and Bell.'

Maria's heart quickened. She had felt the same for a lifetime.

'You were worried that you might not return.'

His eyes widened in surprise.

'Yes. Every day I was away. How did you know?'

'You forget I can see into your soul.'

She placed her hand on his chest. He covered hers with his own.

'You saved my life once, Maria ... and now I feel like you're saving it for a second time,' he said, gazing at her fingers thoughtfully, stroking her hand as though it were ivory. 'You were by my side on the ketch,' he continued, shaking his head in wonder. 'I felt your presence calming me. I heard your voice ...'

Before he had departed, when he had confessed to Maria the true motive behind his trip with Palgrave, he also shared with her his fear of the sea. All water in fact, even the Kennebec River. Pleased he had been truthful, Maria had given him counsel, describing a technique she had often used herself when feeling anxious, when she felt powerless to control events around her. Kirkcaldie was to close his eyes and listen to the waves, the wind, the pounding rain and breathe in their power and strength, the energy nature produced. 'Use it to your own advantage, take it,' she had told him. 'You would never allow a man to best you, then why do you surrender to the sea? This is what I did during the storm that saw the *Whydah* wrecked. I consumed its energy and saved you.'

Maria had observed him attempt to understand what she discovered long ago. She had watched him struggle with the notion that power could be drawn from nature. And at the life that awaited him with a woman such as herself.

'And now? What is your feeling?'

'For many years, I believed I had nothing to live for. In spite of that, I have managed to survive for so long.'

Kirkcaldie looked into her eyes, searching.

'But that has changed. I want to live. I want to be free. And I want you.'

Kirkcaldie twined his fingers with hers and leant in to

kiss her. It was the softest of caresses, as gentle and as cool as a cat's paw, but her heart swelled and her body ached for him.

'Goodnight, my darling,' he whispered.

As he turned away, Maria could bear it no longer. She caught his shirt sleeve and drew him into her chamber.

'TELL ME THE TRUTH,' Leah uttered into the dark.

She turned to face her husband. She could see the whites of his eyes, open and staring at the ceiling.

'We travelled to the Caribbean – Martinique and Trinidad – to secure the molasses needed to make Eight Bells,' Palgrave said plainly as though he was informing Leah of the weather, or a peculiarly coloured finch he had spied in the woods.

'By "secure" do you mean smuggle?'

'I do.'

'Why?'

Palgrave rolled towards her and stroked her arm.

'I didn't have a choice. Almost everything we have I've invested in the distillery. If I were to pay the tax, we would be ruined. But even more troubling is the fact that all those who have invested in me would be ruined as well – Ben Shute and his hospital for one, your friend Riyogi and his boarding house ... these are worthwhile causes that aid the Augusta community. I didn't tell you because you would have attempted to stop me as you did when I first left you in Eastham.'

Leah frowned. In that he was right.

'When I recall your sorrow on that day, your anger and genuine pain, real bodily pain, I could not bear to see you like that again. I would have stayed this time, knowing that to do so would eventually cause you even greater sorrow.'

Leah had not realised the burden her husband had been carrying since the Molasses Act had been introduced. Now she was troubled she'd not given Palgrave the support he had needed. Instead, she had suspected that he set out with Kirkcaldie on a rollick, an escapade to feed his unfathomable need for adventure. She moved towards him, resting her head against his chest.

'I'm sorry. I suspected you of much worse.'

He laughed, a short, surprised sort of laugh.

'Worse than smuggling?'

'It's not the criminality of the act that disturbs me so. I have told you of my crimes, all of which are far greater than smuggling or piracy. It's your motives that I found troubling. For me to imagine that you are not content with this family, with me ... it scares me to the point where I cannot breathe.'

'Leah –'

'I could face Reverend Dent's whipping post one thousand times over if it meant not losing you.'

Palgrave stroked her hair, calming her. She felt her pain begin to ease.

'Leah, you will never lose me,' he said, kissing her forehead.

28

BOSTON, MASSACHUSETTS

Shift, stay, skirt, bodice, stockings and garters ... John enjoyed observing Eliza's body – supple and graceful, every movement exact – so he was thankful for the surfeit of garments. Once she was dressed, he gazed at her in her entirety, everything in perfect proportion. John thought her mother must have been a great beauty because her father was a plain man, making no physical impression on those he came in contact with.

He wondered what she was thinking. Eliza appeared completely composed, poised, certainly not bashful, yet John assumed she would not have been in this situation before, or at least not very often. The morning after an evening with a man were not typical circumstances for a young woman of Eliza's position to find herself in, John assumed.

John, however, *had* been in this situation before, despite an early lack of opportunity or instruction. Kirkcaldie had been a watchful and caring guardian but while he possessed many talents, he was negligent in others. He instructed John in the art of knot tying, fighting and cards.

Having studied Kirkcaldie for years, John quickly adopted his stratagems and improved upon them. His natural acumen with numbers meant he could count cards quickly and with ease. These were necessary skills in Kirkcaldie's world and he passed them on deliberately to his son.

But spending the best part of his life in the company of other men, Kirkcaldie never seemed to realise that a lumbermen's camp or carnival grounds were not necessarily the most suitable environment for a young man approaching adolescence. Even when Kirkcaldie had built their home and was working as the governor's surveyor, John had gone to a school where all his classmates were male.

If Kirkcaldie had ever sought out female companionship, John was never aware. But he certainly noticed women notice Kirkcaldie. Despite his reticence, females flocked to him like pigeons around crumbs.

Luckily, as he matured, John's spindly body broadened and his serious face (which sat oddly on a child's frame) became handsome. He found that by adopting Kirkcaldie's demeanour and many of his mannerisms, he was never short of female companionship. Forming a long, meaningful attachment, however, had eluded him.

'Where to now?' John asked Eliza as she sat tying her shoelaces.

The object of his observation glanced at him, assuming a face that implied she was giving his question some thought. When she was done with her shoes, she looked him in the eyes and shrugged good-naturedly.

'Are you asking if we should marry now the "bundling" has been done?'

John was surprised at the hint of acid in her response,

suggesting, with her reference to old Puritan customs, that he was a prig.

'Of course, not. I would not foist my circumstances upon any woman, let alone one I care such a great deal about.'

Eliza raised an eyebrow.

'You care for me?'

He nodded, puzzled, but also slightly irritated by her off-handedness. He was concerned that all he had shared with her, about himself and Kirkcaldie, could be taken so lightly. He sat up.

'Why did you come here yesterday?'

She rose from the stool and went to him then sat on the edge of the bed.

'I don't know,' she said, cupping his cheek in her palm. Her mouth twitched into a smile.

'I suppose I must care for you, too.'

DESPITE THE KISS that Eliza imprinted on his memory before she left, John was still unsure as to the nature of their relationship. However, he resolved to nurture the attachment. He cared deeply about her and although Eliza's behaviour had been strange, he wanted to see where this sudden union might lead.

Only a few minutes after she had departed, John heard Joshua's familiar, boyish tread on the stairs. He fleetingly wondered if his friend had seen Eliza leave. He scanned the room quickly, ensuring all traces of his lover had vanished with her.

Joshua barged into the room at once, producing a coin purse and placing it on the desk. It was John's cut of the Schleck settlement. He removed his hat and cloak and hurled them onto the chair. John watched as Joshua strutted around the small space, breathing with the ferocity of a lion. It was obvious that he was at sixes and sevens. It was only when his friend produced the morning's edition of the *Gazette* that John could discern why.

Joshua tossed the paper on the bed next to where John was lacing his shoes. He straightened and scanned the front page. The headline read: 'Boston bonesetter bashed within inches of his life by unknown, masked intruder'. John looked at Joshua who frowned, his face tinged with puzzlement and disappointment.

As John read the column inches Joshua continued to roam the room like a caged animal, waiting for his partner to finish reading. Bowman had related the attack to the newspaper accurately. Surprisingly accurately, in fact. The man clearly had a head for detail, outlining the number of punches to his face and describing his attacker's physical appearance – tall (beyond six foot), broad of shoulder with dark hair. He wore a cloak and a mask. John looked up from the page when he had finished.

'What's going on?' Joshua asked, his voice awash with confusion. His partner was intelligent with a lawyer's mind, adept at stratagems and exposing conspiracies, easily able to piece together this simple puzzle. John wondered how he should respond. He was not in the habit of lying to Joshua, but his dark secret was something he could not share with anyone apart from Kirkcaldie.

'Bowman's attack occurred on the evening you went to interview him. Now, suddenly, you are acquainted with his daughter as well. It cannot be a coincidence ...'

He sighed and pushed his fingers through his blond hair.

'What's more, the description of the assailant is remark-ably like you.'

Joshua drew his gaze towards the window. His pained expression indicated that while he wanted to believe no ill of his friend, all the facts stood in the way.

John rose, nodding calmly.

'I went to interview Bowman. Just as I told you, I did not believe him but, within the limits of the law, there was nothing I could do. The following day, I was contemplating the possibility of petitioning the court for Bowman's arrest based on the testimony of Schleck. Realising the court would be unlikely to agree, I decided to visit Bowman once more, on the off chance I might extract information. When I arrived, Eliza was there tending to her father. He had been attacked during the night.'

Joshua did not appear to be convinced.

'I warrant there are many men in Boston with my build who are in possession of dark hair ... The evidence, although hearsay, is incriminating, but in all the years we have been friends, have you ever known me to be a violent man?'

Still clearly troubled, Joshua shook his head.

'I realise that in the past I have dabbled in criminal behaviours, some of which you have also taken part. However, you must agree that organising cock fights and smuggling rum into the dormitories at Harvard do not compare to beating a man almost to death.'

John scanned the article again.

'My guess is that disgruntled by his employment at the East India Company being terminated, Bowman appealed to the newspaper. He's even quoted here saying "The East India Company are not beyond this type of menacing". Perhaps he is right? Most of the labourers and dockers the company hire are immigrants. They might have been attempting to quiet him and his extreme views ... even the most "respectable" organisations employ bullying tactics.'

Although calmed slightly by this explanation, Joshua still seemed wary.

'And Eliza Bowman?'

'She is a friend, nothing more.'

With his relationship with Eliza so young and fragile, John did not want to hear Joshua's counsel regarding the opposite sex.

'Eliza is estranged from her father. He was a difficult man to live with, as she tells it. We met that day at Bowman's and I gave her my calling card should her father remember anything of the attack. Although he did not, she must have remembered the card when troubled by the predicament of her students' family.'

'But why did Bowman not go to the authorities? Why did he take his story to the press?'

'Who can say?' John responded. 'As I said, money, most likely. Perhaps notoriety – to gain an audience for his cause? There could be a million reasons ... I have learnt from his daughter that Bowman is a quarrelsome individual who is not averse to provoking anger among all manner of men, even the most amicable.'

Joshua breathed in deeply and rubbed his eyes.

'Forgive me,' he finally said. 'The description and the timing ... it seemed all so condemning.'

'I understand. We are suspicious by our very natures.' John squeezed his partner's shoulder then added dryly, 'That is why we have such sterling careers in law.'

Joshua laughed at this and relaxed.

'We should spend today following up on our cases, few though they may be,' John continued, eager to change the subject. 'Although we have the Schleck settlement, it would ease my mind to have another case on the boil.'

Alleviated of his suspicions, Joshua took a seat at the desk and began rifling through the documents upon it.

The partners in law worked throughout the day but John's mind kept turning to his friend and his suspicions. John resolved to cease these acts of violence. Somehow, he needed to quench the thirst that spurred him on to these acts. Despite his father's urgings, he did not want to turn to Kirkcaldie for help; he had relied on him too much throughout his life. *Perhaps Maine might prove a tonic to my troubled soul*, he thought. He was looking forward to his upcoming trip to Augusta, looking forward to finally seeing Kirkcaldie settled and happy – another reason why he could not burden the man with his troubles.

Having their typical relations restored, the pair parted company for the day in a cordial fashion. As soon as Joshua left, John immediately went to Eliza's boarding house. After a lengthy conversation with the landlady attempting to convince her that his presence was the result of a legal matter involving the will of Eliza's grandfather, John was finally allowed into the parlour.

Although a fire burned in the hearth, he felt cold as he sat with his hat in his hands waiting for Eliza. Another resident was seated in the parlour also. An older woman with spectacles and a stern demeanour sat knitting with an expression of grim determination on her face. She was introduced as Mistress Bird. John removed his hat and offered her a pleasant 'good evening' which only prompted the woman to knit with an even greater celerity, the *clicking* of her needles resounding like crickets on a still summer evening.

When Eliza entered, she offered John a brief curtsey. The pair sat at opposite ends of a burgundy damask sofa.

It took all John's energy and willpower not to embrace her. Her hair was loose and the top button of her collar was unfastened, as though she had been preparing for bed. When Mistress Forsythe had gone to fetch her, Eliza must have dressed in a hurry. He spied the soft hollow of her neck that only last night he had filled with kisses. The remembrance ignited his craving for her, and his eyes lingered on the rise and fall of her breast. When he lifted his gaze to hers, he noticed her cheeks colour. Still, the mischievous expression she wore told him that her feelings echoed his own.

'Your father spoke to the *Boston Gazette*,' John said in low tones to avoid the earshot of Mistress Bird. 'Do you know why?'

Eliza shrugged, exasperated. 'He called himself a "philosopher" in the article, a "social critic". Did you notice?'

John nodded.

'My instinct tells me he is painting himself a martyr. What better way to muster disciples?'

She closed her eyes then and rubbed her forehead, seemingly exhausted by the last few weeks caring for her father and her worries for Mistress Brown.

'Oh, how I despise the man. I wish he might have died in the attack.'

Mistress Bird looked up from her knitting. Her eyes flashed with disquiet.

Sitting on the edge of the sofa, Eliza appeared too small, too alone to harbour such immense emotions. Bowman's attitudes were extreme and his behaviour barbarous, but for a daughter to loathe her father with such a burning passion seemed to warrant a far more heinous crime than publishing inflammatory pamphlets.

'Will you walk with me?' she asked after a moment.

'Of course.'

Eliza collected her cloak then informed her landlady that she was visiting her father. Mister Kirkcaldie, the lawyer, was to escort her.

Once outside in the cold air of the evening, she clutched John's hands and pulled him to her, kissing him deeply. When they drew apart, her eyes were pooled with tears.

'How can I remedy this, Eliza?' John asked, feeling her warm breath on his cheek. His sole purpose in the world now was to protect her.

'The last few weeks, being back in my father's company … it has unearthed so many memories that I believed I'd buried.' Her voice cracked with the final utterance.

John led her away from the boarding house so they wouldn't be heard. They began to walk.

'Tell me, Eliza,' John pressed. 'Did he beat you? Was he a drunkard?'

She shook her head. John said nothing more for a time until they reached the river where they halted. John did not wish to play the lawyer and harangue her into confiding, so he waited for her to speak. Eventually, she did.

'When I was a child, just a girl … he would touch me.'

'Touch you?'

'In a way that a father should not touch his daughter,' she said, staring straight ahead into the black water.

John was silent, taking in her words, considering Bowman and his actions. He sensed the creature inside him, the animal he was so desperate to tame, awaken and stir.

'How long did this continue?' he said through clenched teeth.

'It stopped when I lost my mother. I have come to believe his vile acts were merely a means of tormenting her ...' she replied pensively, as though recalling a long-forgotten memory.

Knowing that his response, his reaction, the first words that sprung from his mouth after this truth would be the most important of his life, he chose them with great care. He turned to face her.

'Eliza, what would you like me to do?' he uttered earnestly, hoping to convey in his tone *all* that he was capable of.

From the expression on her face, he could see that they were not the words she had been expecting.

'His actions are not a crime ...' she whispered.

'It is true he cannot be prosecuted in the law. But it does not mean what he did to you is not a crime,' John said. 'Do you want to see him punished?'

She lifted her eyes to his, searching, uncertain of his meaning.

'Were you the one?' she asked. 'Were you the one to ... "punish" him before?'

John nodded solemnly.

'He left a man, an immigrant, to die a long, painful death.'

She looked at him with concern.

'Although this poor man was saved, his life will never be the same again. My actions in response were abhorrent, but –'

'No John. What you did was just. My father deserved what you meted out to him.'

She paused, took a deep breath.

'And he deserves whatever more will come to him now.'

29

TAMESINE: ROUGH SEAS

NASSAU, 1705

The voyage to Nassau was far worse than Tamesine had imagined. When she arrived in the port thirty-six days after her departure from Mousehole, she was thin and weak. Her legs felt as though they would snap if she were to put her feet upon dry land. The passengers – inmates, more rightly – waited on deck clutching their belongings, eager to disembark. Tamesine climbed to the deck from below where she had spent the majority of the voyage. The heat struck with the force of her father's mighty fist and, as she waited for her eyes to adjust to the bright sunlight, a wave of nausea overcame her frail body. She found herself swaying listlessly on her feet.

'Take a deep breath, lass.'

A kindly girl named Agatha, not much older than herself, placed her hands on Tamesine's scrawny shoulders to steady her. Agatha had journeyed alone to New Providence Island as well.

Tamesine did as instructed. The air was thick, rank with the stench of waste, rot and blight. Led to the rail, she leant against it and took in the township of Nassau. She had never seen so much colour. She squinted against it. Even in the summertime, a thin grey blanket seemed to cover Mousehole. Nassau was lit by the vibrant yellows of the sun and the sand, and by the activity taking place on the sickle-shaped shore. She wondered if a place such as this could ever be home.

John was waiting at the dock when the *Mary* dropped anchor in the bay. He rowed out to meet her in a small Royal Navy cutter, so eager was he for the reunion with his bride.

Tamesine was glad of John's impatience. The number of passengers who had been clustered like chickens below decks on the *Mary* would take days, Tamesine judged, to be rowed ashore. Women in their skirts, grasping their paltry possessions to their crumpled, stained breasts as though they were Mary's holy belt, would take an age to descend the rope ladders that had been flung over the side.

As military etiquette deemed, John asked permission of the *Mary*'s captain to board. He spotted Tamesine standing alone, away from the disembarking multitudes.

'Where is your baggage?' he asked immediately.

Tamesine raised a knotting bag no bigger than a dab. Apart from Eseld's parting gift, it was all she had.

She kept her grandmother's music box housed in her pocket, close to her always. She patted it gently to reassure herself of its presence and her heart keened with sorrow, bringing to mind thoughts of her beloved sister and the familiarity of Mousehole.

The couple's reunion was awkward. Tamesine felt ill at ease; John seemed like a stranger to her. She could tell from his expression that he was horrified by her appearance. There was none of the affection and curiosity that had filled his eyes when he had first seen her in Penzance. *Was it any wonder?* she asked herself. Her hair was putrid and weighed heavy and lank on her shoulders. The bodice and skirt she wore were soiled and marked, as was her face, she imagined.

Tamesine had seen but four ewers of fresh water in which to wash herself since she departed Cornwall thirty-six days before. When she had approached the captain and requested more – not merely for herself but also for the other women on board, some with small babes – she was rebuffed, albeit quite good-naturedly, as though she were asking for roast partridge and French peas.

And the seasickness had been unrelenting; Tamesine had never experienced such torture. Most times she lay breathless, speechless in her bunk with scarce strength to move. When she did attempt to shift, a dreadful weariness came upon her. She could not even cook the meagre rations she was given. When Agatha had prepared for her a portion of rice, Tamesine could not keep it down. It was simpler to go without food, she decided.

There were very few blessings that Tamesine could count during her time on the *Mary*, but Agatha was one. Delirious with nausea, Agatha wiping her brow with a cool damp clout, she had questioned the girl one evening.

'Why are you going to Nassau?'

'There are opportunities in the town, I have heard, opportunities for business and advancement for women like me. Women who are ... alone.' Agatha smiled.

She was pretty, with a gentle round face. Her golden curls were kept in check with a tartan ribbon.

'Not all of us have a handsome naval lieutenant waiting to save them,' she said, with a wink.

At Agatha's words, Tamesine's thoughts twisted and turned like the movements of the ship. *Is that why I am here? Am I trapped on this fetid frigate with a hundred others because I hope John will save me? Save me from what?* she asked herself, finding some relief in the press of the clout on her forehead and Agatha's low humming. *My father? From Mousehole?*

She decided she would be disappointed with herself if that were the reason, for she would trade her predicament in a heartbeat for the opportunity to return to her home and Eseld. She would give over her life readily to whatever the fates had in store for her to be rid of the constant seasickness she endured.

Her life in Mousehole was so entangled with the sea that she had never imagined the affliction would paralyse her as it did. When she considered it, she realised that although the sea was all around her, she had never really been a part of it as her father had. She remembered him mocking other men, new fishermen, for their unceasing *hwyja* and she wondered if he had somehow wreaked his revenge on her actions by cursing her with it. *How he would love to see my misfortune now*, she thought. *'What a fine example of a fisherman's daughter'*, *he would mock.*

Tamesine was not alone in the ordeal. Many passengers were ill, suffering, making the stench between decks insufferable. Tamesine was trapped and was forced to bear the unbearable. Often, a fear of death would grip her body and soul and she was incapable of thinking of anything else, to the point where her breast seized and she could barely draw breath.

Once, not long into the voyage, Agatha had escorted her onto the deck. It was a 'bonny' day she had told Tamesine, assuring her the fresh air would 'work wonders for her constitution'. However, all Tamesine imagined as she leant on the railing was hurling herself overboard and losing herself in the white, foaming spume. Many of the passengers, after only a few days of torture, would find their sea legs but Tamesine never did. If God or the Devil would not save her then perhaps the choice was hers to make. It was as though Agatha had read her thoughts on that day because she never escorted Tamesine onto the deck again.

Now, standing before her husband and his consternation, she smoothed her skirts and attempted to fix her hair, but her actions were futile. She hung her head in shame and tears stung her eyes. Finally seeing her dismay, John walked to her and took the small knotting bag from her. Although the bag was small it seemed to weigh a ton in Tamesine's hand; it was a relief to her to let it go.

'The passage was harsh, I can see,' he murmured gently, shouldering the bag then sliding an arm around her waist to support her. 'I must reside at the barracks for a time, but I have rented a room for you in a boarding house. It has a view of the mountains and it is clean. The landlady is a jolly sort or woman, from the north.'

He lifted her chin with a finger.

'We will go there now, and I will take care of you.'

At his touch, tears began to fall down her cheeks. John brushed them away. He looked into her eyes and kissed her lightly on the lips.

'Welcome to Nassau, my wife.'

At that instant, Tamesine's legs gave way and she collapsed into his arms.

30

AUGUSTA, MAINE

John had been due to arrive shortly before the ceremony. Kirkcaldie willed the sound of his hasty arrival – a door banging open, heavy footsteps down the hall, hurried apologies – but none were forthcoming. These days Kirkcaldie understood more than ever the desire of Palgrave and Leah to have their children close by. It had seemed like an age, Palgrave had commented to the groom recently, since all his children had been assembled under the one roof.

Now Elizabeth, newly with child, and her husband stood alongside Joseph and his wife. The young couples were watched over by Leah, who appeared radiant in a simple gown of dark emerald. Aside from John, the only other absentee was young Caleb, who had recently turned twenty-one and was en route to Paris where he was to continue his studies in Science. Kirkcaldie observed that despite Caleb's absence, Leah still wore an expression of such happiness that she might have been the one being wed.

The party stood in Palgrave's study before the Reverend

Soloman Belcher, although neither bride nor groom believed in God. In fact, apart from Belcher, neither the bride or groom, nor any of the attendees, had any apparent affinity with God. Sarah's faith was her special secret.

When Bellamy and Maria had visited Belcher earlier in the week, he had chastised them harshly for he had never once seen their faces in church since arriving in Augusta three years before. He argued fiercely against marrying them as they had not had their banns published.

'You must have your banns published for three consecutive weeks in the church,' Belcher had cried more than once during the meeting. Maria had remained silent, her eyes narrowing.

'We have no time for *banns*,' Kirkcaldie had informed him.

Kirkcaldie would have been content to be handfast or have a Kennebec bargeman marry them but Leah had argued that unless they were married by a minister, the marriage would not be recognised. 'Old habits die hard,' Kirkcaldie had commented to Maria at the time.

'I have purchased a marriage licence instead,' Kirkcaldie said, still smarting from the cost of the document.

Belcher appeared displeased, clearly viewing the licence as a short cut of the unholiest kind.

Kirkcaldie noticed Maria wince, her countenance growing graver and her eyes fierier by the second. It was left to him to apologise and seek forgiveness by way of a coin purse containing 25 pounds. All criticism of the betrothed and their hastily purchased licence were instantly silenced.

Now Belcher cleared his throat, indicating he wished to begin. Palgrave and Bell moved to Kirkcaldie's side, Leah and Patience to Maria's. Kirkcaldie had expected his elder son to be by his side as well. He was concerned for John's safety; it was out of character for him to break a promise. Kirkcaldie could not decide whether it was the business of the law, snowfall or something more sinister that delayed his son's arrival. The wedding party had waited the better part of an hour – much to Reverend Belcher's chagrin – but with no sign of John, they finally decided to proceed.

Despite his worry, Kirkcaldie was intent on enjoying this day, one he had thought might never eventuate. He took comfort as he looked at Maria, and then down at his youngest son, so solemn-faced, and his heart welled with emotion.

Bell had come to his chamber early that morning and climbed into his bed, hugging his arms around his neck. He reminded Kirkcaldie of the baby monkey from the cousins' picture book, *A Description of Three Hundred Animals*. The child's warm breath had woken him. When Kirkcaldie opened his eyes, Bell's face was but an inch from his own.

'To what do I owe this unexpected visit?' he asked, smiling.

Bell's brown eyes turned to his, wide and expectant.

'Are you my father?'

Bell's question was as startling as being awoken by a pail of cold water. Kirkcaldie had nodded uncertainly, unsure how the boy would react to the truth but confident it was the right time for it to be revealed.

Bell had squeezed his father even more tightly, until Kirkcaldie could scarce draw breath, then pressed his cold face against his father's cheek. Kirkcaldie breathed in his son's scent. The boy was still young enough to smell sweet and fresh-washed in the morning. When their faces drew apart, his son was sobbing.

'I'm so happy,' he had stammered through his tears.

His child's immense joy had brought Kirkcaldie to tears

as well and the pair had laid there crying side by side, dampening the bed clothes, until they could smell the coffee brewing and bacon cooking on the hearth in Leah's kitchen.

With his son in his arms, it had occurred to Kirkcaldie that he had never felt so close to another person. Perhaps he had shared this type of connection with his own mother or father, though he could not think of a time when love was openly expressed between them. There was his sister, whose sweet-toned voice he could still recall, but the memory of her physical presence had faded like ink on parchment.

Of course, there was John. In their early days together, when Tamesine's death was still fresh, John would often climb onto his lap, or crawl into the hollow of his body when Kirkcaldie was sleeping. It was as though John, grief-stricken and alone, was attempting to lose himself in his new father and, Kirkcaldie supposed, he was trying to do the same. To this day, Kirkcaldie still sensed John's pain as keenly as an archer's dart.

His elder son's absence today of all days produced in Kirkcaldie a mounting sense of unease. He took a deep breath to calm himself. His gaze fell on Bell's face once more and his thoughts returned to that morning.

During the wedding breakfast, Bell had shifted his gaze from his father and mother continuously, his smile glowing all the while like sunlight on the rippling sea.

'Should I call you "Papa"?' the boy had asked suddenly, enthusiastically.

'You may call me whatever you please. But "Papa" may not roll off your tongue naturally for you have known me as "Kirkcaldie" for your entire life. That particular word – "Papa" – always sounded laboured when issued from John's mouth.'

Bell frowned. 'Why is that?'

Maria shot Bellamy a doubtful look.

'I became John's father when he was about your age. He knew me as someone else first, not as "Papa". I'm not his father by blood, as I am yours, Bell, but I am the only one he has ever known. If you do not call me "Papa" I will not be slighted.'

Kirkcaldie wanted to be truthful with his son, but he was concerned that to dive into his past, into the story of Sam Bellamy, would be too much for the child to grasp.

Seeing the confusion on his son's face, he added, 'I do not think there is sound reason for any of us to alter our names unless we wish to. I shall be Kirkcaldie and you Bellamy Joseph Hallett as always, if that is what suits you best.'

Maria had clutched Kirkcaldie's hand beneath the table, smiling at him warmly.

'And you, Sister?' Leah questioned, gaining Maria's attention. 'You have been Maria Hallett your entire life. Will you take your husband's name?'

Everyone at the table was aware that Maria Hallett was not one to hold with convention, but this was different. Not to become Mistress Kirkcaldie would be viewed by the community as an affront to her new husband as well as to tradition.

'I have given the subject much consideration,' she began thoughtfully, laying her knife and fork on the table, then dabbing her mouth with her napkin.

'I never imagined that one day I would be Mistress Kirk-caldie, although I have been in love with the man seated beside me since I was a girl and have dreamt many times of being his wife. My vision of a life with him has fortified me through the most difficult of circumstances. Now, when faced with this choice, many arguments come to mind as to why I should become Mistress Kirkcaldie and only one to the contrary. Even so it is this one lonely contention in which I find myself in agreement.'

Bell and Patience stared at his mother, baffled, while all the others present knew exactly what she meant. Maria was in love with Samuel Bellamy; until the day came when Samuel Bellamy could be reborn, she would remain Maria Hallett. Kirkcaldie understood, too. Just like his bride-to-be, he had never been the type to follow the rules of God, the King or convention.

Now, standing beside his bride, ready to exchange vows, Kirkcaldie realised it did not matter a jot what names they carried. Maria was beyond common labels. She stood beside him, luminous in such a splendidly unusual gown, so unique, that it could only be worn by Maria.

Over an ivory-quilted petticoat sat a bodice and skirt of pine green. The silk was emblazoned with pink peonies and freesias of yellow. The flowers' stems, in varying shades of green, looped and entwined, seemingly reaching beyond the limits of the skirt's short train and along the ground, giving the impression that Maria had awoken that morning and emerged not from her bed but from the earth.

She is a goddess, Kirkcaldie thought, *a pure product of nature.*

Patience had made her aunty a bouquet of evergreen foliage – azaleas and rhododendrons and more – which served to enhance the effect.

'What are you doing there, Patience?' Kirkcaldie had asked the girl a day earlier when, walking by the summer kitchen, he had noticed her through the window. He had been returning from the woods with a rifle and a brace of plump hare.

Patience attempted to conceal her task by throwing her small body theatrically across the table.

'It's a secret, Kirkcaldie!' she replied, bristling. Fronds and foliage poked out in all directions from beneath her. 'It would be ill-omened of me to reveal my endeavour.'

'Are you making your aunty's wedding bouquet?'

The girl sighed in resignation then removed herself from the table. She frowned. It was the same expression of complete vexation that Kirkcaldie had seen on Leah's pretty face a thousand times before.

'Neither your aunty nor I believe in omens. We are not superstitious types.'

Although Maria was once, he thought.

'Tell me, what flowers and plants do you have there?' he asked, dropping his kill by the door and venturing closer for a more thorough examination.

Patience described each bud and leaf and informed Kirkcaldie where she had discovered it.

'This one,' she said, pointing to a slender pale-green leaf, 'is witch-hazel. Aunty Maria asked me to find it. She said you call it "winterbloom" ... do you not?'

Kirkcaldie was not sentimental, but his heart swam in emotion on learning Maria had suggested the plant to her niece. Instantly, his mind skipped like a fleet-footed rabbit back to that summer's day in Eastham by the lake, sitting with Maria in the shade of a weeping willow. Maria had plucked a leaf of witch-hazel from a nearby bush and they had mused over its names. *Why did I ever leave her?* he wondered as Patience talked on.

From that girl under the willow to the woman before him, resplendent and glowing – how Maria had transformed.

Despite the 25-pound cost of the ceremony, Belcher did

nothing to lengthen the proceedings. Within the half hour, Kirkcaldie had slipped the ring onto Maria's finger and the event was concluded. Kirkcaldie and Maria were declared husband and wife. 'Finally,' many would have groaned. And regardless of the brevity of the proceedings, for many years to come Kirkcaldie was able to recall each moment, each word as though time itself had stood still.

ALTHOUGH THEIR NUMBERS WERE SMALL, Leah had cooked a wedding feast fit for the governor's ball. Kirkcaldie's hare were made into a clove-spiced stew with potatoes and carrots, there was roast duck, turnips and cabbage, cornbread and pumpkin casserole. The cake, which Maria had baked herself, was rich, spiced, made with dried fruit and flavoured with Eight Bells rum, and Bell and Patience had spent many hours crafting paper chains with which to decorate the table.

'This day has been a long time in the making,' Palgrave stated merrily, holding his silver cann aloft. 'When I first acquainted each of you with the other, it was obvious there was an affinity present. Why, the affection between you was as thick as blackberries in July.' He grinned. 'And I seem to recall counselling against the match.'

Kirkcaldie nodded, remembering that evening in Palgrave's small home in Eastham. It was the day he had first met Maria.

'But the strangest event has occurred. Even under challenging circumstances, tragedies pulling you apart as they have over the years, that affinity has only grown stronger and more powerful. Believe me when I say that I have known the strength of love, even after twenty-eight years of marriage.' He turned his gaze at Leah and raised his cann in her direction. Then he paused, thinking.

Palgrave looked at Kirkcaldie. His next words addressed him alone.

'Your arrival in Eastham changed the lives of all of us here today. You have grown to become my brother, a man whom I trust beyond all others. When you were lost to me for those eight years, I sensed a hole within me that no accomplishment could fill.' Emotion thickened Palgrave's voice. 'And, while it's a great sorrow to lose my sister to you, I know that you will love her and strive to keep her and my nephew safe always, as you have always done for me.'

Kirkcaldie rose from his seat and gripped Palgrave's hand, pulling him into a hearty embrace. The men stayed that way for some time, each contemplating all the events that had led to this moment in Palgrave Williams's grand dining room. When they broke apart, the feasting began.

As the party ate, Maria drew Kirkcaldie away from the others and held out her slender fingers. On her left hand sat a glorious silver band that replicated a knot.

'Where did you get this ring?' she asked. 'Is it a treasure you saved from the *Whydah*?'

Kirkcaldie laughed and the room turned at the rarely heard strains. It had been an age since the company had been blessed with that rich, honeyed sound.

'You know better than most that the only treasure I had in my arms when I leapt from the *Whydah* was John.' He took her hand and ran his finger over the band. 'Palgrave made this for me.'

'Really? Palgrave has not smithed in years ...' She examined the ring again in amazement. 'Even so, he has lost none of his skill. And the knot?'

'I'm a simple man; I cannot pretend otherwise. The sentiment, I hope, is obvious.'

The couple kissed then, a kiss of such longing and passion that both husband and wife willed the celebration to cease. However, their ardour was interrupted by a knock at the door. The tone of it prompted Kirkcaldie and Palgrave to break away from the party and move towards the sound.

Could it be John? Kirkcaldie thought as he watched Palgrave move to answer it, hoping his son had made it after all.

When Palgrave opened the door, Charlie Purse stood on the doorstep beside a tall, slender man who appeared to dwell in his later years.

'I apologise for interrupting your supper,' Charlie said awkwardly, noticing the wedding party. 'This man came to the tavern looking for someone. Riyogi pointed him in your direction.'

The stranger removed his hat to reveal a startling shock of ginger hair. Although the brightness of it must have faded with age, the tone and texture of the hue was unmistakable. Kirkcaldie stared into the man's eyes – he recognised their blue instantly.

'Good afternoon, gentleman,' said the unexpected guest. 'My name is Ephraim Post. I have been led to believe you are acquainted with my daughter.'

31

BOSTON, MASSACHUSETTS

When John arrived at Summer Street, Bowman's house was dark. He waited an age, but the man did not return home. As he waited, the feeling of rage inside him grew stronger until John could not tolerate the delay any longer. There was a force within him that demanded release.

After some time, John heard a jaunty tune being whistled by a passer-by strolling along the thoroughfare. To his consternation, the whistler appeared to be Ben Franklin. John stepped into an alleyway, struggling to reason why Ben had returned to Boston and why he was in such close proximity to Bowman's house. He watched as his friend knocked on Bowman's door. As John had suspected, there was no answer. Ben checked his pocket watch then knocked a second time, raising his head, clearly hoping to spy a light in an upstairs window.

'Mister Bowman,' he called. 'Are you at home? It is Ben Franklin from the *Philadelphia Gazette*.' Persistence was a quality Ben had in abundance, remembered John. Within a moment, Bowman's neighbour Mister Hardcourt – the neighbour who had fetched Eliza on the evening of the attack – emerged from his house clearly bamboozled by the kerfuffle. Ben introduced himself and offered Hardcourt his card.

'Henry Bowman moved on the day before last, or maybe the day before that,' Hardcourt informed Ben. 'I can't remember exactly, but he gathered his belongings and departed like a shadow.'

At this news John's fury petered out, replaced by an immense concern for Eliza. Had Bowman realised who had beaten him? Had someone told him of John's connection to Eliza? He would not put it past the vile man to seek revenge once recovered, to make his daughter's life a misery. He'd certainly be too much of a coward to face John.

Fortunately, when he had last seen her, John had sent her to his room with a key. There she was to remain until he returned. After hearing her story, he did not want her to be alone any longer. Now that he knew Bowman was on the loose, John was pleased with his decision. Who knew what the man was planning? He could not be sure whether Bowman's flight was motivated by fear or strategy.

Stung by the unexpected misfortune, John hastened north, hoping to avoid Ben and his questions. However, he soon heard behind him the light tread of a man jogging.

'John Kirkcaldie! I thought it was you.'

John's heart tightened. He turned. Rendered speechless, his mind quickly assessed the possible reasons he might have for being near Henry Bowman's residence at that hour. It was left to Ben to begin the discourse.

'You seem ill ease. Are you quite all right?'

Very slowly, John came to his senses, the colour returning to his face and his breathing becoming steady once more.

'Are you still interested in Bowman?' Ben asked.

John nodded, deep in thought. 'I suppose the *Gazette* article brought you here?'

'"The Masked Angel",' Ben said, using the newspaper's nickname for the mysterious attacker, 'has garnered interest in Philly. I'm here to run my own investigation for my publication.'

John's heart tightened again.

'I came to interview Bowman. It looks like you had a similar notion. According to his neighbour, he's moved on.'

'Really? Where?'

Ben shrugged. 'The neighbour could not tell me.'

'Could not or would not?' John replied, hoping to discover the depth of Ben's knowledge.

'Does it matter?'

John gave a wry smile. 'Probably not.'

Ben stared at him for a moment. 'You seem troubled.'

'It's nothing,' John said, attempting to appear composed. 'What will you do now?'

Ben removed his timepiece from his vest pocket, examined it closely for a moment then snapped it closed.

'I will make inquiries. There's the whore who seems quite willing to tell her story and I've also heard talk of a man named Penn ... apparently a witness saw our masked madman hurry from his house.'

John's heart sank. He wondered if Ben was fishing for information. The courtyard and the street had been deserted when he'd left Penn's residence, yet Eliza had mentioned the girls noticing their mother leave the house ... They might have noticed John as well. Was Ben attempting to manufacture a story through will alone or was there some truth in the news?

'Penn?' John queried.

'Yes, the masked maniac entered his premises last week and pummelled him. He told the local tavern owner his story when he was next in for an ale.'

Innkeepers know more than the authorities and newspapers combined, thought John. Of course his friend would know where the richest source of information could be mined. What's more, innkeepers were renowned for their loose lips. Rumour and gossip about Penn's attack would be surging around Boston like a contagion by now.

John's brow suddenly furrowed. 'You call this man a "madman" and "maniac" ...?'

'Bowman was not innocent, neither was the seaman who attacked the whore, but did they deserve the beatings they received?' Ben shrugged, undecided. 'And Penn ... I cannot uncover any crime he may have committed.'

You never will, John thought.

'The attacks,' continued Ben, 'seem completely random and disproportionate to the brutality of the punishment that was administered to the victims.'

Victims? John did not view them as such.

'I believe we have a criminal who enjoys the hunt and the kill in equal measure, speaking metaphorically, of course.'

John knew that Ben would leave no stone unturned in his search for the truth or a winning headline. Until now, the 'Masked Angel' had been portrayed as a hero but John had an inkling that Ben planned a slightly different angle for his story. While Mistress Brown would rather hang than tell of her ordeal and Penn wasn't likely to reveal his crime, once Ben Franklin began interviewing people he would likely put the pieces of the puzzle together.

'Will you join me for an ale?' John asked, pointing in the direction of a tavern he knew to be quiet. He hoped to unearth all Ben knew and perhaps convince him of a less sensationalist angle for his story.

'Perhaps tomorrow, dear friend. I have a lead on Bowman's daughter, one Eliza Bowman. I'm heading to her boarding house now.'

ELIZA BECAME aware of the door opening. The sound, although distant, pulled her from her dream like a rag doll drawn from a washing basket. She heard John's footsteps but, trapped in a strange type of half-sleep, she could not open her eyes. She felt a hand on her forehead, sensed the brushing back of her hair. The covers were drawn higher over her shoulders. Within an instant, she drifted back to sleep, determined to find her place in the dream world.

She sees her childhood home, on Bedford Street. The living room. Her mother is present. Her father, too. Her mother's face is red – burning hot in anger, tears stream down her face. Her father's face is calm, almost content as his wife rages about him. Lifting his hand to ward her off like one might a fly or a demanding, obnoxious child, he returns to the journal he's reading. He cares not that his wife is overwrought, unrestrainable.

Her mother disappears for a moment, returning with a pistol. Her father does not look up, does not notice the weapon. Holding the gun in both hands, aiming at her husband's head, she stands not more than three feet from him. Eliza can see it takes the total sum of her mother's will to prevent her arms from shaking. She watches as her mother cocks the weapon using all the strength in her fine, delicate thumbs. At the moment she fires, her father lifts his head and the bullet enters his neck. The weapon is dropped to the floor and her mother collapses.

Eliza woke with a start to find John seated near her, his worried face gazing at her own.

'My father?'

'He has gone. Disappeared.'

After a moment, Eliza's mind began to clear. Breathing hard, lying on her back, she stared at the web of cracks in the ceiling above her. She could feel strands of her hair, matted with sweat, clinging to her forehead.

'You were dreaming.'

She propped herself up, nodded, still dazed by sleep.

'I saw my mother ... she had a gun ...'

She closed her eyes, concentrated, saw the vision again.

'She tried to kill my father.'

Her eyes sprung open.

'John, I don't think this was a dream. It was real, a memory – my memory.' Tears began to trickle down her cheeks. 'I think she tried to kill my father when she discovered what he was doing to me ...oh John, I wish she'd had better aim,' she said, bitterly.

'Tell me.'

Eliza wiped her eyes. Her brow drew together in concentration, remembering.

'I was hiding. As a child I spent many hours in the small cupboard under the staircase inventing games, hiding from my father, longing to be someplace else. I imagined it a burrow and me a rabbit. Perhaps I was there ...' she said, uncertain, her tone feverish. 'No, I must have only wanted to be. But I could see them clearly ... he was reading. I saw my mother aiming a gun at his head. At the moment my mother pulled the trigger, he looked up and the shot entered his neck. It travelled a clear passage into the wall behind him. There was blood.' Tears came again.

John moved closer, took her hand, stroked her knuckles gently.

'She was taken away ... and I never saw her again. My father had his own wife taken to prison. I didn't know why until tonight. My father led me to believe she was ill, made sly comments about her state of mind. I assumed she'd been taken to hospital, perhaps an asylum. I was frantic, bereft, but he would not tell me more. In fact, he never spoke of it again, never told me what happened to her.'

She clasped John's hand, furtive now.

'For years, I heard her screams ... I still hear them now on occasion. I thought they were screams of pain, but they were from when she was dragged away by Red Coats.'

Eliza's eye's widened, a light slowly dawning in her mind.

'The letter ... I found a letter she wrote to me, hidden in my father's attic. She must have penned it when she decided to kill him. She knew she would be imprisoned somewhere, possibly even hanged, and she wrote me her story so I could know the woman she had been.'

Eliza began to sob. John waited, knowing she needed to release her pain.

Then suddenly, panicked, she pushed back the covers.

'I must get to school ...'

John sensed that to deal with her trauma, Eliza's mind needed a return to order, to what she understood best. He took her hands again, wishing to reassure her.

'It is not time. It is still dark outside,' he said, recalling the image of her as a rabbit hiding from the hunter. He took her in his arms. 'It's safe here.'

She nodded, relieved, then sank into the comfort of his embrace.

DESPITE JOHN'S protestations in the morning, Eliza insisted on going to school. She could not afford to lose the position, she claimed. However, aside from a return to order, John believed Eliza's decision to go was due to her dedication to her profession. He sensed it came from a place similar to his own, the desire to right wrongs, to protect those who could not protect themselves.

Once Eliza had departed, John washed then attempted to corral his thoughts. Bowman was gone and Ben Franklin had arrived, already eager to interview Eliza and Sara McArthur. He would get to Penn, too, eventually. Ben was scrupulous and exceedingly clever – he would speak to the Browns as well, make connections between the Brown girls and Eliza Bowman. All those connections led back to John. But what would Ben – his oldest friend – do with the knowledge? John did not know.

The worst of it was that just the evening before he had been determined to carry out Eliza's wish and kill her father. He could barely believe it of himself. While he stood waiting among the shadows of Summer Street, he had imagined how he would proceed. After some thought, he decided – quite rationally – upon breaking the man's neck.

He had seen Kirkcaldie do it once. He had not known John was watching. There had been a carnival in Concord and Captain Grand had been fighting and doing well. But a man in the crowd recognised him as Sam Bellamy. At first, Kirkcaldie had laughed off the man's suggestion when he had yelled out 'Black Sam' from behind the ropes. But this man, who travelled with the carnival with a dancing bear, had persisted and both Kirkcaldie and John became aware that he was talking to others about his discovery.

Following the bout, Kirkcaldie and John had retired. However, John heard Kirkcaldie rise and steal away from the tent. He had followed, intrigued and half aware of what Kirkcaldie was doing.

Kirkcaldie found the man filling a trough with food scraps for his animal. He had approached from behind and wrapped one arm silently around the man's throat. Without seeming to apply any force at all, and with the least amount of strain, Kirkcaldie had snapped the bear owner's neck. The man had struggled slightly, only dropping the bucket of scraps after John had heard the crack of bone from his hiding place behind the wheel of a wagon. Kirkcaldie lowered the man's body to the ground and John had fled to the tent, feigning sleep when Kirkcaldie eventually returned.

To John, it had seemed like a simple means of murder – silent and clean. It was what he had planned to do to Bowman. Now the memory of it made him retch.

Eliza needed to push all thoughts of her parents from her mind. They were a distraction. The full memory of the day her mother was taken away had come to her in a dream. Having been recently in her father's presence had unearthed it. The flurry of emotions caused by seeing him had blown the soil away on that painful event in her past. He was gone now and she hoped he would never return to Boston. She could put the past behind her. Again.

Priding herself on her rational nature, her complete and

total dedication to reason, Eliza resolved to think no more of either of her parents. She would devote herself to her role as teacher and to John. Thinking of him now, she felt embarrassed and ashamed she had asked him to take action on her behalf. It was not his responsibility to assuage her grief. Shaking her head as though the physical act would dislodge all negative thoughts from her mind, she went about her day and taught her lessons, making a silent vow to herself to be less introspective and consider others more. 'Wallowing never helped anyone,' she often told her class.

Eliza gazed at the students in her room. They were copying a passage from Virgil into their handwriting books. Although she was forbidden to teach Latin, she had concluded that there was nothing wrong with asking her students to transcribe it. Comforted and slightly mesmerised by the scratch of the children's quills against paper, she looked out the window and noticed a light snow fall – its whiteness concealing the grimy, slushy cobblestones. This image, that would seem to most so meagre, somehow warmed her. She sensed her spirit lift.

As she stood by the window watching the snow cover grow denser, she resolved to go immediately to John once lessons were finished for the day. She liked him immensely and she did not want his crimes or the memories of her childhood coming between them. They were both damaged. As such, they could help each other heal.

Thinking back, she realised she had been defensive with him at first. She had been all ramparts and spikes. Even though John had opened his heart to her, she had not trusted him. Yet he still offered his help to her, unexpectedly and in earnest.

Eliza had never been in love but now she wondered, as she watched the snow drift gently to the ground, whether the mix of emotions she was experiencing at that moment – gratitude, desire, care – might be love. The sense of his strong hands on her body and soft lips on her neck remained as vivid now as when they came together in the early morning. She had wanted to stay longer in his bed, curled into the side of the warm, willowy body that seemed to take the shape of her own. But she had to go to school. The headmaster did not tolerate tardiness from neither students nor teachers.

When she finally walked through the school gates at dusk, she was startled to find a man waiting for her. Reginald Spalding. Registering her surprise at seeing him, he tried to explain his presence.

'I hope you are well, Eliza. I have been in Boston for a month. My mother is quite ill, you see. I have done little else than care for her.'

'I am most sorry to hear it.'

Spalding rubbed his gloved hands together and stamped his feet, freeing them of snow. The brim of his hat had collected a healthy dusting. *How long has he been waiting?* Eliza wondered. She had thought little of Spalding since his departure a year ago.

'My sister is seeing to my mother tonight,' he went on. 'I thought I might take the opportunity to leave her house for a time, reacquaint myself with the city.'

She nodded, recalling her recent experience with her father. 'It can be extremely difficult when caring for a parent.'

'My mother is not long for this world, I fear. She was never what one would call doting and I find my duties an immense burden.'

Eliza sighed sympathetically. *Is this why he is here?* she mused. After their sole encounter, he had taken no further romantic interest in her. Perhaps now he sought the comfort of a friend instead.

'Would you mind joining me for a bite to eat?' he asked. 'It would do me the world of good to talk about matters that are not related to my mother's health. I always enjoyed your company. I think we share a similar perspective on matters.'

Her thoughts shot to John but Spalding's piteous expression induced her to consider his invitation for a moment. Perhaps it would do her good as well, to discuss matters that did not involve recent events, to listen to another's woes and to clear her mind before she talked to John again. It would be a step in the right direction, a step towards becoming outward-looking.

She agreed, taking Spalding's arm, and they strolled through the crisp, white street to a tavern.

32

AUGUSTA, MAINE

'So you see, good people, it has taken me some time to put my head on straight,' said Ephraim Post to his stunned audience. 'Achak found me in New France about four years ago. A finer tracker you will never meet, yet it still took him the better part of six years to find me. I kept moving constantly, hoping to disappear, so he had a job of it.

'But in the end, I am glad he found me. When he told me all that had happened – it seemed a confession of sorts – I was angry and could have strangled him where he stood. I believe he would have allowed it, too. But we had been friends once, and based on our history and his friendship with my daughter, I came to a strange conclusion. When I thought about his actions, I understood them. There was a time when I was just as mercenary – I realised he could have done nothing else but to kill my brother in that situation.

'When he had informed me that Tabby had protected him, that she had pinned the crime on Cool at her trial – why, I realised that Tabby also knew this, so I thought if Tabby could see good in Achak, then so could I. She's clever, always has been. She could see exactly where justice needed to be meted and it wasn't on Achak.

Ephraim sighed at the recollection of events so long ago.

'After Achak explained everything, it took me some time to pull myself together. Well, what amounts to a decade in total seems like an inordinate amount of time, I admit, but when you consider that I was convinced I had murdered my brother ... well, perhaps for some it might be understandable. But now that I am recovered, needless to say, I feel it's fine time I was back in Tabby's life.'

There was no mistaking that this man was Tabby's father. The resemblance lay not only in his appearance and the resolute glimmer in his clear blue eyes but in his means of expression as well. It was so reminiscent of Tabby that Palgrave was forced to swallow hard; the lump in his throat was close to choking him.

Earlier, Patience and Bell had been sent to their room and Sarah was asked to look after Charlie. Joseph, Elizabeth and their partners had taken their leave, sensing the import of Mister Post's visit. The rest of the wedding party had gone to Palgrave's study to talk. The gathered company now sat in silence. After listening to his story and hearing of his desire to see Tabby, how could they tell this father, who was so determined to reunite with his daughter, that she was gone, missing, vanished from the world?

Palgrave was the first to speak.

'No-one has seen or heard from Tabby since her trial. She disappeared on that day.'

Ephraim's face grew serious at this news.

'I went to Moosehead Lake in search of her,' Kirkcaldie continued. 'Her Indian friends had not seen her. For my work, I travel throughout Maine and beyond. For several years after Tabby disappeared, I asked many I came across if they might remember seeing her. I believe they would have, and recognise her easily – she was such a singular, striking woman. Yet no-one ever had. Tabby is a huntress. She is better at concealment than most and she clearly wanted to remain hidden from the world.'

Ephraim Post nodded in agreement, saddened by what he had heard. His voice cracked as he began to speak.

'You were my last port of call. I have travelled the length of the Kennebec many times over in search of her and you people were my last hope. I even went as far as Quebec, the convent where she was schooled. All correspondence ceased with the trial, the Sisters informed me. The Oriental at the tavern, who I learnt she was close to, has not heard from her either.' He sighed. 'I was a fool. She begged me for years, pleaded with me to speak to her but, like an obstinate pig, I was stuck so deep in my own misery that I was blind to her own.'

He sighed again and rubbed his forehead, contemplating the thousands of possibilities, his thoughts coming to rest at one.

'I just hope that she is still alive. I can live without ever seeing her again, as long as I know she is well.'

As he rose to leave, Leah spoke.

'Will you not stay for supper? I have made such an inordinate amount of food, enough to feed ...' She clutched at his arm. Ephraim Post stared at her white knuckles for a moment then patted her hand gently.

'I appreciate your hospitality, Mistress, but I will leave you to your celebrations. My presence here will only be a grim pall, a dark cloud over the festivities.'

Post shook the hands of Palgrave and Kirkcaldie and walked towards the door of the study. He was deep in thought as he placed his hat on his head and straightened the brim, an expression of such sorrow etched onto his face, a face so similar to Tabby's that it made the entire party wretched.

'I suppose it's a blessing,' he muttered eventually, 'that while talking of Tabby to all these people in the towns and settlements around the Kennebec, I have learnt her story. She helped people. She saved lives. She was courageous. Tabby somehow acquired all the attributes that I had lost when my brother was killed, or perhaps was never in possession of in the first place.'

He wiped his eyes with his palms.

'And now I am full of sorrow at the thought that it was my own self-pity that stopped me from knowing such a remarkable woman. I just pray she is safe and happy, wherever she is in the world.'

There was nothing anyone could say to ease this poor man's guilt, his regrets.

'Mister Post ...'

The group turned to Leah. She took a step towards the man, a strange look of panic and sorrow on her face.

'I know where Tabby is. She is both safe and well.'

WHEN HER PARENTS and the newly married couple ventured into her father's study with Mister Post, Sarah offered Charlie some supper. He ate a healthy selection of everything on offer on the expansive table. Sarah did not attempt to prevent him, predicting the others may no longer be in the mood for celebrating after Mister Post's unexpected visit. Charlie was as tall as her father although seemingly twice as gangly; to her mind, he needed a little fleshing out.

After a few minutes, Charlie looked up from his plate,

his black hair falling across his brow. He pushed it back and noticed Sarah observing him. He reddened.

'Lions, I have read, gormandise when they can, after a hunt for instance, because they do not know when they might eat again. That is me, I'm afraid. My life has been a series of feasts and famines. I'm a lion, I suppose.' He smiled, but did not apologise for his behaviour.

Sarah nodded, wondering about his past. When her father was away, when she was a child, she was aware of her mother's burden to protect and provide for the family. However, Sarah had never gone hungry. There was always food on the table.

Charlie slowed his eating after a while and the pair were quiet. Sarah sipped her punch, observing him. The cough that had placed Charlie Purse in hospital had disappeared entirely. However, a scar remained above his lip from the beating he received. She had stitched that wound herself. He had been unconscious at the time, allowing Sarah to take immense care with her stitches. They were neat and, although still prominent, the scar was as straight as an angel's flight.

'The man your aunt married is not from Augusta, is he?' Charlie asked.

'Kirkcaldie?' Sarah replied. 'He's from everywhere, really. Kirkcaldie is the governor's surveyor. He travels a great deal but he has a home near Hallowell.'

Charlie nodded, wiping his plate clean with a heel of bread.

'He and my father have been friends for twenty years or so,' she said, hoping to prolong the conversation.

'Have you always lived in this house?' Charlie asked when he was finished. He leant back in his chair and took a deep, satisfied breath.

Sarah shook her head. 'We moved here some time ago from Cape Cod. When I was a girl, our home was Eastham and then, for a short time, Wellfleet.'

'I know those towns. I worked on a whaling ship for a year.'

'A lucrative profession.'

'For those who can stomach it.'

Despite his lion-like appetite, Sarah surmised that Charlie Purse was not a predator at heart. He seemed to possess a sensitive soul.

Within the half-hour, the rest of the party emerged, congregating outside the dining room. A foreboding tension emerged along with them. Sensing the changed atmosphere, Charlie rose, wiping his mouth on a napkin. Sarah looked at her mother's ashen face and her father's clenched jaw. Hands were shaken. Charlie smiled a sweet farewell at Sarah, thanking her for supper, then the visitors departed. The door was closed.

Sarah heard her parents ascend the staircase. Maria entered the dining room where her niece waited.

'I'll help you clear the table,' said Maria, but then noticed the questioning look on Sarah's face.

'Tabby Post is alive and living in New Orleans.'

Sarah's hands clenched tight around the plates she was holding. Her heart rose into her throat.

'Ben will surely go to her,' she said in a low voice.

Maria moved to her niece and gently eased the plates from her grasp.

'No doubt.'

33

———

Leah had never known her husband to be an angry man. He was placid by nature and it took a great deal to provoke him to even raise his voice. However, he had killed men, many men, so she knew there must be a kernel of rage in him capable of erupting. But Leah's concerns did not involve physical violence. Unlike many other men, who beat their wives for the slightest misdemeanour, Palgrave had never raised a hand against her. It was the mask of disappointment that cast his usually pleasant countenance in a wholly despondent light that was crushing her like the weight of a thousand boulders. Nothing she had done in the past – the lies she had told to protect her family, the murder of Dent – had provoked this reaction in her husband. At those times, he had been understanding, even sympathetic of her motives.

Once Mister Post departed, Palgrave had sent everyone away. Doing so was an action so unlike him that Maria and Kirkcaldie had stood frozen for a moment, staring at each other hopelessly. His tone had not been offensive, but it had been hammer blunt.

Indicating the staircase, Palgrave had watched as Leah climbed each step like a convict ascending to the gallows. Once in their chamber he asked her to sit. He walked the perimeter of the room as she waited. As time drew on, Leah grew increasingly fretful. Clearly attempting to contain his rage before he spoke, Leah believed she would rather have been struck with his fist than wait a moment longer.

'How could you? How could you keep this a secret?' he said finally, exasperated. 'Poor Ben has been grief stricken – heartbroken – for years. Convinced she was dead or worse, he has wasted his talents and his life in a charity hospital, slaving like a pauper with the hope of honouring her memory. And Kirkcaldie ...' Palgrave shook his head. 'You allowed him to ride off in search of her. Who knows what dangers he might have faced along the way in all the time he did so? And, like a fool, I have been managing her money and investments for years – to what purpose? Your actions are unfathomable ... I cannot even begin to grasp your motives.'

There was an edge to his voice that she did not recognise. It was as cold as iron and as bitter as gall. He grew silent and Leah was uncertain whether she should speak.

'I didn't know for some time,' she said, hesitant, miserable. 'It was six months after she disappeared that I received her first letter. Tabby asked me not to reveal her whereabouts, even that she was alive. I didn't know what to do ... Ben had gone, and Kirkcaldie was away ... I had no opportunity to tell them, even if I felt I could. She did not want to be found, Palgrave.' Leah said, anguish filling her words.

'It's selfishness, pure and simple,' he declared. 'From both you and Tabby. Did whatever she was experiencing warrant the torture Ben has endured all these years on her behalf? First joining the army to save her, hoping on his return that she would be his, then returning only to discover her gone ... Tabby Post is no different from her father, wallowing in her own self-pity ... And you, delighting in the drama of it all, possessing a secret that is yours alone!'

Leah rose, coloured.

'That's untrue and unwarranted. Tabby saved my life. I am beholden to her for my life! Was I to deny her the only thing she has ever asked of me?'

Palgrave seemed to calm slightly then. Lost in their own thoughts and struggles, the couple stood face to face for a time, breathing hard, eyes locked like fighters in a ring.

'Does she have any intention of returning?' Palgrave eventually asked when he regained his composed.

'I don't believe so. She has made a life with the Sisters of Ursuline in New Orleans. It's a cloistered life, away from the world, but it is what she desires. She teaches and heals – Tabby is doing exactly what she was born to do.'

'Why did she tell you?'

Leah lowered herself onto the sofa, exhausted from the day's events. The day had begun so happily with a wedding breakfast and then a wedding. Remembering Palgrave's toast, she sighed in an effort to stem her tears. To have the day end this way was excruciating. She wondered if she might have handled the matter differently knowing the consequences. She did not believe so.

'I have asked myself the same question many times.' Leah paused in order to choose her words carefully. 'In that first letter, Tabby wrote to me that it was after the trial, after she had disappeared that she discovered she was with child.'

Palgrave eyes grew wide. Leah could see the anger colouring his cheeks once more, but she pressed on.

'The baby, a daughter, was born in New Orleans. She didn't dare to travel to Quebec, knowing how easily she would be found. Tabby had heard news the Sisters were establishing a second convent in Louisiana and took it upon herself to head there for sanctuary. This is where the child has been raised. It occurs to me now that Tabby may have wanted someone to know that a child belonging to her existed in the world, in case anything happened to her. That is the only reason I can think of for Tabby telling me.'

He frowned. 'And the father?'

'I asked several times but she never answered me. I have long assumed the father was either Kirkcaldie or Ben but I don't know for certain. It could be anyone ...Tabby never discussed that aspect of her life with me. But does it even matter now? The child is nine years old. ... I beg you Palgrave, please do not tell either of them. It would ruin Maria and Kirkcaldie, and as for Ben ... what good would it do to know?'

Palgrave slumped onto a chair.

'Oh, Leah,' he sighed, removing his spectacles and rubbing his tired eyes.

IT WAS NOT LATE, perhaps just seven o'clock, but Kirkcaldie and Maria prepared for bed. It was a sombre occasion. Ephraim Post's arrival and Leah's revelation had left them with a feeling of loss and a sense of injustice. They could not reason out Leah's motives for keeping Tabby's secret for so long, yet the knowledge that she was alive and in reach left them both with a multitude of questions and a nagging sense of 'what if?'.

They changed out of their wedding clothes in silence. Kirkcaldie lit the candles then sat down on their bed.

'Did you know where she was, Maria?' he asked his wife,

a touch of melancholy in his voice. 'You were connected to her.'

'Our connection was through you. Once she severed your attachment, I could not sense her anymore.'

Kirkcaldie nodded, satisfied.

Maria sat to brush out her hair. 'You called her "a singular woman".'

'There was a time,' he said, speaking to Maria's reflection in the looking glass, 'that I confess to having given some thought to a life with Tabby. I had even resolved to free her if Dummer had found her guilty. And I will also confess that when I went in search of her, the emotion that drove me was love.'

Maria glanced in the mirror at her husband.

'But that seems like a lifetime ago and so much has occurred that has altered and focused my priorities. Recalling that time and the way Tabby was, I realise that she was too wild, too free-willed for me. Tabby Post could never have been tamed. My heart, my body, no longer yearns for her.'

Maria paused in the brushing of her long golden hair. 'And me? Am I not wild and free-willed?' she asked.

'You were. Now you are tethered.'

She continued brushing. 'By Bell?'

Kirkcaldie nodded to himself. 'Yes. And by me, I hope.'

Maria placed her hairbrush on the dresser and walked to her husband. As she stood before him, she caressed his face with her palms. Kirkcaldie felt their heat – it was as if she had captured the sun under her skin. She pressed her hands against his cheeks more tightly. Her eyes were wild as she looked upon him; Kirkcaldie sensed her force surge through his body. Their faces were close, almost touching. Her breasts pressed against him through her shift.

'If you play false with me, Samuel Bellamy, I will rip out your heart and feed it to the pigs.'

She kissed him hard on the mouth, biting his lip, drawing blood. Within him, all around him, her spirit was a whirlwind, consuming him. If he didn't have her now, he would surely perish.

'I swear to you, Maria, I will never deceive you.' He wiped the blood from his lips. 'We are of one blood now.'

He rose, lifted her into his arms and then onto the bed.

34

TAMESINE: ITZEL'S COTTAGE

NASSAU, 1705

Tamesine had been in Nassau a fortnight. The landlady, as John had advised, was a merry woman who, never having had daughters of her own, took Tamesine into her care and companionship. Mistress Landry found Tamesine a number of new petticoats, bodices and skirts and even a pretty bonnet to wear when she was brave enough to venture outside into the township.

'People are forgetful. They leave things behind,' she explained, rifling through a mahogany chest of assorted belongings.

'I have never been so well attired,' Tamesine said, staring in the looking glass, twirling a particularly becoming cream skirt that featured embroidered pink roses.

'Now we have fattened you up, we need to have you looking pretty as a picture for that fetching husband of yours,' she smiled. 'Your hair is glorious and would look fine in braids. You are also most fortunate to possess a firm bosom. Once you and the Lieutenant have a babe, that will all change, however,' she finished sulkily, lamenting the fate of her own.

Tamesine warmed at the notion of having John's baby. She felt sure it was likely to happen sooner than either of them expected. Although he was assigned to the barracks, John visited her frequently. He would often bring food and madeira with him and they would picnic on the floor of her chamber. Then they would come together, exploring one another as only a man and woman are able. Intoxicated from the wine, the heat and each other, they would lie glistening, naked for hours in each other's arms, the netting covering the bed creating an idyllic haven of sorts for the lovers. By morning, when the low, early rays penetrated their sanctuary, John would depart still delirious, languid and completely overcome.

She had last seen her flow on board the *Mary* then not again, but Agatha had explained this was most likely a symptom of her seasickness and weight loss, not of pregnancy. Before she had boarded the ship, Tamesine and John had only laid together once – at St Maderne's Bed on the day they were handfast.

John hoped for a child as well. He spoke of a son often. He told her that once she had a baby, he would seek permission to reside with her. It was not unheard of, he explained, for officers to live with their wives and families in cottages behind the town, in the hinterlands. Then, when the baby was older and stronger, he would request leave for a period and travel with her and their child to Surrey. He told her of his family's lands there.

In Surrey, he would introduce her to his mother, older brother and sister. His father – also John King – had died some years before when John was a boy. His sister had two children of her own and his mother was a devoted grandmother, John informed her. 'She has extremely strong opinions on raising children. However, I believe as she has brought up three very successfully herself, she should be listened to.'

Tamesine did not relish the day she would have to step foot on another ship but she enjoyed hearing of her husband's plans and imagined a reunion with Eseld. John informed her it was seven days travel from Mousehole to his family's lands in Surrey, and his mother's expectation would be for them to stay with her for a considerable length of time. To Tamesine, she sounded like a formidable woman.

'What have you told your mother of me?' she asked John one day as she lay in his arms.

'I have written of your beauty and courage and your life in Mousehole.'

Tamesine frowned. 'Have you told her that I am ...'

What am I? Common, poor, a labourer, she thought. She worried that none of these options would be palatable to a woman like John's mother.

'I believe I wrote that you helped your father who was a fisherman.'

Tamesine rested uneasily that night. Difference was fascinating to John. He adored her turn of phrase and unfamiliar accent, seeing them as exotic, rather than common. Similarly, when they ventured out in Nassau, he watched in awe as men were tattooed, admiring the skill of the artist in equal measure as the courage of the man being worked on. But Tamesine was aware that difference terrified most people, especially those wealthy enough to see difference as a threat. She suspected John's mother was one of those people.

She embraced John more tightly and pushed her thoughts to the back of her mind.

Over the next few weeks, Tamesine waited to flower and, when she did not, she discussed her situation with both Agatha and Mistress Landry. The latter advised a visit to a midwife who lived in the hinterland, a Lucayan woman who returned to New Providence when the Spanish departed. Her name was Itzel.

At dawn the trio embarked into the hinterland. It was not a long distance but it was slow and tedious in the heat. Masses of tiny midge-like creatures swarmed, seemingly blocking their passage, but Mistress Landry cut through them as though they were freshly churned butter, carving a path for Tamesine and Agatha in her wake. But Tamesine remained wary. Her first week in Nassau had seen her bitten red and raw by mosquitoes. Mistress Landry assured her these minuscule flying creatures were not mosquitoes and would do her no harm.

Larger, hand-sized insects – colourful caterpillars and butterflies – distracted Tamesine from the rigours of the trek. Mostly, they seemed gentle beasts, content to rest on a lush, full leaf, no doubt keeping a watchful eye on the trespassers. Tamesine and Agatha gasped when they came upon a flock of striking flame-coloured birds standing in and around a shallow mountain lake.

'They are flamingos,' Mistress Landry informed them. 'Harmless and quite beautiful.'

Tamesine gazed at them in wonder. Even the prettiest birds in Cornwall were whey-faced and puny by comparison to these incredible creatures.

As they made their way higher into the mountains the air thinned and grew cooler and, much to Tamesine's delight, more sweet-smelling. The air in the township of Nassau was noxious. The change the slight altitude brought with it was a welcome relief and made the last few miles of the journey almost bearable. Itzel's white cottage sat nestled in a small valley, among trees and shrubs of every shade of green, the blooms of which were dewy and pregnant with life. The entire picture resonated with growth. Tamesine imagined a similar cottage she might share with John one day, with whitewashed walls and blue gingham curtains hanging in the windows. Hearing the chatter as they approached, Itzel walked out onto the long terrace that surrounded her home and inspected the visitors.

She was an immensely handsome woman, broad-faced and bronze-skinned, who might have been (to Tamesine's eye) anywhere between sixteen and sixty. There was simply no telling her years but there was an air of gentleness and peace about her that seemed to render her ageless.

'Welcome,' she called, gesturing for them to step onto the terrace. 'I will fetch you water. *Las agua. Subiendo.*'

The women rested in the shade, waiting for Itzel to return. The water she poured from a clay jug was as cold as that of Madron Well and, if the reviving nature of the tonic was any indication, it was just as magical. Tamesine instantly felt restored. Itzel stared at her as she drank down large gulps of the liquid.

'You are the pregnant one, then, aye?'

Her voice was a strange and rich combination of tones and accents, thick and fleshy, just like the jungle she was surrounded by.

Tamesine nodded. 'I hope so. You can tell just by looking at me?'

'I can tell from here that you have the colours of a woman with child. You're buzzin' orange and silvery all over as bright as a firefly.'

Itzel moved towards the door and led the women inside.

'Pregnant women glow on the outside with all the life

that is bubbling within. You are a ripe, juicy peach waiting to burst. I will be wanting to look you over, if that is your intent in walking all the miles to my home here.'

Once inside the cottage, Itzel examined Tamesine. She kept her black eyes closed as she pressed into Tamesine's soft flesh. The woman's warm, large hands traversing her belly felt as soft as a lady's glove.

'A March baby, at a guess,' she finally confirmed when done. She looked Tamesine in the eye. 'When it's time, I will come to you. Find Galy. He'll bring me.'

'Galy?' Tamesine asked.

'A boy in town.'

'I know him,' Mistress Landry said. 'He works for Tom and Garrett at the Three Irishmen.'

TAMESINE WASHED and braided her hair, waiting for John to arrive, barely able to keep her hands from her belly now she was certain there was a life inside it. Her prospects, so bleak just a few months ago, now festooned before her like a whirling maypole. John lifted her from her feet when she told him the news, twirling her in the air. Tamesine's heart brimmed with happiness in the knowledge that her decision to leave Mousehole was the right one. John resolved immediately to write to his mother of the news.

GALY WAS prompt when he was sent for by Mistress Landry. Once instructions were issued, he took off like the east wind through the streets of Nassau and into the hinterland, his little black feet fleet and nimble. Within the hour Itzel had arrived in Tamesine's room. Within minutes after that, a baby boy slid into the world and was placed in Tamesine's arms; she was in love with her son in an instant. As the new mother gazed at her creation, Itzel went about the duties of a midwife. Tamesine barely felt the force of Itzel's large hands on her abdomen as she expelled the afterbirth.

Soon, with his eyes still closed, the baby's tiny mouth pursed and he nuzzled his head against Tamesine's chest.

'Put him to your tit,' Itzel advised. 'He be hungry.'

The child latched on immediately and began suckling ferociously on Tamesine's nipple. She smiled at the expression of peace and contentment on her son's mottled pink face that belied his ravening nature. Mistress Landry and Agatha, who had been waiting for the heartening sound of a baby's cry, entered the room and stared lovingly at the child in Tamesine's arms, with Mistress Landry insisting the boy was the image of his father. Agatha, who took some time to cast her judgement, believed she saw only the mother in the child.

'Mistress Landry, will you fetch my husband?' Tamesine asked, still gazing at her baby. 'Tell him he has a son – John King.'

Mistress Landry arrived at the barracks and found them empty. The makeshift home for the *Greyhound*'s crew was being disassembled piece by piece by two young seaman. Mistress Landry made it a habit not to walk on sand; she loathed the stuff. It was the bane of her life. But for Tamesine, she made an exception. She hoisted her petticoats and skirts and, with an audible sigh, trod her way along the beach towards the barracks.

'Do you know where I might find Lieutenant John King?' she asked one of the men. 'Of the *Greyhound*,' she added so there would be no mistake made.

'The *Greyhound* sailed this morning for Jamaica. From there it is heading to Florida.'

The seaman waited for Mistress Landry to find speech.

'And Lieutenant John King was on board?'

The seaman nodded. 'If he was a member of the crew then yes, of course.'

Mistress Landry was not a naive woman. She had buried her third husband only a year ago and had been successful at business on the island for fifteen years, among thieves and pirates – the draff. And, if she were completely honest, most naval officers she had met were not far above these grouts in both morals and behaviour. But John King seemed different. A blind man could see he was utterly ensorcelled by Tamesine and she by him. For the Lieutenant to leave without a word seemed out of character and it took the woman, who had witnessed a lifetime's worth of strange and inexplicable events in the years she had been on Nassau, completely by surprise.

WHEN BABY JOHN KING was six months old, Tamesine decided to send his grandmother a letter. Despite Agatha and Mistress Landry's pleas that her husband may have been killed or lost at sea, Tamesine knew in her heart of hearts – in the same spot that told her she had to flee Mousehole – that he had deserted her and his son. Awareness led to grief. However, Tamesine was not surprised. Disappointment was an old friend.

She was angry, too, and concerned for her and her son's

future. Mistress Landry and Agatha seemed to excuse John for his actions, making it difficult for Tamesine to cut him loose. If John had planned to return to Nassau after completing his work in Florida, then surely he would have told her of his departure in the first instance. Mistress Landry and Agatha only wanted to see good in John because he *had* been good – handsome, moral, loving to Tamesine – and neither of them remembered nor realised the influence a parent could have on a child, even a grown child. Hatred of her father had driven Tamesine to the far ends of the world.

Itzel could see her anger, saying her colour was clouded red as though a fire raged deep within. Tamesine could sense it, too – its persistent, unforgiving heat. She realised that while she was furious with John, she was more furious with herself. She had trusted him completely. How could she have been so foolish? Her heartache only eased when she remembered how John had abandoned them in the most cowardly of ways. With that realisation, she instantly hoped Agatha and Mistress Landry were correct and he was dead – run through by a pirate or eaten alive by sharks. Imagining his suffering gave her some comfort.

Each day she would wind her granny's music box then sit staring at the jouncing ships as she nursed her son, cataloguing her options. Return to Mousehole she could not. Humiliation in the face of her father's ridicule was an option not even worth considering, even though he, her mother and Eseld were her only family.

But no, she had John, her son. He was her family now. As was Agatha and Itzel and dear, sweet, well-meaning Mistress Landry. New Providence would be her home, she decided. All three women were alone in the world, making a life for themselves on the island. Who was to stop Tamesine from doing the same? It mattered not that she was just sixteen. It mattered not that she was a mother now.

Itzel, who had grown into a mother figure in Tamesine's life, advised her to pen the letter if the writing of it would help her move forward. It took her days to complete her correspondence, but once she had, she was satisfied with the result.

Dearest Mistress John King,

My name is Tamesine King and I am your Daughter by way of Marriage to your Son – Lieutenant John King of the Greyhound.

We two were Handfast in Mousehole at Midsummer when he was in Cornwall hunting Smugglers. You may say that to be Handfast is not to be Married because a Minister of the Church of England did not perform the Rights. Forgive me for saying so, but you are wrong to think it. The Ceremony is ages old and solemn by anyone's thinking.

I loved your Son with all my Heart and, I believe, he loved me in return. This is why I abandoned my own Family and followed my Beloved to this Island over squally Seas. Here, I gave birth to his Son – who I have named John, after him. He is a grand Child. His Eyes are presently a mottled Hue, but I am sure, given time, they will become his Father's Emerald. There will be no mistaking that your Son is his Father, although I pray he is more constant and steadfast in his Affections.

Convincing John to abandon me was your doing, I suspect. And although I have always been a distrustful Soul, I do believe I am right to be so in this instance for I know it would not do for a Surrey Lady to invite a Fisherwoman like me into her Family. However, in truthful Fact, I am your family. There is nothing I hope to gain from the writing of this Letter, except the Opportunity to Unburden myself and gain a Modicum of Freedom from my Woes. For although my Union with your Son was brief, it was passionate and I doubt whether I will ever love so strongly again. I pray this Letter might go some way in severing my Feelings.

Yours Sincerely,

Tamesine King

After Agatha, Mistress Landry and Itzel approved her words, she folded the pages, placed them in an envelope and addressed her letter to Mistress John King, Petworth House, Surrey.

35

BOSTON, MASSACHUSETTS

The moment John learnt that Henry Bowman had vacated his house and disappeared, he knew he could not travel to Augusta for his father's wedding. To leave Eliza alone in the city was unthinkable. He wrote Kirkcaldie a letter, explaining as much as he was able without alarming his father. Despite his concern that the letter would not arrive in time – thereby causing Kirkcaldie unnecessary worry – John could not leave Eliza.

Since that night, however, John had not seen her for three days. He had visited the boarding house each morning, but Mistress Forsythe always informed him that Eliza was unwell, feeling too poorly to leave her room to see him. Although John realised that people became ill, it was unlike Eliza not to have sent him a message and he was becoming anxious with concern for her. Ben Franklin had been told the same story by the headmaster at the Writing School.

'Both father and daughter have vanished,' Ben remarked as he strolled with John towards his rooms after the two had shared supper at a nearby tavern. 'Slightly suspicious, would you not say?'

His friend's words did nothing to ease his concern, but John remained calm in his response, keen to throw Ben off his line of inquiry.

'Henry Bowman I cannot comment on, but Eliza Bowman is ill. You have been told so by her headmaster – news that only confirms what I discovered from her landlady. You are looking too closely for clues, my friend, and in the process seeing everything as sign of mischief and deceit.'

'You may be right, but I don't plan to depart Boston without a story. I'm meeting with Penn tomorrow.'

John knew Ben would be good to his word. Dismayed, wanting to see Eliza, the need to speak with her became more pressing; he must do so before Ben Franklin met with Penn. That excursion would surely result in Ben interviewing the Brown family as well.

JOHN WAITED until almost midnight before returning to Eliza's boarding house. During the afternoon, the temperature had dropped, driving people into their homes. Now the moon was concealed by a dense layer of cloud and not a soul stirred on the street. Both factors worked to John's advantage.

He lifted his scarf over his mouth and made his way to the back of the house, through the narrow gap between buildings. Standing in the small courtyard, rhythmically tapping his gloved fingers on the boiler where Eliza's landlady carried out the washing, John looked up at the window he knew to be Eliza's. He considered the safest passage. The two-storey wall at the back of the house was completely flush – barely a windowsill to grip. Nevertheless, he took a foothold on the narrow sill on the ground floor window and, stretching beyond his full height, managed to grip the sill of Eliza's room. Following this, he hauled himself up the shingled wall, finding he could use the small overlaps of wood to push his weight further forwards with his feet.

Clinging to the wall like weed on a cliff face, he tapped on Eliza's window.

'It's John,' he called in a low voice.

Within a minute, the curtain moved aside and she was lifting the sash, helping him through the window. He collapsed on the floor panting, his arms burning with the exertion. Eliza stepped back from the window into the darkness of her chamber.

All he was able to see was the shape of her, clothed in a shift, feet bare. Her face was entirely in darkness. He had hoped to embrace her. Whether she suffered from rheumatism or smallpox, he cared not. He needed to hold her; the few days they'd been apart seemed like years to John. It pained him that her first instinct was to step back, away from him.

He rose, concerned. She seemed to recoil from him, retreating further into the corner of her pitch-black chamber. John lowered his scarf.

'It's me, John. You do not need to fear,' he murmured.

'I know.'

He could not see her, but somehow John could sense her fear – he could almost see it shrouding her in the bitterly cold room.

'It's deathly cold in here, Eliza. Will you allow me to light you a fire?'

'Go, John. I implore you, go.'

Fear was in her voice, her gestures, the blenching of her body.

'But why ...' he took a step towards her. 'I don't understand.'

She turned, cowering, shielding her face. John too grew frightened, terrified of what Eliza thought she must conceal. What could possibly be the cause of this alteration? He pulled back the curtain to allow entrance to the meagre light of midnight then moved towards her slowly, as one might approach a skittish horse. He touched her arm gently, easing her body towards him. He gazed at her face.

Tears fell from her blackened eyes. There was further bruising on her lovely face and down her neck. He examined her more closely, shifting her slightly into the scant moonlight that petered into her room. Someone had attempted to strangle her.

He took her in his arms. She sobbed more freely, then violently, gulping air. He felt her body convulse, seizing against his, her chest rising and falling like a swan upon rough waters.

'Hush, my love, you are safe,' he said, stroking her hair, desperate to ease her distress. Eventually, she began to settle and he led her to the chair in her room. It was a tattered object, the chintz ragged, almost threadbare. John could see by the carved mahogany arms that it had once been a grand piece of furniture.

He drew a blanket from her bed and wrapped it around her shaking shoulders. He knelt before her, rubbing her arms through the wool, attempting to warm her.

'Was it your father?'

She shook her head wretchedly.

John frowned. A random attack? Surely not. The coincidence was too great. Moving towards her small stove, even smaller than his meagre hearth, he stacked it with kindling and lit a fire. Once the fire was ablaze, he squatted there for some minutes, inciting a more intense flame, wondering how to best proceed.

He lay the poker down then turned to her.

'If not Bowman, then who?'

Although her tears had ceased, she was still trembling. Throughout his life John had been confronted with the worst of humanity. As a child, he was witness to it. As a man, a lawyer, he had listened to people tell their miserable stories of violence and brutal undoing. However, apart from his mother, he had not loved any of those people. He wasn't entirely certain he wanted to hear Eliza's tale, but he knew she needed it told.

'When my mother was taken away, I pleaded with my father to take me to her. I only wanted to see her, know she was well. I still believed she was in hospital at that point. But even as a child, I could sense he was agitated by my requests. After a few months, he ordered me never to ask again. He told me she had left us, that she was gone forever and should be forgotten. I could not believe she would do such a thing, but there was nothing I could do to change his mind. So slowly, miserably, I accepted she was gone. I never asked to see my mother again.

'Later, after I became a teacher and left his house, I tried to look for her. If she had been ill but had recovered, I reasoned she would have been released from whatever hospital or institution she had been committed to. I was determined to find her, convinced it was her shame, embarrassment or my father's threats that had prevented her from seeking me out herself. So I went looking for her on my own, trying every place I could think of.

'For months, I walked the length and breadth of this town whenever I could, searching everywhere. Her appearance had been so striking and her French accent so distinct,

I was certain someone would recall her. Soon, the months turned into years and still I could not find her. But I never gave up hope.

'Then two years ago, I came across my father in Union Square. He was speaking to a gathering about the economic and moral danger of immigrants. He likened the spread of these workers to a disease, I recall.' She paused and closed her eyes for a second. 'His ignorant, hate-filled vitriol made my blood boil. I could not hold my tongue. I pushed my way to the front of the crowd and raised my voice, reminding him of the dockers and the teachers and the myriad of other foreign workers in the city who were of upstanding character who played a necessary role in Boston's prosperity. I reminded him of my mother, his wife ... who was, in fact, an immigrant.

'Recognising the sense in what I had said, suddenly hearing the hypocrisy that laced every one of his spite-filled ideas, the crowd dispersed. That was when he approached me. He came so close that I could feel his embittered breath on my cheek. "Your mother was a miserable bitch, a whore who invited men's glances and flattery. I can see that the apple hasn't fallen far from the tree."'

John's stomach turned in disgust. Hearing Eliza's words, he hated Bowman all the more.

Eliza continued. 'Then he told me that she was dead.'

She lifted her face to John, her expression steeped in loss.

'Despite my father's cruelty, his past lies, I knew he was telling the truth. After so many years, I realised that the only person in the world who loved me was gone, because I knew beyond the shadow of a doubt that my father did not.'

John squeezed her hands. They were still icy.

'Even though she had been taken away, the thought that

my mother was somewhere, anywhere, helped me withstand the horrors of living with my father. It was because of her that I studied, worked hard to make something of myself so that one day I could find her. But when my father told me she was dead – had died alone and in the worst of pain only two years previous – I was bereft, unmoored. It dawned on me that I had no-one ... And that in her dying hours, my mother had likely been just as alone as I was.'

Eliza let out a sob. 'The worst of it was that my mother had never been taken to hospital, had she? From what I learnt in my dream, I realise now she must have died at Bridewell prison. All those years, she would have had nothing to comfort her – not her only daughter, not her freedom.' Eliza shook her head. 'The prison ... it was the one place I didn't think to look. I expect her body was hurled into a lime pit, no doubt,' she said bitterly, her face wet with tears.

Determined to finish her story, Eliza wiped her eyes, steeling herself before continuing.

'In the days following my father's revelation, I dreamt constantly about my mother – her suffering, her misery. The thought hollowed me out and there was not a person I could turn to.'

John took her hands. Eliza stared at their intertwined fingers.

'I began to seek out men. I thought a man might offer me a scrap of comfort in my distress.' She captured his gaze, anxious. 'But not since we met, John. You must believe me. Our first night together was not sparked by my loneliness, but by my deep affection for you.'

Silent, John was in no position to judge this woman. He had seen far worse. He had experienced the extremes of human behaviour. He had witnessed Kirkcaldie break a man's neck then had nestled into the crook of his father's warm body as they slept. There was no black and white in the world, only grey. Instead, hearing Eliza tell her story made him realise that he loved her.

'What I have done in the past is wrong, amoral. Believe me when I say that I was not blind to the consequences of my actions. But I did it nonetheless.'

'But your injuries ...?'

'A former teacher at the Writing School, a married man – someone I thought a gentle man. I had laid with him in the past ... two years ago, and only once. He was waiting for me after school on Tuesday. His told me his mother was near death. She'd been a tyrant all his life, yet he felt a responsibility to care for her in her final weeks. I suppose I saw the similarity in our predicaments ... He sought out a sympathetic ear, someone who might understand his moral dilemma.'

She stared into the flames for a moment, shadows dancing against her face. He could read the regret and sorrow in the depths of her liquid brown eyes.

Witnessing Eliza's distress incited the first stirrings of the darkness inside him.

'This is what I assumed, but it eventuated that he needed comfort of a different kind. When I told him I was attached, he ...' Eliza pushed her face into her hands. 'He called me the most loathsome names, hit me then forced himself upon me. He left me in an alley behind the school.'

'What is this man's name?

'John, I am responsible!' Eliza cried, panicked. 'I have brought this on myself!'

He believed he might burst if he could not place his hands around this man's scrawny neck immediately and wring the life from his worthless body. But Eliza needed him. She needed to be consoled. He moved closer to her, taking her in his arms. She instinctively rested her face against his chest.

'I have told you my mother was a madam when I was a boy,' he began. 'When I recall her today, I understand her more and more. She had two identities, you see. We would spend the day together in the cottage she had built. There, she was my mother, teacher, friend and nurse. She would wear an apron and her hair loose with a ribbon around her head keeping her errant locks in check.

'Then, when the sun sunk below the horizon, she donned luridly coloured satin skirts, jewels, face paint ... She became a different person entirely. This she did to survive and build a future for us. But she demanded respect. Her occupation and appearance did not mean that she asked for men to take advantage of her.

'So you see, Eliza, it does not matter that you had invited this man into your bed in the past. You did not bring this attack on yourself.'

As John said the words he believed them, but knew that a judge and jury would not. Just as Mistress Brown and her own mother would have been judged, Eliza would be portrayed as a harlot. This was the reason John needed to act. Now.

'Tell me this man's name.'

Eliza shook her head, refusing to meet his eyes.

With great tenderness, John tilted her chin towards him so he could see her face. He ran his fingers gently over her bruises, over the violence that had been inflicted on her, as if committing it to memory.

'Eliza, please ...'

'Reginald. Reginald Spalding,' she said, finally.

'Where is his mother's house?'

'On Bueller Street, next to the tannery.'

DESPITE THE OVERWHELMING hunger building inside him, John waited by Eliza's bedside until she was asleep then exited her room in the same manner as he had entered, landing in the courtyard with a loud thump. He took off at a blistering pace towards Bueller Street. As he ran through the empty streets, John pursued only one goal – to punish Spalding in the severest manner possible. *How can a man, an educated man, take such vile advantage of a woman?* he thought as he ran. He wondered what hatred simmered inside Spalding to lead him to unleash all his masculine force on Eliza, once his colleague and friend.

When he arrived outside the wooden cottage next to the tannery, he stopped. He wanted nothing more than to break down the door immediately. But he resisted; instead, John took in the scene, measuring his options. Through the gauze curtains on the front window, he could see a faint light flickering beyond the darkened room, somewhere at the back of the house. He moved around to the side of the humble dwelling and reached an alleyway. From there he scaled a fence and found himself, once more, in a small courtyard where he found the tanner's workshop: pelts – rabbit and fox – hung from strings that crisscrossed the enclosed yard, lending the space a spectral atmosphere in the mist-soaked moonlight. For an instant – a mere moment – John had second thoughts about how he must proceed. Then, as though rising from a fiery and hellish pit, the beast he had tried so hard to suppress overcame all his good reason, rose from deep within him with an unstoppable force and pushed him forward.

Stooping low, he spied a man through the window. From Eliza's description, he reasoned it could be no other than Spalding. The man sat by the hearth smoking a pipe, his stockinged feet resting on a low stool. With his thinning hair brushed over his crown to cover a balding pate, he appeared a harmless sort.

But John had learnt long ago that appearances were always deceiving.

Spalding had a book open on his lap and wire-rimmed spectacles perched on his nose. He was reading. John squinted, needing to see the subject matter of the book, but he was not able for he had already placed his own spectacles in the pocket of his cloak. It struck John that he too had assumed this same position on many occasions by his own hearth; waistcoat unbuttoned, shoes removed, enjoying the pleasures of a much-treasured book following a hard day at work. Perhaps he and Spalding were not so dissimilar.

Then his mind returned to Eliza and fury surged through his body once more.

36

AUGUSTA, MAINE

Palgrave was typically an early riser, although since he had married Leah, he enjoyed lying beside her in the morning until she woke, listening to the sounds of her breath and watching her peacefulness in sleep. This is how it had been since they wed. Often when she woke, she would smile a vague sort of smile and roll towards him, spending the few final delicious moments of slumber in his arms. He would breathe in the scent of her hair and trace the contours of her body with his hands.

Occasionally they would come together in this state of blissful half-waking. When they did, it was like a wonderful dream – slow and rapturous, as if they were under an enchantment. The warmth of her, the longing he sensed in her were irresistible. Even when he had been away from her, he had always woken before sunrise, yearning to have her beside him. He had loved Leah since she was just a girl and neither time nor distance nor the shock and sting of biting truths had ever lessened his feelings for her. In fact, he had only grown to love her more.

However, this morning when he woke he felt not

warmth or rapture, but a sense of loss. Since learning of her betrayal, he had begun to see her in a different light, a slightly dimmer, less attractive light. This sudden consciousness of his changed sentiments distressed him to the point of choler. Palgrave still loved her of course, but since Ephraim Post's visit, his anger with her had only grown, dousing the fire he had once felt. Now a different flame burned within him. The more he considered her actions, the more furious he became.

He had not forgiven his wife and he was not certain the matter could be forgotten. Aside from the lie, what troubled Palgrave more was the lack of remorse Leah displayed for her actions. Although she had apologised to himself and Kirkcaldie, Leah stood by her initial decision to keep Tabby's secret. How could she betray the woman who had saved her life? she had asked. But to Palgrave the true question of the matter was how could she betray her husband; they had promised long ago there would be no more lies between them.

While he understood her position, he could not empathise with her. It seemed to him there was more behind the stance she had taken – pride, arrogance, the knowledge that she was Tabby Post's most-trusted confidante. Vainglory. Palgrave knew his wife was a proud woman but pride without good judgement was dangerous. What's more, Leah's actions had wounded his own pride. Palgrave was not a square-toed husband by any means; he realised Leah possessed her own mind and opinions and he loved her all the more for them. But to have her conceal Tabby's whereabouts from him for nearly ten years undermined his position in his house and his role as her husband, her confidante.

So that morning when he woke, he dressed hastily in the

clothes he'd laid out the night before, slipped on the boots he'd placed in the hall after Leah had fallen asleep, and propped a letter to his wife on the shelf above the hearth. As he did so he recalled his correspondences of the past from Nassau. He had penned lengthy essays to her, hoping they might serve as a connection, a link to each other – his hand reaching for her across the ocean. Leah had not replied to any of his letters. Yet she had been corresponding with Tabby Post for a decade. Shunting his bitterness aside, he gazed on his slumbering wife then departed the house alone.

He had not told Kirkcaldie of his plans. His friend would want to join him but that was impossible. He was only ten-days wed. In any case, Palgrave was confident he could captain a second voyage to the Caribbean alone.

It was first light when Palgrave reached the hospital. He walked along the corridor, past sleeping patients and a nurse who silently indicated with a lift of her chin that Doctor Shute was in his office. He wasn't sure what he would say to his friend or even if there was any value in telling him that Tabby was alive and well. A lengthy list of consequences flowed through Palgrave's mind as he stepped lightly along the deserted corridor.

He knew Ben would be awake and in his small office. It was the quiet time, when the busy doctor preferred to get work done. When Palgrave knocked quietly and pushed open the door, he saw that his friend was leant over a table with a scalpel in his hand. It was one Palgrave had fashioned for him after their first meeting. He could see that it was still razor sharp – Ben's fingers were stained pink with blood. He glanced at Palgrave but continued with his task.

'What can I do for you so early in the morning?' Ben asked merrily, without lifting his gaze from the heart he was dissecting.

Palgrave entered and glanced at the lonely pallet in the corner of the room, still crumpled from the night before. He wondered how a man, raised in the rarefied world of a governor's mansion, could tolerate sleeping in such a lowly space, among jars of human organs, the detritus of his profession. Palgrave was immediately reminded of what Ben had sacrificed in the memory of Tabby Post; the thought strengthened his resolve.

He did not know where to begin. Leah had refused to tell Ben the truth when Palgrave had pleaded with her to do so. She had explained with a coolness Palgrave found mortifying that it would be a further betrayal of her friendship. Tabby had been adamant for a decade that Ben should not know the truth. Palgrave was still at a loss as to why. But he had learnt long ago that to attempt to understand a woman's reasoning was a futile task. Just as Leah would never comprehend his hunger for adventure, he would never fathom her motives, or those of Tabby Post for that matter. Did Tabby feel responsible for Ben joining the army, an act she knew he would have loathed? Had that driven her into hiding? Or was she so uncertain of her child's father that she was saving Ben from a further sacrifice he would surely wish to make? Palgrave would never know. The workings of women's minds were inscrutable to men.

He had promised his wife he would keep the secret, however, he had made the vow without ever intending to uphold it. It would be the first promise to his wife he had broken since meeting Leah Hallett.

Now Palgrave pulled out a stool and sat on the opposite side of the table, concentrating on Ben's nimble fingers as he sliced and probed. He was just as curious and eager as he was when they had first met in Wellfleet, when Palgrave had made the young doctor his first set of instruments. Ben's hope, his optimism, had inspired Palgrave Williams, just as Samuel Bellamy's had many years before.

'Ephraim Post appeared unexpectedly at the house these ten days past.'

Ben lifted his head and placed his instruments in a porcelain dish. He leant against the table as though to brace himself.

'He's quite well now, it seems,' Palgrave met Ben's gaze. 'He was looking for Tabby ... He has been looking for her for quite some time.'

Ben nodded, considering the information. 'I see.'

Although Palgrave had no knowledge of Leah's secret before Post had knocked on his door, he somehow felt responsible. He kept telling himself he should have known.

After a pause, Ben spoke.

'And does Mister Post know where to find his daughter?' he asked.

'He did not know when he came to our house.' Palgrave cleared his throat. 'But he does now. Leah told Mister Post where Tabby can be found. She has known for much of the time Tabby has been gone. They've been corresponding.'

A strange sorrow washed over Ben's face, one Palgrave had not been expecting, one he had never witnessed in his friend before. Ben had worked closely with Leah since the hospital had been established. They had worked side by side. Furthermore, it was not only Tabby who had saved Leah's life; Ben had been at Tabby's side during the operation and had cared for Leah diligently in the weeks following. He had overseen her recovery with the kindness and sympathy of a saint.

'This heart,' Ben began, using his scalpel to point at the organ, 'is quite diseased. You can see here – this artery is entirely blocked meaning blood cannot travel freely through it. The poor man died yesterday. There was not a thing I could do. His heart seemed to seize, his wife said. He clutched at his chest and within moments, he was dead.'

He suddenly threw the scalpel harshly onto the table. It slid onto the floor at Palgrave's feet. Ben turned and plunged his hands into a basin of soapy water. He scrubbed them vigorously. Palgrave remained silent.

As Ben dried his hands, Palgrave finally spoke.

'I know you love Tabby still and your heart will not mend until you are able to see her, be with her. And I am grievously saddened that this information has been withheld from you all this time.'

Palgrave reached out a hand and place it on his friend's shoulder.

'Tabby is in New Orleans. She lives at the convent of the Sisters of Ursuline ... with her daughter.'

Ben turned his face from the wash basin and stared at Palgrave. He closed his eyes for an instant then lowered his head in grief, Palgrave thought, as though he'd just heard news of Tabby's death rather than her existence.

LEAH WAS SEATED in the kitchen clutching Palgrave's letter when Patience entered. Sarah had risen early and had already begun on the day's baking rituals. It was not a chore she typically had a hand in. It appeared that her daughter did not intend working at the hospital this day either, Leah noted sadly. Sarah had not returned to the hospital since the wedding. Leah realised Sarah would not pursue Ben knowing Tabby was alive.

Initially, Leah's motives for keeping Tabby's secret had been crystal clear – friendship and gratitude. But over the years, as Sarah began to mature and her affections for Ben Shute and the couple's suitability became obvious, her motives, Leah admitted to herself, had grown cloudy. This realisation troubled her. If she was brutally honest with herself, she had wanted Tabby to stay away and she had hoped Ben never discovered her whereabouts. Now, as she gazed on Sarah's blighted countenance, she wondered if she had been selfish or merely carrying out a mother's responsibility.

Her youngest child was also mournful and had been since the loss of her beloved cousin, who had left for his new home the week before. Patience seemed exhausted and bedraggled, not her usual gladsome self. She had been courageous, helping Bell pack his bag and boasting how she would now have a chamber all to herself. But as the newly formed family departed down the long drive, Patience had broken apart, fragile as an eggshell, sobbing miserably.

'We will see them constantly,' Leah had comforted her daughter. 'Kirkcaldie's house is such a short distance away. It takes less than an hour and when the river has thawed, even less time. Kirkcaldie, as you know, is a fine carpenter, I'm certain he will make a canoe for you both.'

At the mention of 'canoe' Leah had locked eyes with her husband and thoughts of her deceit silenced her good intentions.

Now she sat feeling humiliated and alone, despite the presence of her daughters. Aware Palgrave had been disappointed in her actions, Leah was certain the rift they had opened between them could be repaired. Surely, he, of all people, understood her motives? The bond he shared with Kirkcaldie was a treasure Palgrave would never risk losing, more valuable than the total riches with which he'd returned to Wellfleet. They had done each other's bidding since the day they met; they had been a shield for each other for almost as long.

Instead of striving to sympathise with her reasons, Palgrave had gone, stolen away, leaving only a brief note. Her heart ached, knowing she had disappointed him so. It was penned with a painfully truthful hand. Nothing he wrote was false or overstated. She had 'lied to him for a decade', he'd said. And it was true.

Now she was left wondering again whether she had been abandoned. She worried both for his safety and their marriage. According to his missive, Palgrave was heading to Boston and then on to Trinidad and Martinique in order to secure a further shipment of molasses, alone. It would be his first sea journey without Kirkcaldie since he had returned to her. The trip would allow him the time, he wrote, 'to clear his head and order his thoughts after such an immense disappointment'.

Each time she read those words, her heart broke all over again.

❧

WHEN SARAH ARRIVED at the Green Dragon, Charlie Purse was shovelling snow. There had been a heavy snowfall overnight, leaving no clear path to the entrance. She watched him for some minutes, admiring the clean, straight lines he carved through the white. He was humming as he worked, a merry tune she did not recognise.

When he turned and noticed her, Charlie smiled.

'On your way to the hospital?' he asked, brushing back the hair that had fallen over his eye with the back of his gloved hand.

Sarah shook her head and stepped a little closer. 'I'm collecting my family's mail.'

Charlie nodded, thinking, leaning on his shovel. 'I haven't seen you pass for a while ... not since your aunt's wedding in fact.'

'I have been busy. My father is away and ...' she paused, searching for a believable falsehood. 'Let's just say events have not turned out as I had hoped.'

Charlie laughed, an exuberant howl. 'They never do, Sarah. They never do.'

Her mother had informed her that a doctor from Portland had arrived yesterday to assume Ben's duties while he was away. But with Ben gone, to be at the hospital would only remind her of his absence.

'I'll only be a few more minutes and the path will be clear,' Charlie went on, offering her a bow.

'Oh, I can go around back.'

'I don't mind you waiting, if you don't.'

She laughed quietly at his turn of phrase, realising she had not laughed in many days. She decided to wait.

Charlie continued with his task. Sarah observed his movements. She noticed he was graceful for a tall man. While rangy, he seemed comfortable in his body rather than ungainly ... but to imagine him on a whaling ship was impossible. He seemed too gentle and good humoured. Sarah wondered why he had joined the crew. Desperation, perhaps? He had suggested as much on the day of the wedding.

Charlie seemed vastly different to Benjamin Shute, in

every way. Then again, perhaps he wasn't. Ben had sacrificed his wealth, career and prospects to honour Tabby's memory. His home was a small corner of his office at the hospital. Charlie had made sacrifices of his own. Perhaps what separated the men was choice.

Sarah realised she had devoted almost half her life to loving Ben Shute and he hadn't given her a second thought when he departed Augusta. And while her mother criticised her quietly for not attending to her duties at the hospital, Sarah could tell by her tender tone that she understood her daughter's heartbreak.

'All done, Your Highness. The path is clear.' Charlie bowed once more, dramatically.

Sarah felt laughter bubbling up inside her once more. She judged the sensation pleasant.

37

TAMESINE: THE THREE JOLLY IRISHMEN
NASSAU, 1716

As she circled rouge on her cheeks, she stared into the looking glass wondering where that girl had gone – Eseld's sister, the fisherwoman, the girl who had fallen in love with a handsome naval officer when she was fifteen; Tamesine. The time since she had arrived in Nassau bedraggled and desperate, while not brief, had flown by in a flurry of industry and endeavour. Yet in those fast-flowing years, she had transformed into an entirely different person. *Would Eseld even recognise me now?* she wondered. Tamesine tried to imagine her sister's life. *She'd be a wife and mother, no doubt, and a wonderful one at that,* she thought. Even as a child, her sister's loving and nurturing instinct had been obvious.

John was nine now, just a little younger than Eseld when Tamesine had left her. She considered them for a moment – both sensible with an insight far beyond their meagre years. But unlike Eseld, John had dreams so far-reaching that she was frightened where they would lead him.

Tamesine examined her face in the looking glass a final time then rose from the stool and readied herself, ensuring her bosom was lifted, pronounced and powdered above the neckline of her gown. She touched her granny's music box gently, as she did each evening before she departed.

'We must leave, Johnny,' she called from her chamber.

A faint sound of rummaging came from behind her. Moving to the kitchen, she found her son chewing on an end of bread.

'Hungry? I wonder what delight Tom will have waiting for you this evening?'

Her son stopped chewing and swallowed. 'Turtle stew,' he replied wryly. 'It's the same every night. I feel that soon I might sprout flippers and find a shell upon my back.'

Tamesine laughed as she gathered her belongings. 'Then at least you would have a ready place to hide.'

It was the boy's turn to laugh as they left the lime-washed cottage Tamesine had built and headed towards the town.

'Do you think Captain Jennings will be there?' John asked as they travelled along the path, the lights of Nassau town visible through the trees.

Tamesine shrugged, not wanting to encourage her son's obsession with the sea.

A Spanish treasure fleet had recently been wrecked and news of the opportunity had attracted a wave of rogues, adventurers and pirates from across the globe. All of Nassau could speak of nothing else. Talk was that the Spanish had got to it first, salvaging what they could with the aid of Indian divers, then burying the treasure, waiting for reinforcements to arrive to ensure its safe and speedy exhumation. However, the English captain, Henry Jennings, had assembled a crew and had sailed northwards along the Florida coast to where the treasure was stashed. Talk of him was rampant on the island.

'Jennings marched three regiments along the beach,' John informed her breathlessly as they walked. 'Each one was led by a flag-bearer and a drummer.'

Tamesine nodded.

'Apparently the Spanish admiral strode, all pride and puff, along the beach to Jennings and asked, "Is this war?"' John continued.

'"Not at all," Jennings replied, not blinking an eye. "We have come to claim the mountain of wealth that was fished from the wrecks that you have buried in the sand." The admiral surrendered at once.'

'It's mere gossip, John.' Tamesine replied. 'You chatter like a flock of daws.'

TAMESINE SCANNED the clientele of the Three Jolly Irishmen from her position at the entrance. The smoke-filled tavern was thick with ship captains and sailors, mostly drunk, many of whom she recognised. Regular customers. Taking John's hand, she guided him through the patrons. As they passed, she nodded a 'good evening' to the musician who stood in the corner of the establishment playing *The King's Ballad* on his fiddle.

Brushing against a stool, Tamesine stopped and curt-seyed theatrically, one hand sweeping the dirt floor while the other held out the skirt of her pale blue mantua.

'Do beg pardon, Sir,' she said.

'Pay it no mind,' said the patron, as he and his companion rose from their seat.

As she lifted her face, her eyes locked momentarily with the man who had spoken and she saw his gaze shift to her son and back again. Tamesine felt his look in every nerve of her body. Nodding politely at both men, she clutched her son's hand and continued on her way to the back of the tavern and through a door to the outside. Here, a canvas had been erected sheltering a galley of sorts. A brick of a man with a bald head tussled the boy's hair playfully. The boy looked at the man and smiled with sincere affection.

'Be mindful of Tom,' Tamesine said as she turned towards the tavern.

'Turtle stew for supper, Johnny Boy?' Tom asked. Into a bowl, he ladled a generous portion of steaming broth from the cauldron that hung above the open fire.

John shot his mother a dry look.

A faint smile glided across her lips then she exhaled and walked back inside.

She strolled dispassionately in and around the tables. Most of the men were too drunk to notice her, indulging in their winnings from a Spanish raid. A barely discernible sneer darkened her pretty, open face for an instant.

Now Tamesine stopped and studied each table closely, seeking out the English captain of whom John had spoken. Disappointed by his absence, she continued on her saunter, smiling archly as men grabbed at her buttocks and thighs. A black Spanish lace fan, given to her by a boastful admirer, concealed her revulsion. She halted for a moment and passed the time with Garrett the innkeeper, Tom's brother. The friendship she'd built up with the siblings over the years had allowed Tamesine to pursue her ambitions in their tavern at no cost.

'What do you consider a fair cut?' she had asked when their deal was struck almost a decade before. Numerous taverns had sprouted in Nassau during the Spanish War. At the time, Tamesine had chosen this particular establishment because she had heard it was one of the only saloons not to offer the service of whores.

Garrett had looked down at the baby in her arms.

'How long has this little pup been in the world?'

'Not yet a month.'

'And you? You're but a babe yourself …' Garrett smiled.

'I've been here long enough,' she had replied coolly. 'I'm not green. How much?'

After a minute's consideration of both the mother and the baby, he answered Tamesine's question. 'Why, nothing. The additional commerce your pretty presence will attract is payment enough.'

It had never been her intention to tend to the clientele herself. She had a son, after all, and could not be cursed with syphilis or burdened with the cost of a beating. It struck her that there was a larger sum to be had as the overseer of the operation. It was then but a simple task to attain the employment of three young women who, by hope or circumstance, had found themselves marooned on New Providence as well. One of them was her friend Agatha. She had been such a support to her after John King had deserted them. Discovering that Agatha's 'profession' leant itself to her endeavour, it was the least she could do to offer her support in return.

When Tamesine had first founded the business, the custom had been mainly British Royal Navy seamen and the occasional officer who drank more, but also paid more, than a regular sailor. She soon learnt that was just their way; officers relished flaunting their rank, even if only to a whore. Now her trade was made up of pirates, or 'privateers' as many of them, reluctant to jettison their wartime credentials, preferred to be called.

The raucous laughter at a nearby table made her start.

'I fear it will be quiet for you this evening,' Garrett said. 'But tomorrow will be more profitable, once they've grown accustomed to their success and their sore heads hinder such imbibing as is taking place tonight.' He raised his bushy eyebrows and chuckled.

Tamesine nodded, aware that Garrett's forecast was accurate.

'There are those two over there,' he said, indicating the men she had first talked to that evening. 'Curious, they are. They've not yet finished one ale between them. The tall one, the one who resembles a farmer, is good humoured, although I warrant it's his chum who has the deeper pockets.'

Tamesine's brow furrowed as she pondered Garrett's words and recalled the concern that she and her son had provoked in the handsome man. She found the two men disturbing; their sobriety and poise were ill-suited to this environment. However, casting her eye around the room, she thought they were the only likely prospects in a rank den of thieves and freebooters. She made her way slowly to their table.

The man with the dark hair turned and appraised her when he felt her light touch on his shoulder. His eyes went to her mahogany curls, which she had piled loosely on the crown of her head. A rose-shaped pin helped secure the wayward locks. He waited for her to speak.

'Your dark eyes brim with sorrow,' she said, leaning closer to be heard above the din of the tavern.

'As do yours,' he replied.

'Let me brighten them.' She ran her fingertips the length of the handsome man's arm and took his hand. 'There is a girl,' she gestured towards a door with her head, 'in that room. A very pretty girl. If she does not take your fancy then there is another ...'

'You're from the south aren't you, Cornwall?' he broke in, recognising her accent.

She nodded and looked at him suspiciously for a moment before remembering her purpose. 'You're a fine-looking man,' she continued.

'Thank you,' he replied, impressed with her persistence. 'But my friend here, Mister Williams, is a fine man all over – outside and in.'

Mister Williams's eyes rolled in exasperation as Tamesine took him in. He wasn't an attractive man by any means – thin, angular face and long nose – but his pale blue eyes shone with kindness, buoying his appeal.

'When we set sail tomorrow morning it will be for a long time, many months perhaps,' said the dark-haired man, lifting Tamesine's hand and offering it to his friend.

Without judgement, Mister Williams shook his head casually and finished the remnants of his ale.

'I wish you both a pleasant evening,' he said, rising and placing his hat on his head. 'I will see you at first light, Samuel Bellamy.'

When he departed, Tamesine glided seamlessly into Williams's seat. 'So ... Samuel is your name. "Black Sam" I will call you,' she said, teasing.

'You have seen inside my soul and seen the colour of my heart,' he responded, smiling wryly.

'Nay,' she whispered. 'I speak of your eyes. They're pitch black. Your heart,' she continued softly, laying her palm on his chest, 'is the colour of sunlight. I can feel its warmth.'

She hoped he could feel her breath on his face. He glanced at her hand.

'You are mistaken good lady. The eyes are the window to

the soul, are they not?' he offered, clearly enjoying the exchange. 'My heart, if I may lay claim to one, is as dark as my visage – as black as coal.'

'I pray thee, allow me to spark that cold, hard rock that lies at your core.' She edged even closer.

He gazed into her hazel eyes and gently fixed one of her curls behind her ear. He laughed lightly, uncertainly, she thought.

Then Tamesine felt the tingle of goosebumps on her bare arms.

LATER, when Tamesine watched Samuel's passage through the tavern and out the door, she was left to wonder, despite her good sense, when she might meet him again.

38

HALLOWELL, MAINE

When he heard the knock, Kirkcaldie looked towards the door in surprise. He rarely received visitors in the backwoods of Hallowell and he certainly wasn't expecting any so soon after his wedding. He, Maria and Bell were only just settling into their new life together.

Kirkcaldie smiled at his wife, winked at his son, then slipped the knife by his plate unseen into the sleeve of his shirt. Thus prepared, he moved towards the door.

It was John.

His heart leapt. Despite John's letter, Kirkcaldie had been worried. He made a movement towards his son, eager to embrace him, then stopped. Next to John stood a young woman. Kirkcaldie took the couple in for a moment and saw that both were ashen, desperate.

'You do not need to knock, John. This is your home,' he said, stepping back and allowing the pair entrance.

Kirkcaldie could see John wasn't himself. 'I was concerned when you did not attend the wedding,' he said gently, without accusation. 'Your letter arrived a few days after.'

John glanced at Eliza before responding. 'I'm sorry, Kirkcaldie. It had been my intention to be there, but circumstances did not allow.'

'Pay it no mind,' Kirkcaldie responded, leading the couple to the kitchen. 'I'm pleased you're here now.'

As introductions were made, Kirkcaldie examined the woman's face. Dark bruises were apparent, the edges yellowing against her olive skin.

Bell ran from the kitchen and leapt into John's arms.

'John!' cried the boy, embracing him heartily. The child was bursting with happiness. 'We are brothers, you know!'

John shot Kirkcaldie a look of apology over the boy's shoulder. He realised he had not been there when the boy had discovered their connection.

'We are indeed and how thrilled I am to have a brother, especially one as handy with his hands as you are, Bell. You must teach me those knots. I have forgotten most of them ...'

The group moved into the kitchen where Maria was waiting. She took in the scene for an instant before greeting the newcomers, taking Eliza's hand. The younger woman's skin was cold as ice. She sensed something in her touch.

'Come, sit closest to the hearth. You are frozen.'

As Maria laid two more plates on the table, a stilted conversation followed. Kirkcaldie could see that John was holding something back due to Bell's presence. They spoke of the wedding and Kirkcaldie told them of their new life as a family together. John smiled and nodded, uttered appropriate responses, but when Kirkcaldie gazed at him from across the table, he was aware of a dark undertone colouring his elder son's entire demeanour.

Eliza was quiet, chewing small morsels of her food as

though they were distasteful, as though she would be ill. Maria gazed at her, watching her, noting each forced smile, frown and flinch.

Bell took up the conversation when it ebbed, discussing his new home as though John, Kirkcaldie and Maria were not acquainted with it. His enthusiasm for his brother's return seemed to fit oddly with the strained atmosphere in the kitchen. It was like a pleasant but overwhelming scent designed to mask a far worse odour.

Maria began to clear the table. Kirkcaldie followed suit, walking to the basin on the bench under the window, while John and Bell chatted on. Maria and Kirkcaldie glanced at one another, then, heads brought close together, Maria whispered to her husband.

'Eliza has been hurt. Recently. In the same way as I was by Silas.' Kirkcaldie swallowed. 'I can feel her torment as though I am living it again.'

Kirkcaldie nodded sombrely, hastily attempting to construct the reason for his son's visit home. He turned to the table, smiling.

'Bell. It's time you fed the chickens. They will be famished.'

Maria handed her son a pail, half-filled with turnip peelings and the like.

'John shall come with me,' Bell stated.

'Not today, my son. Tomorrow. He is far too exhausted for such an arduous labour.'

Bell laughed, shaking his head in admiration at his father's extraordinary wit. Once the boy had departed in the direction of the coop, Kirkcaldie approached the couple. He placed his hands on John's shoulders. In an instant, he rose and slumped into his father's arms, as though finally given leave to breathe. Kirkcaldie could feel the tension drain from his son's body.

'What has happened?'

John and Eliza looked at each other, pained, anguished.

'Eliza,' Maria said gently, taking the young woman's hand. 'You seem to be of an artistic temperament. Would you enjoy seeing my sketches and paintings?'

Eliza looked uncertainly at John.

'Maria is an artist. She is very good,' John said.

The young woman rose and was led from the room. Her gait was as listless as summer-stricken air.

As soon as they were gone, Kirkcaldie asked John to sit. He looked at his son intently, waiting.

'I killed a man,' said John, then buried his face in his hands.

Kirkcaldie took a deep breath then sighed. 'The man who raped Eliza?'

Startled, John lifted his head in question.

'Maria. She has a sense for such matters.'

John's faced crumpled. 'I went to see him when I found out. I watched him through his window. The man was a teacher, a father, a son caring for an ailing mother – an upright member of the community. He was reading Dante ... how could the man who had attacked and raped Eliza read Dante, Kirkcaldie? As I watched him and thought of what he did to her, all control left me. Her injuries, Sam ...' He groaned at the memory.

'And now, she is so different, much changed from the experience and I do not know whether she will ever heal. Worse still, I do not know how to help her.'

Kirkcaldie nodded, taking in the breadth of John's admissions.

'I beat this man in his mother's kitchen. I pushed his

head into the stone hearth. He begged for mercy and I paid his cries no heed. I was a wild animal.'

Kirkcaldie's heart reached out for the boy, desperate to remove his pain. John was not made for killing.

'It was the beast inside you ...'

'No, it was me!' cried John. 'It was my doing alone ...'

Kirkcaldie nodded, recalling his own bloodlust after Hornigold had murdered Tamesine.

'What is wrong with me? I feel as though there's a part of my soul missing and rage has filled the space that is left. It is consuming me.'

Kirkcaldie knew exactly of what John spoke. After Tamesine, half of him had disappeared, cleaved away by grief. He was lost. But he eventually found himself again, in John. John had given him purpose, an identity. He left Bellamy behind and became Kirkcaldie. Looking at his son now, it occurred to him that John was but a shell, as he himself had once been. He needed answers to questions that Kirkcaldie was not able to provide.

In John's mind, his life began when he and Sam Bellamy had leapt from the *Whydah*. But he had a life before that in Nassau with Tamesine, and she had one before that in Cornwall. Kirkcaldie wondered whether this was the part of John that was missing. Perhaps he needed to discover what and who he was made from. Kirkcaldie had done his best, but could he have been mistaken in believing that their bond was stronger than blood?

All John had of his early life was a brass button, a trifle. Now, considering his relationship with Bell, Kirkcaldie quickly came to realise that John needed to know his birthright.

He inhaled deeply. It was time he told John all he knew. He took his distressed son's hands in his.

'Tamesine hailed from Mousehole in Cornwall. She did not speak very often of her family, but she told me once of a younger sister named Eseld, who she loved dearly. Do you remember that your mother kept a music box in her bedroom? Eseld had given it to her when she had sailed to Nassau.'

John's brow furrowed in recognition, a spark of memory lit. He closed his eyes and an expression of warmth came over his troubled countenance. Soon he began to hum a tune, a melancholy strain.

'I recall it. The music box was her granny's. Mama told me she would often play it when I was a babe, to help me sleep.' John smiled wearily. 'She blamed the device for my love of the sea.'

'Of your father, I can offer you nothing more than what that brass button you carry can tell you. Only that he abandoned her on the island the day you were born.'

John nodded, regretfully.

'I have never wished for a father other than you, Kirkcaldie ... But I admit I have carried with me a feeling since childhood that there may be a man living somewhere in the world who shares my eyes, or temperament ... or my passion for Latin,' he laughed dryly, attempting to show cheer to his father.

'And your idealism,' Kirkcaldie concluded.

KIRKCALDIE HAD GIVEN over a room of his house to a studio where Maria was able to paint and sketch, a private space only for her. Kirkcaldie, Maria had discovered, was very good in that regard, sensing that although they enjoyed their time together, they also valued the hours they spent apart. She supposed they had both led rather solitary existences before uniting as a family; over the years, each had grown comfortable with their private pursuits.

She had thought she knew this man, but in just the few weeks they had been husband and wife, Maria discovered Kirkcaldie was also an extremely capable cook and seamstress, bringing to each task his surveyor's exactitude. Maria enjoyed observing him cut a carrot into equal parts or mend Bell's breeches with precise, uniform stitches. It came from so many years of doing for only himself and John, she supposed. He had to be mother and father both and he cared not a jot for carrying out tasks other men would label 'women's work'. She wondered whether Kirkcaldie had been so open-minded when he was Samuel Bellamy.

And the room.

He had presented this room to her quite proudly, she thought, on the day she and Bell arrived. It sat on the south side of the house and, being so well situated, was filled with light and warmth. Her cloth cupboard stood against the wall, housing her paints, pastels and brushes, and on the walls hung her art. An easel, which Kirkcaldie had constructed from a pine that grew behind the house, stood by the window. It was not the perfect place for an easel for the light was too bright, but she had not wished to tell her new husband this fact, figuring she would ease it slowly over to the centre of the room, inch by inch, without him noticing.

Now Eliza wandered Maria's collection, admiring the various styles the artist had adopted over the years. For a long time, she examined the portrait Maria had drawn in charcoal of the willow, Silas's face emerging phantom-like from the branches. Maria had kept it. Leah had not understood why, but Maria had come to learn that to bury the past was of little benefit – it needed to be confronted, tiny battles fought every day.

'I had an experience similar to yours a long time ago,' Maria told Eliza as the young woman examined the work.

Eliza turned to her, shocked.

'The man was a childhood friend who hoped to marry me. I had, for many years, held him close to my heart. However, one summer's day he forced himself on me by this willow tree, hoping the act would alter my affections.' Maria smiled, ruefully. 'Of course, he failed to change my mind.'

In an instant, tears sprung to Eliza's eyes.

'At the time, I journeyed into myself in the hope I would be safe. But I ventured into such blackness it was as though I had travelled to the depths of my core, into the very centre of my suffering.'

Eliza nodded, understanding.

'I took many years to emerge again completely.'

For the next few minutes, the women were silent as Eliza absorbed Maria's words. When Maria began to order her paints and brushes, Eliza stepped closer to help.

JOHN AND ELIZA stayed with Kirkcaldie for a week, during the course of which all of John's crimes spilled from his mouth and into the lap of his father. Bowman, the seaman, Penn and, of course, Spalding. John was at last entirely sympathetic towards Kirkcaldie, who had spent two decades as a wanted man.

The day after Spalding's murder, John had fled Boston with Eliza. He left a note for Joshua advising him to seek out another partner or go forward alone as he would not be returning for some time. He also left Joshua his share of the Schleck settlement.

When they left, John felt he needed to be as far away from his crimes as possible. He could not foresee returning, ever. Seven days later, returning to Boston and confessing to the crime was at the forefront of his mind. Kirkcaldie read it every day, etched in his son's creased brow, watching as John pored over the latest gazettes from Boston and Philadelphia.

'It would do no good to confess your crimes,' Kirkcaldie advised one day as they chopped wood behind the house. 'And if your clever friend Ben Franklin solves this mystery, as you seem to think is inevitable, he will not pursue it.'

John looked at him, uncertainty clouding his face.

'Ben is a good man, John. He's your friend. Would I betray Palgrave Williams for a headline?'

John leant the axe against his thigh and wiped his brow with his gloved hand.

'How have you lived with your crimes all these years?' he asked. John had not intended the question to be accusatory and Kirkcaldie did not take it as such.

'Truth be told, there is no man's life I have taken which I regret. But there are many lives I regret not saving – Thomas Baker, Hendrick Quintor, Peter Hoff, John Julian ...' Kirkcaldie paused at the thought of his shipmates who had been executed for piracy. He sighed.

'And, of course, your mother.'

John felt a sting in his eyes. He knew that Tamesine's death weighed more on Kirkcaldie than the all the others put together.

'And what of Benjamin Hornigold?' John asked. In his confession to Kirkcaldie, he had told of the death of the man who had caused them both so much pain.

Kirkcaldie raised the axe above his head and brought it

down with a thump, splitting the pine log in half. 'I wish I'd had the pleasure.'

'I too,' John muttered quietly.

As they worked, John's thoughts moved to Eliza.

'Sam, I love Eliza, but I fear I cannot be a husband to her with this animal inside me. My actions have already put her in danger. What will I do if I fail to control this monster?'

Kirkcaldie nodded, considering. 'Needless to say, for now you must stay away from Boston, as should Eliza. You both need time to heal.'

The men gathered the wood and walked towards the house. They added their efforts to the woodpile then took a deep draught of water from a nearby pail, a thin layer of ice bobbing on the surface like a ship at sea. Kirkcaldie gazed at it for moment, lowering himself to his haunches then gently poked one side of the thin, cold platform with his finger.

'What is it?' John asked.

'I have been thinking on what you told me. There is nothing more I can offer you that will ease your pain. You need to know your mother fully and find your father, if you choose. You must journey to England, to Mousehole,' he instructed, looking squarely at his son. 'That's the only way you will be whole.'

39

I n England, when Kirkcaldie had been a child of eight years old, his father had always told him that mucking out the stable was boys' work. So when he had arrived at the age when he believed he was a man, the chore irritated him beyond reason. He could still recall how his skin had bristled with anger and contempt, growing flushed, hot and itchy. If he left the job half-done or expressed his frustration, he received a beating. He had soon learnt how to contain his irritation.

Now, nearly forty years later, he found the task meditative, even calming. His father had been wrong – mucking out the stables was most definitely the work of a man. Although he would never voice his opinion, it was a chore he relished. Focusing on the sharp, even lines left from the shovel in the hay allowed for a deeper level of contemplation, or so Kirkcaldie believed. Once clean, the raking of unsoiled hay onto the floor of each stall left him with a feeling of great satisfaction. It was such a simple task and not such an odorous one if performed daily.

Bell approached the task with the same level of unbridled enthusiasm with which he approached every task. However, after a short duration, he would find a distraction. A bug or other small creature that he'd capture in a jar then remove to his chamber in order to sketch it. Kirkcaldie frequently entered the stable to find both rake and shovel on the ground and his son missing. But Kirkcaldie never punished the boy for his poor attention. After all, he was but a child and Kirkcaldie was a half-hearted disciplinarian.

On the other hand, John had never grown weary of the task. Like his father, he enjoyed the thinking time the activity afforded him. His elder son had acquired the sensibilities of a man when he was still so young.

John had confided in Kirkcaldie late one evening as they shared a bottle of Palgrave's rum. He told him the entirety of Eliza's story – her father's depravity and her mother's retaliation. Kirkcaldie had listened to his son's release, desperately wanting to relieve his burden. But he could not. John was in love; Eliza's worries had become his own and he bore them courageously. That was the sign of a man.

'Oh, Johnny,' Kirkcaldie sighed as they drained the last of the bottle. 'There are wicked people in this world and you have had dealings with more than your fair share, as have I. Eliza will be right again and so will you, but, like all good things, it will take time and patience. However, I can say without a doubt that your mother would be proud of you, of the man you have become.'

Father and son stood and embraced.

'But in the future, leave the killing to me.'

John had laughed at his father's comment. Kirkcaldie took it as perhaps the first sign of his son's healing.

Now, Kirkcaldie leant his rake against the wall and led Dobbin back into his stall. The Spalding situation had been resolved to Kirkcaldie's satisfaction. John would travel over the sea to Portsmouth, find his way to Cornwall and then to Mousehole. He guessed that Eseld would be in her late thirties. Hopefully, she would still be living in the same fishing village where she was raised with her sister. If not, surely some person in the hamlet would know her whereabouts. Kirkcaldie hoped Eseld might recall Lieutenant John King and know from where he hailed.

Besides, John was intelligent with a lawyer's gift for investigation. He would find his aunt and, more than likely, his father as well. Kirkcaldie's heart ached a little at the notion, but he realised it would be best for John. Perhaps Tamesine's parents – John's grandparents – were still alive; while Tamesine had never spoken of her mother and father (Kirkcaldie had sensed a great discord between them) they may wish to know their grandson.

Together, the family had agreed that Eliza would stay in Hallowell while John was absent and act as Bell's tutor. Maria had been feeling the loss of her sister and looked forward to the female companionship. She sensed an affinity with the young woman and she was confident she could help Eliza rebuild herself.

All parties were sorted, the stables had been mucked and Kirkcaldie was satisfied. By the time John returned to Massachusetts, Spalding and the others would be long forgotten. John could continue with his life with Eliza by his side.

Kirkcaldie's road to happiness had been paved with tragedies and obstacles. Finally, at five and forty, he had found the state of being that had constantly eluded him. If he had a say in the life of his eldest son, John would not have to wait so long. This is what Kirkcaldie resolved as he scanned the stable a final time, admiring the result.

His appreciation was interrupted by the soft crunch of

hay under foot. Lifting his gaze, he turned towards the entrance.

'Mister Kirkcaldie,' said the man in the doorway. 'My name is Henry Bowman.'

Kirkcaldie gripped his shovel tightly. A spark caught in his belly, a stirring.

Bowman continued. 'I believe you are harbouring my daughter.'

The man was a nondescript gent, seemingly harmless. Sizing him up, Kirkcaldie nodded.

'How did you find her here?'

'Eliza is such a diligent young woman,' Bowman said, walking further into the stable. 'When she departed Boston, she asked her landlady to forward her mail to the post-master in Hallowell. In her room, I also found a lawyer's calling card. Your son's, I believe. Once I reached Hallowell, it was easy to find her ... and your son. He is a lawyer, is he not?'

'You should know the answer to that question, Sir, seeing as he came to your house to interview you following an incident with an immigrant docker.'

Bowman appeared to be startled at the depth of Kirk-caldie's knowledge.

'Of course,' he said. 'Of course. How forgetful of me.'

Kirkcaldie raised an eyebrow. He was uncertain of how much the man knew, but he could see Bowman was begin-ning to make connections. This odious man could be the source of John's undoing.

'Why are you looking for her?' Kirkcaldie said. He waited for a response, observing Bowman closely.

'The wellbeing of a child is a father's sole concern. I love my daughter with all my heart.'

Kirkcaldie snorted in disgust. He was reminded of

Maria's explanation of Silas's loathsome behaviour. *You say you love Eliza, but you hate her*, he thought. Men like Bowman and Silas used love to justify evil. Bowman had destroyed the mother, now he wanted to wreak destruction on the daughter ... *And on my son*, he concluded.

Kirkcaldie sensed something in him awaken fully, stretching after a long slumber. Bowman had travelled to Hallowell seeking revenge. Kirkcaldie would recognise it in the heart of any man. He was sure that Bowman knew John was the one who had attacked him. He must blame John and Eliza for his current circumstances – unemployed and adrift. Men like Bowman never took responsibility for their actions.

'Eliza's inside.' He gestured for Bowman to lead. 'I'm sure she'll be pleased to see you.' The other man turned and began to make his way to the house.

In one quick, decisive movement, Kirkcaldie had the shaft of the shovel over Bowman's head and pressed tight against his neck. Within seconds, he was dragging the man deeper into the darkness of the stable and then into a stall. Bowman's hands gripped his, attempting to uncurl his fingers from the tool. But Kirkcaldie tightened his hold, pressing Bowman's back into his own body. Bowman's feet tried to find purchase on the freshly raked hay as he struggled, but Kirkcaldie's purpose was clear: the man in his arms deserved to die. He'd once been complacent and refused to heed Palgrave's warnings; as a result, Hornigold died with his sins unpunished. Kirkcaldie wasn't going to make the same mistake twice.

Once he was positioned firmly against a wall, Kirkcaldie yanked hard a final time and heard Bowman's neck break. Breathing deeply, regaining control, it took a minute for Kirkcaldie to release his hands. His fingers ached as he watched Bowman's body fall to the ground. He gazed at the body for a moment, satisfied with a job well done.

KNEELING ON THE COLD GROUND, John gripped his brother tight. Bell's small arms clung about his neck warming him, and the tune of the child's shallow breathing against his cheek was the most melodic sound John had ever heard.

'I will return, little brother. In no time at all. But you must understand that I need to make this trip. We have different mothers, you know, and I need to discover where mine came from.'

Bell released him. Tears pooled in his brown eyes. He nodded. 'I know.'

John embraced Maria, thanking her for her care and her kindness, insisting on a guarantee that she would keep Kirkcaldie safe.

'Always the man of law,' she muttered drolly. 'Keeping him safe is all I have ever done.'

He and Eliza had uttered their farewells earlier that day. Lying close together before dawn, they had whispered assurances to one another, planning for the future, mapping out a pathway forward they would traverse together.

Kirkcaldie led the horse – already saddled, John's baggage attached – from the stable to his son.

'Tessa is an old mare,' he said, stroking her mane. 'Once you get to Boston, sell her for what you can. Use the profits as well as this,' Kirkcaldie said, pressing a heavy purse into his hand, 'to secure your passage to England. There's also enough there for expenses once you arrive.' He paused for a moment, reaching into his pocket. 'And there is this, too.'

Kirkcaldie handed John his compass.

John hesitated, staring at the instrument he knew so well. He looked at Kirkcaldie.

'Go on, take it, Johnny,' he said gently. 'I plan to stay put for a while.' He looked towards Maria and Bell before returning his gaze to John.

Finally, understanding the significance and meaning of the parting gift, he tightened his hand around the object.

The men stood face to face for a time, each contemplating how they should proceed, Tessa's reins still clutched tight in Kirkcaldie's fist. Finally, he released the horse and drew John to him in a heartfelt embrace.

'Good luck to you, son.'

'I will miss you, Sam. I could not have wished for a better father.'

After the women returned to the house – Eliza had been keen to retire, still exhausted from her travails and already missing John – Kirkcaldie and Bell stood for some time by the bluestone wall watching John's passage into the woods.

When he could no longer be seen, Bell looked at his father.

'Why did John call you "Sam"?'

Kirkcaldie rubbed his chin as he sat atop the wall. Bell climbed up beside him.

'Because that is my name.'

The boy looked at his father in confusion.

'Would you like to hear a story?'

Bell nodded.

'There is much of this that your mother should be privy to as well.'

Father and son ventured inside the house. Along with Maria, the family sat together by the hearth until supper as they listened to Kirkcaldie tell the remarkable tale of Samuel Bellamy.

EPILOGUE

irkcaldie lay in bed considering his good fortune. The sun would not rise for another hour. Maria was still asleep beside him, her expression serene, as peaceful as an angel. Although he could never be Sam Bellamy to the world again, he believed he had finally gained what all men desire: freedom. It had taken him almost two decades to achieve what he had begun when he sailed away from Eastham and Maria as a young man. Now he had wealth and a family. Only the night before, after he and Maria had come together, she had mentioned the notion of them having another child. It had been a notion Kirkcaldie had contemplated himself, but he had not dared to dream of the possibility.

'I am not yet forty,' Maria had whispered in the dark, taking his silence for reluctance. 'And Bell would get such great pleasure from a brother or sister.'

Kirkcaldie's heart rose into his throat.

'If you are hesitant,' she went on, 'I understand.'

They had come together again in silence, in a different

way, taking care with one another, lingering over each kiss and touch.

Now he gazed at her in dawn's first light, taking in her silhouette, the shape of her lips and nose, all at once relishing the moment and all the moments they would have together in the future. Kirkcaldie heard the first bright carol of a song sparrow breaking through the silence of the early morn.

Then another noise; the sigh of a horse.

Kirkcaldie rose in a heartbeat and pulled on his breeches, peering through the gap in the curtain. He could only see the horse, tied to a pole. But where was the rider? More importantly, who was the rider? His thoughts seesawed as he searched for an answer.

Tabby? Surely not Tabby.

Moving towards the door of the chamber he grabbed the poker from the grate then descended the staircase lightly, so as not to wake the house or alert the unexpected visitor. When he reached the front door, he clutched the poker firmly, concealing it behind his thigh. He listened for a moment, his ear pressed against the wood. Then he grasped the door handle and pulled.

A young man stood before him, his fist poised, ready to knock on the door. He smiled and removed his hat.

Disarmed by the visitor's friendly countenance, Kirkcaldie looked at him more closely. It was Charlie Purse – the fellow who had escorted Ephraim Post to Palgrave's house on the afternoon of the wedding. He felt his muscles relax.

'Mister Purse. To what do I owe the pleasure?'

'Good morning, Mister Bellamy,' said the young man.

Bellamy ...?

Instantly on alert, Kirkcaldie tightened his grip on the poker. He could kill Purse now, quietly. Drag him into the woods. If he worked fast, he would be buried before breakfast. Bowman had been in the ground within the hour of his death.

The visitor smiled again.

'In truth, Mister Bellamy, my name is not Purse.'

Kirkcaldie frowned, momentarily confused.

'It is Driver. Charlie Driver. I believe you were acquainted with my father Jack.'

Understanding dawned. Jack Driver. The stroller, the teller of tales. Kirkcaldie remembered his crewmate from the *Whydah* immediately.

Charlie pulled himself up a little straighter.

'Sir, I have come to claim my father's share of the prize.'

AFTERWORD

My inspiration for *The Lark's Call* came from Tamesine, Bellamy's second love interest in *The Hummingbird and the Sea.*

I had a vague idea what I wanted Book 3 to be about, but needed a strong thread to pull the elements together. That thread became Tamesine's storyline in the novel.

I also wanted to explore her background further, as well as her bond with her son. Tamesine is such an independent and uncompromising single mother and businesswoman who has survived and thrived through all manner of disappointment and hardship. From where did her determination and strength come? Her story needed to be told.

Finally, by setting her chapters in Cornwall, I knew I'd have fun researching an area of Britain with such a deeply rooted sense of history, culture and tradition. I visited Cornwall some years ago when we were living in the UK. However, that was before my author career, so places such as Madron Carn and Boswarthen Chapel were neither on my radar nor my itinerary.

Never fear! YouTube to the rescue. There are some

awesome videos that take viewers on a tour through these places. From these as well as a selection of wonderful Pinterest images I was able to soak up the atmosphere of these Cornish locations, albeit second hand.

As for the appearance of Ben Franklin in the story ... readers probably know Benjamin Franklin as one of the founding fathers of the United States, or perhaps as the inventor of (among other things) the lightning rod, bifocal glasses, the Franklin Stove (remember his ridicule of John's smoky lodgings...) and swim fins! However, I discovered during the research phase that Franklin's attendance at the Boston Latin School overlapped with John Kirkcaldie's. I simply couldn't resist making them childhood buddies and including this renowned historical figure in the story!

I read Walter Isaacson's biography and was astounded by Franklin's accomplishments, and his intelligence. What I write about his education in the book is all true – as far as book learning went, Franklin had very little. What's more, no one in the story is quite as clever as John. I needed a character who was capable of outwitting him (and he nearly does!).

My research extended to Boston and Harvard University as well. I read Mark Peterson's history of Boston, The City-State of Boston. The reading took me a while but Peterson's evocative writing and the primary sources used throughout gave me a great feel for the city during the time of John Kirkcaldie's 'nocturnal wanderings'.

ACKNOWLEDGMENTS

Thank you so much for reading this story. I hope you found the journeys of the ever-increasing cast of characters engaging and moving. As I was writing the novel, I came to realise that despite science and technology and the advancements of the 21st century, women and men are the same now as they were in the 18th century. Likewise, cruel injustices still occur every day.

As ever, I would like to thank my trusty team of editors - Sylvia Balog and Jo Egan. I've said it before and I'll say it again, the editing process is absolutely fundamental when producing a book for publication. No matter how wonderful a writer you think you are, there will always be improvements an author can make to a manuscript. Most of the flaws in our work we cannot see. It takes a few pairs of eagle eyes to uncover them all for us.

Finally, the love, support, patience and guidance of my husband, Chris, is always and forever appreciated.

ENJOYED THE LARK'S CALL?

Thanks for reading *The Lark's Call*. If you enjoyed the story, share a review where you bought the e-book, on Goodreads, or contact me at jennybondbooks.com and share your thoughts.

BONUS SHORT STORY

THE LARK'S CALL

Get a free copy of the short story, *The Good Shepherd* when you sign up for my newsletter via this link: https://BookHip.com/SCMMHWS

You'll also be notified of giveaways and new releases and receive updates of my author journey

SOAR FURTHER INTO THE WORLD OF THE LARK'S CALL

Check out my *The Lark's Call* Pinterest board - images that provided inspiration and information during the writing process.

Listen to the Spotify playlist of the novel. Music, past and present, aimed to reflect the themes and atmosphere of the story.

To access either of the above, on the relevant platform search 'jennybondbooks'.

ABOUT THE AUTHOR

I'm an author of contemporary fiction, historical fiction and non-fiction. I have published my books in Australia, New Zealand, USA and Europe.

I'm also an English teacher and I've been lucky enough to introduce the love of language to many students around the world.

I guess this also planted the seed of an idea that I should give writing a go, myself

Sydney, Australia, is where I was born and raised, but prior to my reinvention as a writer (which had something to do with a friendly argument with my husband!), I held the position of Head of English at Eaton House The Manor in London's Clapham Common. I also taught English and Drama for eight years at a selective high school in Sydney, and for five years at a private girls' college in Canberra.

Whether I've been at home, living and working in another country, or travelling for the sake of adventure, I have never spent a single day without a book by my side. This meant slipping from the act of reading into the act of writing didn't actually seem that much of a change.

I've long been a fan of great historical fiction writers such as Hilary Mantel, but I also spend quality time with books by authors from other genres, such as Margaret Atwood, Kate Atkinson, Tim Winton, Ian McEwan, Jane Austen, John Irving and E. Annie Proulx.

When I'm not writing, I enjoy keeping fit and love to

travel. I live in Canberra, Australia with my husband, two sons, and a lively Staffordshire Bull Terrier named Mick.

I enjoy running, swimming and yoga daily, as I believe staying active is an integral component of a happy writing life. You can visit me at www.jennybondbooks.com.au.

Jenny